Book of Darkness

A.N. Sage

OLIVERHEBERBOOKS

CONTENTS

Chapter One

Light trickled in through the half-shut blinds in my room, and I groaned as they blasted their incessant rays into my sleepy eyes. I've been up for half the night, tossing and turning, unable to sleep. It was almost two weeks since Peyton's return from her meeting with the shadower resistance leaders, and it'd been absolute Hell ever since. Between trying to calm down River's constant need to protect me and my best friend's insistence to go undercover again, I've had my hands full. Not to mention the witch hunters that treated me like enemy number one, though that was mainly Savannah's doing. No matter how hard I tried to picture it, I couldn't imagine ever being friends with her, but most days, that didn't bother me one bit. I had other things to worry about. Like the weird shadows that slithered amid my magic that I still had zero information on, and I sure as hell couldn't ask the High Coven about it. They were riding me hard enough after what happened with River's mom. I needed no more of their attention drilled in my direction.

I had no idea how this happened, but somehow, I went

from hiding the fact that I was a witch from everyone in Shadowhurst to being the most talked about gossip in town. It was exhausting.

My phone buzzed on the nightstand next to my comfy bed and I rolled my eyes before turning the screen over. It was likely River checking in again because, Goddess forbid, I didn't text him every ten minutes of the day to let him know I was safe and not being chewed to pieces by a shifter or some shit. Don't get me wrong, his concern was sweet, but I've spent most of my life fending for myself with no one's help. I should have told him to back off weeks ago, but I didn't have the heart to do it. Besides, his worry only meant that he was around all that much more and having myself a piece of River was not something I could say no to. The boy was just too yummy to pass up.

By the time I dragged my sorry ass from bed and showered, it was already past seven. Moving with extra speed, I tossed on a clean band tee and jeans, threw my hair in a messy bun, and bolted for the door. My eyes were still foggy from lack of sleep and as I made my way down the long hallway of the main house, I could hear Imala's laughter fill the kitchen. Her infectious happiness tugged at my heart, and I couldn't help but smile each time she was around. Since they took me in, the Chandlers have become a second family of sorts, one I didn't want to take for granted, and I made certain they knew how much I appreciated them letting me stay in their guest house. For people who thought they were harboring a troubled teen from the city, they definitely treated me awful nice, and I vowed to do nothing to make them regret taking me in.

My clumsy feet creaked on the hardwood of the posh Victorian-style house as I walked to the front door, and I cringed as the sound echoed down the hall.

"Billie, dear? Is that you?" Thomas' voice called after me and I froze in my tracks.

"Uh, yeah?" I yelled back. "Be right there!"

Despite walking the fine line of being late to school this morning, I couldn't say no to Thomas' signature lattes and scones. Sure enough, as soon as I walked into the kitchen, the smell of baked blueberry rushed by me, and my stomach growled in anticipation. I rounded the corner to the open-concept kitchen and plastered on the most welcoming smile I could manage, which for me, was likely more of a scowl, but whatever. It was the best I could do at the moment.

"I know you're late," Imala cooed and wrapped an arm around my shoulder before leading us to the kitchen counter, "but you absolutely must take a scone to go. Thomas got up early to bake enough for the entire neighborhood, it seems!"

She eyed her husband, narrowing her beautiful brown eyes his way before shaking her head.

"Any time you want me to stop cooking for you, just say the word," Thomas teased. "But last I remember, it was why you married me."

"That, among many other things." Imala winked at me, and I stifled the laughter that bubbled in my throat. Those two were so in love, you'd never know they've been married for ages.

I shoved the undeserving jealousy back down into my gut and reached out to Thomas, grabbing the paper bag full of scones and a to go coffee cup from his hands. My stomach did somersaults thinking about digging into both when I got to the Shadowhurst Academy.

"Thanks," I said, smelling the contents of the bag. "This smells delicious, as always. You guys are the best!"

"I'm quite certain she's talking about me," Thomas joked and elbowed Imala in the ribs before pulling her in for a kiss.

They were still kissing when I made a beeline for the front door and surprisingly, I didn't feel like upchucking last night's dinner at their display. Most kids would hate seeing their parents all over each other, but the Chandlers weren't my parents, hell, they weren't even my foster parents, and their affection toward each other made me smile. I could only wish to be that in love with someone after years of being together. It was adorable and I was all for it. But today, I was more for not being late to registration for fall classes.

The cool and familiar breeze of Shadowhurst hit my face as I stepped onto the front porch, waking me up with a jolt of icy air. Unable to wait, I dug my teeth into one of Thomas' infamous scones and hopped on my bike. *Shadowhurst Academy, here I come!*

"B! Over here!" Peyton yelled out as I pulled my bike into the campus car lot.

My best friend's face was beet red like she'd been running for hours, and her hair was unusually messy. Today, she sported her token leather shorts and a tank top held together by a hundred pins. Even from where I stood, I could see her neon-pink sports bra peek out through the holes, and I wondered how she could be so comfortable in her body to show it off without a care. But Peyton was a shadower, a soul sucker, and if there's anything I learned about shadowers while being friends with Peyton, it was that they never took life for granted. If there was something they wanted to do, they did it without question. I was positive that having the High Coven and all the witches of the world on your ass and trying to kill you had a lot to do with that. If someone threatened my existence daily, I'd be living life pretty wild too.

Peyton's cheeks puffed and she narrowed her black lined eyes in my direction before running to catch up with me. "Girl, finally! We thought you weren't gonna make it in time."

"We?" I asked, looking around the lot.

It took only a second for me to spot River behind her. His wind-blown hair fell over his forehead as he strode toward us, and I had to all but wipe the drool from my face as my eyes trailed the taut muscles of his chest while he walked. The unfairly tight button-up he wore hugged his chest in all the right places, and I had to curse the Goddess for the distraction she was blatantly shoving my way. River was nothing if not a fine piece of man and I still couldn't believe that by some luck, I somehow ended up dating him. Mostly because he was a witch hunter and I was, you know, a freaking witch. But we made it work, and I wasn't complaining about getting some one-on-one time with the sexiest boy in school. Don't get me wrong, I was still freaking out like crazy, but that was mostly because River was so sure of me and our relationship. I, on the other hand, had no idea how to act like a normal person around him. Until River, my dating pool has been limited at best, and I found myself playing the role of a girlfriend without a script to go by. If a girlfriend was even what I was to him. I seriously had no clue.

"Dude, you're drooling..." Peyton whispered between clenched teeth. "Get a handle on it."

I stepped past her to meet River halfway. As soon as he was near me, my body was set ablaze and I felt my thighs quiver with the need to wrap themselves around him. *Calm your shit. You're in school.* I forced my gaze from his biceps to meet a set of brilliant green eyes and choked back a gasp. He was damn perfect. Like I said, no clue.

"Hey, gorgeous," River whispered, and I died. Like actually, dead. "Glad you made it."

He wrapped one arm around me, his fingers tracing the waistband of my jeans, and crashed his lips to mine. On instinct, my fingers reached for the back of his head, and I ran them through the silky waves. River's tongue brushed against mine and I moaned into him, unable to stop myself.

"Get it, boy!" someone yelled out behind us, and I froze, my lips still pressed to River's, body as stiff as a surfboard.

I pulled back and peered over his shoulder to find Jayden climbing out of the passenger seat of Tyler's truck. The token jester of the witch hunter group had grown on me since we first met, and despite his arrogant attitude and ill-timed jokes, he was one of my favorite people in Shadowhurst. Jayden tossed his backpack on his shoulder and zipped up his varsity jacket before coming our way. Behind him, Tyler helped Abigail out of the car, and she flashed me a fake smile before dragging her boyfriend away from us. I guess I still had some work to do to gain her trust, but that wasn't surprising. It wasn't every day that witch hunters befriended a witch, and I knew it would be a long while before they accepted me into their group.

River brushed his lips against my ear, and I jolted my attention back to him. "They'll come around, don't worry," he whispered, making me relax into his arms. This guy knew just the right things to say to make me feel safe and I loved every second of it.

"Don't stop the make out sesh on my account," Jayden teased. "Some of us haven't had action in months. Am I right, Peyton?"

"Speak for yourself!" Peyton chuckled before looping her arm under his to lead him into the quad up the hill.

She was kidding, of course. If my best friend got any action, I'd be the first to know it. Unfortunately, Shadowhurst had a limited number of bachelorettes, and I was fairly certain Peyton had no interest in any girl at the school. I wished I knew someone to set her up with, but the last time we talked about it, all she said was that she had bigger things on her plate at the moment. I couldn't blame her. If a shadower resistance wanted to recruit me into their ranks and was threatening to kill my best friend, I wouldn't worry over dating either. Except, it was me they wanted dead and somehow, I couldn't keep my mind off River and that damn dimple on his left cheek, no matter what I tried. What the hell was seriously wrong with me? *Ew.*

"Couldn't sleep again?" River asked, running a thumb under my chin to tilt my head up to face him.

I sighed. "Nope. Can't get my stupid mind to stop reeling."

"You know I have your back in this. You don't have to worry so much."

"I'm not worried, hunter," I hissed, unable to keep my annoyance under control. "If those shadowers come after me, I can handle myself."

River's laugh echoed down the lot, and I noticed Peyton glance back ahead of us. Her eyes studied me, making sure I was all right before turning her attention back to Jayden. Somewhere along the line, everyone in my life started treating me like I was breakable, and I was sick of it.

"I know you can," River said. "I'm just saying that you don't have to go it alone. That's what my job here is. You can dump your shit on me, and I'll take it."

"Thanks," I said, embarrassed by my earlier outburst. "Sorry. Guess I'm not used to having people around that care."

"Well, get used to it! Because we do care and we'll be around whether you like it or not."

My eyes narrowed at Peyton's retreating back. "Yeah, don't I know it," I scoffed. "Do you think she's right? That we should let her go meet the resistance again and see what's up?"

A frigid gust of wind wrapped around me, and I scooted in closer to River's side as we walked. His arm pressed against my hip, pulling me in until there was no space between us, and the warmth of his solid body filled my bones. *Perfection.*

"I don't know. But it might be a good call. She's the only

one that can get close to them, and we need to know if their threat to kill you is anything we should worry about or if it's empty talk."

"I don't feel comfortable putting her in that kind of danger without being there to protect her."

"I'm positive she feels the same way about you," he said. "I think you have to let her do this."

I grimaced. Mostly because I knew he was right. There was no stopping my best friend once she had her mind made up and fighting against it would only put a rift between us I didn't want. I had to let Peyton go back to the shadowers and the thought tore me apart. The resistance had rubbed me the wrong way since we found out it existed. It was rare to have all three shadower types work together, and having them all unite to fight against the High Coven's oppression scared me to no small degree. What was even worse were those damn leaders Peyton was so eager to meet again. Anyone strong enough to lead a group of uncontrollable shadowers had to be super, like scary, strong and one wrong move could cost Peyton her life. Unfortunately for us, they wanted my best friend to join them, and as it turns out, to kill me in the process.

"You know," River said as we made our way to the main quad, "at some point, you'll have to stop second-guessing yourself. You need to trust yourself and your choices and you have to trust your friends. It's the only way you won't drive yourself insane."

"I'm not driving myself insane."

His lips pressed to my forehead, and I felt him smile against my skin. "You can't fool me, witch."

My skin crawled and I forced a smile to my lips, but it never reached my eyes. Trusting people was easier said than done, especially since this was the first time I even had friends. Trusting *myself* was way the hell out of the question. There was too much doubt in my past choices for me to let myself go like that again. I trusted Beatrix, and she turned out to be the worst damn mom ever. I trusted the High Coven, and they lied to me every chance they got. So far, the only people in my life that haven't broken my trust were Peyton and River, and I wondered how long it would be until the other shoe dropped. How long until one of them betrayed me?

The bell rang out and panic filled my chest. I pulled back from River, tugging on his shirt to pull him behind me. We darted through the groups of students that littered the quad, jogging to the Main Hall like our lives depended on it. As we ran, I promised myself to spend the rest of the day figuring out how to calm my shit and not spin out of control. Trust may have been off the table, but I didn't need to be a walking time bomb. All I had to do was worry about getting through registration and take it one hour at a time. Lucky for me, Shadowhurst Academy worked on its own weird schedule and once we got our schedules and sat through a day of boring assemblies, classes didn't actually start for another few weeks. It was a weird break to have in between two semesters, but I wasn't complaining. Any chance to sleep in was fine by me.

Beside me, River's fingers squeezed my own and the woodsy scent of his cologne invaded my senses. *I can do this. It's just school, no biggie.*

"B! Hurry your skinny ass up!" Peyton yelled out, holding the front doors of the main building ajar for us.

My smile widened as I sprinted up the steps, River right behind me. Just another day at Shadowhurst.

Chapter Two

"I think I got something!" Jayden shouted in excitement and slid a dusty, old tome across the table.

We'd been huddled in the secret hunter room in the academy's library for most of lunch to get as much as we could done while the library was still open. With the break coming up, we'd make sure to haul the books we needed home with us, but I knew I'd miss the cramped witch hunter vault. Despite being smaller than my walk-in closet at the guest house, the secret room was the only place we somehow managed not to argue. And by 'we', I mean Savannah and myself, though, that was probably thanks to the fact that I kept my distance from her, and she seemed to be okay with that arrangement. Today, she sprawled on the floor in a tight, turquoise mini dress with her long legs a little too close to River for my comfort. I pushed my raging thoughts back into my throat and reached to grab the book from Jayden, reading over the passage he pointed to.

My eyes widened as I took in the words, and I scowled in his direction. "This is nothing but more instructions on beheading, Jayden." I glared at him and shut the book with a loud thud. "We're trying to find something on the resistance leaders Peyton told us about. Not start a freaking war here."

"Well, I thought it might be useful," Jayden said, smirking.

"Geez, dude," Tyler whispered. "You are one twisted bastard."

Jayden rolled his shoulders and flashed his teeth, his inky hair falling into his eyes. "Proud of it, bruh!" He extended a fist, but not one of us dared bump it. We all knew not to indulge his behavior unless we wanted to spend the remainder of the afternoon practicing proper stabbing like little serial killers in training.

"Just don't try to use that shit on me or you'll be finding yourself on the other side of a spell," I hissed.

Beside me, River smiled, but I noticed Abigail and Savannah tense at my words. *Right, too soon.* I wished Peyton and Morgan were here today. Other than Jayden, they were both very comfortable joking around about me being a witch, and I missed their support. As if sensing my discomfort, River scooted closer to me and wrapped an arm around my shoulder, squeezing me closer to his body. My muscles relaxed and I sank into a puddle at his side.

"Anyone else have anything that might actually be useful?" he asked the group.

River was met with blank stares and the standard grimace from Savannah. That girl did not know how to look anything other than pissed off, and if her hatred wasn't mainly directed at me, I would have enjoyed having her on our side. If there was one thing I learned from my time in the academy, it was that you were better off not messing with Savannah Michaels. She was as hard as they came.

There was a clutter of items falling to the floor and we all turned to see Abigail fumble with her purse. Her full lips tightened into a line and the creases on her brow thickened as she searched for whatever it was that required her immediate attention. Beneath her, Tyler's body grew rigid as she ground her hips over his lap, oblivious to his obvious arousal. The girl was a walking sex-bomb, and I had no clue how Tyler kept himself together with her around. If I was riding River that way, he'd be all hands and no control. Tyler, on the other hand, was as cool as stone and I had the distinct feeling he had grown used to Abigail's hotness over the years. It was still awkward as hell to watch, and I looked away with a blush.

A few moments later, Abigail yelped in excitement, holding up the item she'd been searching for. It was lip gloss. Of course. She smoothed the berry stained color over her lips and grinned triumphantly before turning to face us. "What?"

"Careful you don't get knocked up while beautifying," Savannah scoffed.

At her words, Abigail turned back to Tyler and wiggled her hips a few times before her grin spread wider. "Anything for a good lip day." She winked.

Before I could stop myself, I burst out laughing, my hands slapping my thighs in full force. This chick was something else. It took only a second for Jayden and River to join me, cackling like kids on the floor of the dimly lit room. When we finally stopped laughing, I wiped the tears from my eyes and squared my shoulders, regaining whatever composure I still had left. "You're a champ, Tyler," I noted and reached out to high five him. "A serious champ."

"If you want to see a champ," Jayden said, "you should see what I can—"

River slapped a hand over his mouth before he could finish. "End that sentence and you're dead."

His arm pulled me closer, exuding dominance over me like I was some property he owned. It pissed me right the hell off and I wiggled out of his grasp, brushing dirt off the back of my jeans and crossing the room to put some distance between us. River's eyebrows raised and an adorable confused look flashed over his features. My posture stiffened and I shot my best 'we'll talk about this later' look his way, hoping he got the point. He did not. *Ugh. Boys! Idiots, all of them.*

"So, no one has anything so far?" I asked, changing the subject. "This isn't good. We can't have Peyton go in there unprepared and who knows what the shadowers will do once she's there. She said they're trying to recruit her and if the leaders are involved, I'm willing to bet they're much stronger than the average shadower."

"Can't you like use your magic or whatever?" Savannah asked. "What's the point of being a witch if you can't do anything?"

My lips crashed together, and I snapped my attention to her. "We already went over this. I'm not a superhero. Magic doesn't work like that. It has to have a point. A balance. I can't just manifest information out of thin air."

"So, what good are you?"

"Watch it, Sav," River said through clenched teeth.

Savannah's hazel eyes narrowed, and she tucked a curl behind her ear before reaching over to rest her hand on his arm. She smoothed her fingers over his bicep, gaze never leaving mine. "Don't worry, babe," she said with a wolf's grin, "no one's going to hurt your precious."

Fire exploded in me, and I could feel my magic roar under my skin. The shadows I've been holding hostage rushed to the surface and their power overtook me. My eyes were glued to her hand that still rested on River's arm and I could picture myself leaping over and ripping it right off her body. I had never been the jealous type, but something about Savannah made me go wild. Granted, that was likely my idiotic insecurities coming out to play. I knew River would never do anything to hurt me, but Savannah's self-assured attitude riled me up every time. Maybe I was the jealous type after all? My blue eyes darkened as the shadows crept outward, begging me to let them loose. In the corner of my vision, sparkles of light danced familiarly as magic consumed me and I had to grind my teeth to keep myself steady. My gaze trailed Savannah's face and it surprised me to see no fear there. She wasn't in the least bit bothered with the energy I was throwing down and it made me that much more pissed. Deep down, I knew she was toying with me. Hoping I would lash out and scare the crap out of everyone in the room as a way of turning them against me and I wasn't about to let her succeed. Despite myself, I pulled the shadows back in, tucking them away from the world. My eyes lightened and my breathing slowed to a normal pace as I steadied myself against the bookcase behind me. *Deep breaths, deep breaths, deep breaths.* I recited until my body followed my words.

River's eyes observed me, and his body shifted away from Savannah, shaking off her pathetic grip on him. As soon as there was some distance between them, I let myself relax. *Great, now I'm the possessive idiot. Lovely.*

"Think your coven can help?" Tyler asked.

Everyone turned his way, shock across our faces.

"You want me to ask the witches that want everyone in this room dead for help?" I asked, baffled at the suggestion. "I don't think that's the best idea."

"Well, we're getting nowhere on our own and if anyone has information on the shadower leaders, it would be them, no?"

His face scrunched and Abigail brushed a finger over his bottom lip. "See?" she said to the room. "Not just a pretty face, this one."

Ignoring the flush that rose over her boyfriend's neck, she

ran her hand down his short hair and placed a kiss on his cheek. Everyone pretended not to notice the other hand she slipped under his sweatshirt as she caressed his chest. When they pulled apart, Tyler looked like we caught him robbing a bank. His eyes wide and his jaw slacked.

"Anyway," he said, clearing his throat, "what do you think?"

"I'll try, but no promises. I can't risk letting them know who you are or that I have any contact with the hunters in this town. It's too dangerous."

"Guys!" Jayden yelped. "We got ourselves a bodyguard. And a hot one at that!"

Without pause, River smacked his friend upside the head and pushed him over. "Seriously, dude?"

Jayden shrugged and sent a wink my way before getting back up to crouch next to River. His puppy dog eyes sparkled in the low light of the single bulb hanging over our heads and I shook my head, smiling in his direction. You really couldn't stay mad at the dumbass.

Before anyone else could come up with more requests I didn't want to agree to, River got to his feet and opened the hidden door that led back into the school's library. A gust of fresh air rushed by us and my lungs inhaled it greedily, craving the air-conditioned goodness. As the air flowed through my body, the amethyst pendant on my neck hummed against my skin and I let it relax the tight muscles that have formed in my back. My shoulders slouched and I followed River out of the room, checking the clock on the wall to make sure we weren't late for our next assembly.

"You are the only person in the academy that cares about being on time. You know that, right?" River said.

I nodded. "Well, you better catch up, 'cause if you think I'm bad about punctuality, you should see Thomas. He's a stickler for timing."

"I better not be late for dinner tonight then."

"It's in your best interest to show up at least a half-hour early."

His fingers burrowed into the back pocket of my jeans, and he squeezed the soft skin of my ass, making me jump in surprise. "Whatever will we do with the extra half hour?" he purred.

It was all I could do not to melt at his feet, but I slapped on my best indifferent expression and shoved him off. "We're going to do more research on the resistance. You've been spending way too much time with Jayden."

Before he could throw back another smart remark, I pulled him out of the library, ignoring the vicious glares Savannah threw our way as we walked past her. River made me happy, happier than I've been in years, and I would not let anyone get in the way of that. Not even Savannah Michaels.

Chapter Three

Scents of roasted turkey and grilled vegetables drifted through the house as River, Imala, and me waited for Thomas to finish the last touches on the dinner. We had settled in the living room, sinking into the plush leather of the sofas and watching the fire dance in the fireplace set alight in the corner. The longer I lived with the Chandlers, the braver I became with venturing out of the guest house to spend time with them in their home. The fireplace was my favorite part and in the last few weeks, I have ended many nights falling asleep in front of the flames as Imala and Thomas lounged on the couch next to me. It was peaceful and I had begun to look forward to our evenings together.

Light footsteps sounded behind me, and I turned to find Silas making his way toward us with a tray of drinks on a silver platter. His gold-rimmed glasses slipped down his nose and I could see he was having trouble balancing the drinks. His hands were full and since he couldn't object, I hopped from the couch and darted toward him. As soon as I reached him, my hands went straight for the tray, and I was surprised at the lack of resistance when I took it from him. Silas, the maître d' of the Chandler residence, was not keen on people helping him do his job, but he was coming around. I think I did a pretty decent job of convincing him I will not be waited on and after many battles, I wore him down.

His fingers slipped off the tray and he gave me a single nod before returning to the kitchen to help Thomas with dinner.

"Wonderful!" Imala exclaimed, her fingers reaching for the tray. "The wine has arrived!"

She snatched a crystal glass and brought it to her lips, taking a small sip and relaxing deep into the folds of the couch. "Pure Heaven," she cooed.

"We'll take your word for it," I said, gulping down the orange juice in my hands.

"You sure will," Imala said, grinning. "No alcohol for minors in this house. I don't want people to think we're raising a troublemaker."

The way she said it made the hairs stand on my arms. No one had raised me before, at least not as far as I was aware, and it was nice to have someone care enough about how I turned out. Refreshing, really.

"So, River," Imala started, "Billie tells me you're quite the athlete at school."

River arched one eyebrow and flashed a dimple my way. "Does she now?"

"Okay, get over yourself. I only said you like sports, not that you're winning gold medals at the Olympics."

"Not yet," he teased.

"Only if there's a division for biggest cocky bastard," I hissed.

Laughter burst from Imala and she shook her head, taking another sip of her drink. "You two are adorable. Just like me and Thomas back in the day."

"How did the two of you meet?"

"Oh, geez. You do not want to hear that story!" Imala laughed. "Let's just say wine was involved. As always."

I giggled, remembering the story Thomas told me about meeting Imala at her friend's bachelorette party. He made it sound so innocent but hearing her now, I was certain it was likely a drunken disaster that ended up working out in the end. I always liked love stories that didn't start with all guns blazing. They seemed much more real somehow.

"Dinner is ready, my hungry fiends!" Thomas called out from the kitchen.

One by one, we filed out of the living room to join him at the massive marble dining table while Silas and Thomas plopped dish upon dish of whatever goodness had been prepared. My mouth salivated as I took in the selection, and I tugged excitedly at River's sleeve. His smile widened and he jogged past me to pull out my chair, waiting until I settled before taking a seat next to me.

"This one's a keeper," Imala whispered as she walked by me. "Quite the looker too."

Her words barely reached me and though I was grateful for her positivity, my mind was only on one thing. The overflowing plates of food in front of me. I dug in first, fighting River for the mashed potatoes like a savage. Around us, Thomas and Imala laughed at our competitive exchanges, and even Silas threw a few grins our way. Somehow, amid all the craziness that was Shadowhurst, I managed to find these amazing people. I was the luckiest witch in the world.

Two hours of stuffing our faces later and I could barely move. When River suggested we sit on the porch, I was convinced he'd have to roll me there and then rub butter on the doorframe to scoot me out. I was *that* full! No complaints though, the dinner was delicious. Thomas outdid himself this time, and I couldn't wait to see what else the hidden chef had in store.

My back curved and I fit myself into River's chest as we shared one of the larger chairs on the porch. The Chandlers' front yard was a perfect oasis. Between the enormous fountain in the center of the curved driveway that led to the house and the serene rows of trees on the horizon, it was like having a vacation home. Back in Stamwick, I never had quiet nights like this. Mostly because my nights were usually filled with shadower hunts in the filthy alleys of the city. Here in Shadowhurst, not one evening went by where I didn't get to sit in silence one or another. It was perfection.

Around us, the elements swirled in the air and my magic called to them, relaxing my bones as I settled in. I could feel River's heartbeat at my back, his chest rising and falling behind me and lulling me into surrender. He was the sea to my water, always calling me home.

My eyes drifted past the dark trees and up to the night sky, settling on the crescent moon that hung upside down in the distance. Clouds rolled over it and I could smell the chill in the air. *Rain would be here tomorrow.*

"What's on your mind?" River asked, draping his arms around me.

"The moon is stunning tonight," I whispered. "Really beautiful."

His gaze searched for the silver light in the sky, and he relaxed behind me. "I always loved it when it was like this. A perfect crescent."

"Wet moon," I said. "It's when the points face up, like little horns."

He smiled and I mimicked the gesture, my eyes never

leaving the sky. Something about the shape above me drew me in. It was calling to me, but I didn't know why. My mind raced, searching for some long-lost memory that I had forgotten, but nothing came forward. Frustrated, I shook my head and ripped my gaze away from the crescent, turning to face River.

"Thanks for coming tonight," I whispered. "And thanks for not being late."

"You know, you still owe me for those extra twenty minutes..." he grinned.

I slapped his shoulder and chuckled. "One-track mind. Always."

River looked me over and I melted under his gaze. His eyes took in every inch of me as he drank me in, memorizing every freckle on my face. As his gaze drifted lower, I froze.

"Do you blame me?" River asked. "You're gorgeous."

Air stilled around us and the magic inside me exploded. River leaned in, brushing his lips against mine, his warm breath covering my face. My lids fluttered and I gulped as he pulled me in, crashing his lips to mine. Our kiss was fire and passion and it burned me up hotter than the energy boiling under my skin. River didn't waste any time. His hands grabbed for my waist, and he swung me around, wrapping my legs around him until I was straddling him in the chair. My weight pressed into him as I pulled my fingers through his hair, tilting his head back to deepen our kiss. His teeth sunk into my bottom lip, and I moaned against him, riling the fire in him even more. River's hands were everywhere and if I wasn't so preoccupied with how much I wanted him, I would have worried about the Chandlers coming outside to find us all over each other. But they were the last thing on my mind.

I pulled back, taking in the sight that was River Hunting. It wasn't the fact that he was drop dead gorgeous that drew me in, though don't get me wrong, he sure as hell was. What I liked most about River was the way he always put me first. No matter what happened, I knew he had my back. It was the closest I felt to the security I had with the coven since I moved to Shadowhurst, and having him near made the place seem that much more like home. Damn, I was seriously falling for this goof.

River's hands moved up my shirt and I leaned into him, banishing any air between us. The shadows in me exploded, shooting out of my skin and wrapping themselves around us in a thick cocoon. On my finger, the moonstone ring vibrated and buzzed against my skin, and I could feel its cool energy creep inside. My brain was liquid, and my heart was mush. I wanted more. More River. More kissing. More... everything.

"Ohmygodohmygodohmygod!" someone shrieked next to us, and I jumped back from River. "I'll come back!"

I willed my shadows inward, clearing the space between us and whoever chose that particular moment to invade my happiness. As they retreated, the air filled with the icy cold of Shadowhurst weather, clearing the path for us to find a blushing Peyton in the front yard. Her eyes were so wide, they looked like perfect circles, and she shifted her weight from one foot to the other like she wasn't sure if she should stay or run. My head snapped to River, who was still breathless beneath me, his lips puffy from my attacks.

"Hey, Peyton," he growled, clearly unhappy with the interruption. "What's up?"

My best friend looked from me to him, then back to me again. "I'm so sorry! If I knew you guys were, you know, I would have come another time."

"It's fine," I said. "What's going on? You look frazzled."

She took a tiny step toward us, enough that it made me wonder what she was hiding. No one tiptoes around like that unless they were about to drop a bomb of dog shit on your head.

"Spit it out, Peyton," I warned.

"Okay. Okay, don't be mad," she said as though that would work on me. "But I kinda did something you're not gonna like."

I slapped my forehead in frustration. Somehow, I had a pretty good idea what it was Peyton did. "You told the resistance leaders you'll see them, didn't you?"

"Sort of..."

"What does that mean?" River asked, his hands holding me protectively.

"Well, yeah, you're on point. I did set up a meeting with the resistance leaders," she said, biting her lip nervously. "And I kinda set it up for both of us. They want to meet you. Like yesterday."

Above us, the moon got brighter, and I could all but feel the tips of its horns crush into my chest. This was it. This was the beginning of my end.

Chapter Four

"You did WHAT?" I roared. My body shook and my nails dug into the soft skin of my palms as I tightened fists at my side. Peyton's face scrunched and I tried to soften my features, but all I could see was red. "Why the hell would you do that? They want me dead!"

Behind me, River pulled on the belt loop of my jeans to keep me from killing my best friend. "Babe. Breathe. Let her explain." His eyes focused on Peyton's trembling form, and I could sense the agitation in him from where I stood. "Wanna tell us why you did that?"

She nodded but didn't speak. Her mouth opened and closed like a fish out of water.

"Well?" I urged.

"Okay, look," Peyton finally said. "I know you said not to go see them yet, but I didn't have a choice. They rolled up at the house and my dad let them in."

"What? Why?"

The thought of Mr. Ling putting his daughter in the line of fire didn't sit right by me. I knew he was a soul sucker like

Peyton, but from what she told me, he wanted nothing to do with the resistance or any shadower business. The Lings kept to themselves, and they excepted their daughter to do the same. It took us days to even convince him to get on board with me being her best friend and if I was honest, I still wasn't sure he was all there. So why would he let the damn leaders of the resistance into his house? It didn't make any sense.

Peyton looked like she agreed with me, and her eyebrows kissed as she trained her puzzled eyes on mine. "My thoughts exactly! I was like 'Dad, not cool'!"

"And what did he say?"

"That I should hear them out. You know how he is, no drama."

My head hurt just thinking about it, and I took a few deep breaths to calm down. The crescent shapes my nails left in the skin stung as I uncurled my fists, and I rubbed them over and over to give myself something to do. Something other than yell at my best friend in the front yard. "So, you went from meeting them to what? Setting up a slumber party for all of us?"

Peyton laughed but the look I gave her stopped her cold. She recovered with a fake cough and an apologetic grin, taking a step toward me.

"It's not like that. They said they don't actually want to kill you."

"And you believe them?" River asked. *My thoughts exactly.*

"I do."

"Peyton, that's ridiculous. She's a witch and her coven has been hunting them for years. They're the reason the resistance even exists. Why wouldn't the leaders want her dead?" He pressed his chin to my shoulder. "Sorry, babe."

"It's fine," I choked out. "But what he said."

"Okay, yes," Peyton agreed, "some of them want her dead. But not the leaders. They said there's been some unease in the ranks, and the shifters are the ones that pose the threat. They're looking into it."

"And you believed them?"

River's body grew rigid at my side, and he let out a low growl. "Yeah, whether these damn leaders are looking into it or not, Billie's not going in there while there's a pack of shifters that wants to kill her."

"Billie's right here and can talk for herself," I bit out.

"So, you're considering it?" Peyton asked.

I shrugged. "I don't know. Maybe. No, that would crazy, right?"

"Yes!" River yelled out, only slightly overshadowing Peyton's 'no'. "It's nuts, Billie. You can't go in there."

As far as an argument went, I had none. River was correct to assume the worst, and there was a decent chance that if I agreed to meet the resistance leaders, I'd be dead as soon as I set foot on their turf. But what choice did I have here? They've had their claws in Peyton for a while now, and there was no telling what these bastards would do to my friend if I refused.

"Why do they want to meet with me?" I asked because it was the only thing I could think of. "Why do they want to meet a witch?"

"They heard about what happened with Evanora. You're kind of a legend in the resistance right now, B! A witch that went against her own? That's not something that happens every day."

"The High Coven has rules," I said. "Anyone who disobeys them gets handled. Witch or not."

"See?" Peyton exclaimed. "This is why you need to meet them! To show them that not everyone in the High Coven is psycho. I mean, you should have seen their faces when I told them you were my best friend. Their eyes almost popped right out of their freaking skulls!"

"Oh, Goddess, Peyton," I groaned. "What else did you tell them?"

"Nothing, I swear!"

"So, they don't know that I don't one hundred percent trust the coven right now? Because we can't have that get back to the high priestesses. Not when I'm not sure what's going on over there."

River's gaze darkened. "Wait, we're back to trusting the High Coven again?"

"No," I shook my head. "I don't know. They lied. About a lot of stuff, but I can't just jump to conclusions. There are witches I care about there, witches I grew up with. After Beatrix, I had no one. They took me in and treated me like family. I can't forget that."

"I know, babe. And I know shit's complicated, but that doesn't mean you should throw yourself in the middle of a dangerous situation either. First, this crap with my mom, and now, the resistance, and then, all the lies the coven told you? It's too much too soon to be coincidental. I don't like it."

No. Freaking. Kidding. I didn't like it either, but it was starting to look that me liking things was not what life had in store. In the end, all of this was on me. I was the one that chose to stay in Shadowhurst and lie to the High Coven about my friends. I was the one that started hooking up with a hunter and now, I would have to be the one that threw more gasoline to the flames. Maybe there was a way I could play this to my advantage? Infiltrate the resistance to get their location and then spill the beans to the coven. If I managed to do that, the witches would be too busy with taking down the shadowers to worry about my friends, and I'd get Peyton out of the impossible situation she was in. No more resistance meant no more shadowers barging into her house to recruit her into their ranks. Everyone would win.

My heartbeat raced as I ran through scenarios where my plan to play double operative could backfire and knots twisted into tight balls in my stomach. Knowing my luck, the High Coven would roll up in Shadowhurst all guns firing, and my friends and I would end up right in the center of a war. Not to mention the other people in town that were innocent in all of this.

This was a damned mess.

Peyton opened her mouth to speak but before she could utter a word, heavy, warm air blew past us. My eyes widened and I snatched my gaze from her to the shadowy trees near the driveway. Ears perked, I listened for any disturbance, though deep down, I already knew we were in serious shit. Something was coming. A shifter. There was no mistaking their scent when it was this thick in the air.

Slowly, I raised my leg, pulling out the dagger stashed in the secret compartment of my boot. My breath quickened and I could feel River square his shoulders beside me.

"What is it?"

I narrowed my eyes. "Shifter. A big one."

Without another word, I shook my hand to get Peyton on our side of the porch and waited. *Any day now, asshole.*

Trees rustled, whispering at first, then louder and with more force. Just over the horizon, a shadowy figure emerged, creeping toward us and picking up speed as it inched closer. It was so dark, I could barely make out its shape in the distance, but it didn't take the shifter long to close the space between us. My jaw slacked and I heard Peyton whimper at my side as the muscled form of a black bear unrolled before us.

It was so large that its body obscured the fountain behind it, and I could see the matted knots of its fur in the moonlight. The shifter growled, flashing a row of man-eating teeth our way, and I had to will myself to stand still. To my left, River moved, but I pressed my side into him with caution. "No sudden movements," I hissed, my teeth so tight, I could feel each ridge in my mouth. "Don't piss it off any more than we have to."

He nodded and looked back to the shifter. Its chest rose and fell, steam shooting from its nostrils as it breathed. I could smell its foulness even from where I stood, gagging from the stench. But that wasn't the part that gave me the most pause or the part that made me almost piss myself on the Chandlers' front porch. What drew me in were the shifter's eyes. Piercing red dots filled with only hatred and the desire to kill. They were sharp and petrifying and glowing brighter than the crescent in the sky above it. And they were looking right at me.

Chapter Five

It took less than a second for the bear to lunge for us, its thick paws overshadowing the driveway tiles as it barreled in our direction. My heart leaped in my throat, and I curled my fingers around the rune-etched hilt of the dagger to tighten my hold. Beside me, River stood in a defensive position while Peyton outstretched both her arms. I knew my best friend was hoping to get a hold on the shifter with her powers, but she'd need to be close enough to touch it and I was almost one hundred percent certain that if that thing got anywhere near us, we'd be dead before she had a chance. Judging by the doubt in her eyes, she agreed.

Sweat pooled down my back, staining the new silk blouse Imala got me a darker shade. I shifted my feet, putting more weight on my heels, and flipped the dagger to point at the running shifter. The moon's light hit the silver and the bear's eyes locked on my weapon. It slowed its stride, screeching to a stop a few feet from us.

Ah, you know what this can do then. Good! I moved fast, pushing River back with one hand and jumping for the shifter.

"BILLIE!" he screamed, but it was too late. I was already soaring.

The force of my jump carried me through the air, and I landed in a crouch at the bear's feet. Hair whipped around my face, falling in loose tendrils and covering my eyes from it. Over me, the shifter roared, and the sour smell of its breath filled the air. In a flash, I ripped the amber crystal from my pocket and rose to stand.

Magic filled me as my fingers gripped the crystal and flickering lights appeared in my vision. My body heated and cooled at the same time as I forced my energy to collide with the amber, pulling on its power to strengthen my own. The shifter rose on its hind legs and let out another wild roar. Its eyes went from me to my hand, which was now burning in a blazing flame of magic. The fire rose and my smile widened as I stared it down, ready to take on my opponent. Muscles taut, I lifted the dagger in the air to bury it in the bear's wide chest. Behind me, footsteps neared, and I glanced back to find River running toward us. Panic rose inside me, and my mind clouded with fear for him.

"Stay back!" I shouted.

That was all the time it took for the shifter to get the upper hand. It swung out at me, sharp claws slashing the skin of my arm. The weight of its massive paw sent my hand sideways, and I yelled out from the pain as I watched the blood flow from the wounds it inflicted. My entire arm grew numb and my face paled until I was the same light color as the asphalt below. I tried to stay steady, but my fingers wouldn't cooperate, and they uncurled against my wishes. The amber fell from my hand, its energy leaving my body in an instant. I cursed under breath and jumped back from the shifter, my back colliding with River's chest.

His arms wrapped around me, and he pulled me away,

pressing on the wound as he dragged me backward. Blood was everywhere. On my arm. On his hands. In my vision.

The bear dropped to all fours and the ground shook as its weight hit the pavement. It dug its claws into the asphalt, blew out scorching air from its nostrils, and charged again.

"You son of a..."

Peyton's loud screech ran by us, and I choked back a sob as my friend pushed her way to the shifter. They ran toward each other, each on a direct path to the other and ready to collide. My pulse drummed in my veins, and I turned to my friend in horror. "Peyton, no!" I screamed, but she was oblivious to my protests.

Before she could reach the bear, I swung my hand back and threw the dagger at the shifter. It sliced the air, embedding itself in the bear's fur-covered thigh. The shifter yelped, and though my wound was not enough to kill it, it slowed it down. Tumbling backward, it altered its path, barely missing Peyton. I could see my best friend's resolve as she skidded to a stop, turning around to attack again. Her hands reached out and she was inches away from the shifter's side when it kicked its leg back and straight into her stomach. Air left Peyton's lungs and I could see it form a puff of white smoke as she flew back. She landed on her back with a thud, her arms limp at her sides.

"Peyton!" I yelled and tried to wrestle out of River's hold, but he was too strong. His arms tightened around me in a vice, and he continued to drag me away, back to the porch. "Stop! We can't leave her there!"

"You're bleeding!" he snapped and it felt like a slap in the face. "You can't help her like that."

The bear stumbled, turning in circles and swinging at the dagger impaled in its skin. It was moaning and the sound carried through the front yard like a siren call, beckoning whatever Hell was about to unleash.

"Peyton!" I shouted again, and this time, I saw her arm move.

A breath of relief left me just as the front door flew open.

"Billie?" Silas asked, his glasses crooked on his nose. "What in the name of..."

His voice trailed off as he took in the bear that clumsily waddled in our front yard and his jaw hit the ground. I couldn't be sure, but I could have sworn that Silas' hair got even whiter at that moment. I could feel the fear roll off him in waves and my heart couldn't handle it. The last thing I wanted was to put anyone else I loved in danger, but there was no getting around it now. Silas stumbled down the steps of the porch, his body rigid and his back straight. What the hell is he doing? Does he seriously think he can protect us from this thing?

"Get the hell out! Shoo!" he screamed.

Shoo? Really, Silas? That's definitely not going to work. "Don't draw him in!" I yelled.

As if on cue, the shifter stopped trying to free itself of my dagger and snapped its eyes to Silas. It slammed one paw to the ground, then the other, establishing dominance. That would have been enough to have any other human running for the hills, but not Silas. He stood his ground like a damn fool. I huffed, pushing back on River to get to my feet. "We have to help him. NOW!"

"I have this. Stay here," he instructed and stepped around me.

Like hell!

I used my good arm to knock him out of the way and ran for Silas. Blood stained the driveway behind me and the pain in my arm was suffocating, but I pushed it aside, using it instead to rile my emotions. I needed the shadows and I needed them now. I still hadn't the slightest idea how they worked, but they seemed to respond when I was running high on emotion, and I was full to the brim of that now. Pissed was the better term for what I was. Livid.

Body shaking, I pulled for them, beckoning them to make their appearance and come out to play. My heart was full of so much rage, I thought I might explode. *No one hurts my people, you piece of shit!* I flung my arms forward, ignoring the shooting bursts of pain that exploded like lightening behind my lids. The shadows crept to the surface and exploded from my outreached hands. The power was intoxicating, and I could taste every bit of it on my tongue. Before me, the shifter puffed its chest and snapped its teeth, but I wasn't scared of the bastard. The shadows wrapped over my fingers, slithering down the rest of my body until they covered me in a thick mass. On my command, they catapulted at the shifter. Arms spreading, I wrapped my magic around its colossal body, twisting and turning the shadows until they had the shifter trapped in their grasp.

The bear roared and thrashed, but my hold was too strong now. I squeezed the shadows, tightening the prison they created until I could see the bear's eyes bulge from the pressure. It opened its mouth, but no sound came out, only a light breath leaving its body. The thrashing slowed until the bear was lifeless in the hold of my magic, and I could finally hear my own heavy breathing. Everything went still. The air thinned out around me, and I reeled the shadows back into myself, releasing the body of the shifter to fall to the ground.

Without looking back, I closed the distance between myself and the bear, reaching down to pull the dagger out of its thigh. My arm strained as I slammed the tip into its chest, twisting it for good measure when it reached the heart. My eyes scanned the driveway until I saw the amber crystal lying at the edge of the fountain. Snatching it up, I hurried back to the shifter and placed it on its forehead. Magic soared within me, slashing through my veins and into the crystal. In one swoop motion, I pulled the dagger from the bear's chest, grabbed the crystal, and jumped back.

"Finally," I choked out when the shifter's body began its return to original form.

I turned back, not willing to see who it was. River and Silas did not follow suit. Their eyes widened and a gasp left Silas' mouth as the shifter transitioned back to a man. The sound of bones cracking filled the driveway and soon, I heard the familiar whoosh of ash blowing off in the wind. The shifter had been vanquished.

"Wha... How..." Silas tried to form words, but nothing made sense. This was the first time I've ever seen the man stumble, and it unnerved me. Silas saw something he shouldn't have and now, we had to clean up this mess.

"Silas, listen," I whispered, but my eyes were on River. He knew what to do. "I'll explain everything."

"Hey, man," River said from behind Silas. "Come sit."

As Silas turned to face him, River was one step ahead. His fist met the man's nose, and I heard a crunch as River's knuckles connected with bone. Silas' body went limp, and I jumped behind him before he could faceplant on the ground. I carefully lowered him, then looked back to River. "He's out cold."

"Still got it," River joked, but I could hear his voice tremble. He didn't like hurting Silas any more than I liked watching it, but we didn't have a choice. No one could know about the shadowers or my magic. I had to spell him to forget, and it was easier to do if he wasn't conscious.

"What happened to Silas?" Peyton asked, limping over to us. "Did the shifter get him?"

I ran to my friend, pulling her into the tightest hug and

dangling her in my arms like a ragdoll. "Don't you ever do that again! You could have been killed!"

"Please," she scoffed, "that thing had nothing on me. But seriously, what's with the butler?"

"River had to clock him. I need to erase his memories of tonight and we'll need to make up a story about why his nose is broken."

"Holy Batman!" Peyton yelped and punched River on the shoulder. "That's some serious punching."

River's gaze dropped. "Thanks? I think..." He walked over, raising my arm in front of him to inspect it. "What about this?"

"I'll heal. It barely hurts anymore," I said.

That was a lie. It hurt like a mother, but I didn't want to worry him further, so I forced a smile and yanked my arm back, ignoring the sharp pain the motion sent all the way down my side.

"Let's get him back to the guest house. I have everything there I need for the spell. At least Thomas and Imala are out cold by now, so we don't have to worry about them."

As the three of us tiptoed through the house with Silas in between us, I had a distinct feeling that what happened tonight was not a random attack. Peyton said the shifters in the resistance wanted me dead. It was no coincidence this big bastard showed up tonight. Something was going on, something that wouldn't end well for anybody and there was one thing I knew for sure. Everyone around me was in danger.

Chapter Six

An anointing of brown jasper and mugwort oil mixed with my magic was all it took to delete any memory of the night from Silas' mind. The trouble with a memory altering spell was that it was strong as heck and knocked the victim out for a solid few hours. Which was why I now had a snoring butler passed out on the small couch of the guest house. He scrunched his nose and let out another loud groan and I grimaced, turning to face River. "This is a disaster."

Sharp, green eyes met mine and I shook off the indecent thoughts that rushed to the surface. Not now, brain.

"You want a pop?" he asked, grinning as he cut across the room to the kitchenette.

Before I could respond, an ice-cold metal can flew at my face. I caught it, barely, and popped the lid. The cool liquid felt amazing, and I was starting to relax when my gaze caught Peyton's awkward face.

"What?" I asked, with more bite than I intended.

My best friend's face hid nothing away as she looked over at Silas. "I feel bad for him. It's a lot to find out."

"He won't remember it," I said. "It'll be like it never happened."

"Maybe that's even worse."

The three of us stayed silent for a few moments, and I wondered if Peyton was right. Maybe I should have let Silas keep his memories? I mean, yeah, shifters were crazy scary, but someone messing with your memories wasn't much better. If I thought about it, I was just as bad as the mind reapers I couldn't stand. Taking his memories was a no-brainer, but that didn't make it hurt any less. It wasn't my choice to make. At least, it shouldn't have been.

Something vibrated in my back pocket and I jumped from the armrest in surprise. Everyone's eyes snapped to me, and I smiled, waving my cellphone in the air to let them know it was just a phone call.

My eyes narrowed on the caller ID and I grimaced. "Shit!"

"What is it?" River asked, already crossing back to me.

"High Coven," I whispered. "I gotta take this. Can you keep an eye out on Silas?"

He nodded and I jogged into my bedroom, locking the door behind me. My fingers fumbled over the keys, and I nearly dropped the phone twice before answering. "Hello?"

"Hello, Wilhemina," Sebyl's icy tone sounded on the other end. "I hope this isn't a bad time."

"Uh..." My mind flashed back to Silas' limp body on the couch. "No, not at all. Is everything all right?"

"Yes, yes. Everything is fine here. I'm only calling to check in since we haven't heard from you in a few days."

Of course. Of course, she had to check in. I promised the High Coven that staying in Shadowhurst meant I would not keep them in the dark again, which apparently meant calling every other day. If I knew they would keep such a short leash on me, I might have reconsidered the entire thing altogether.

Not that I didn't want to talk to them. Quite the opposite, really. Despite their frustrating insistence on keeping things from me I felt I should know about, I loved my coven mates. They had been a part of my life for so long that I didn't know how to be me without them, and I had to admit, hearing Sebyl's voice, cold as it was, left me with a hole in my heart. Even with River and Peyton by my side, I missed the witches. There were no others like me in Shadowhurst, at least none I knew of, and my kind always functioned best as part of a team. We required the energy from one another like air to breathe. It strengthened us and our magic in a way nothing else could. It gave us a center and having mine so far away weakened me in ways I wasn't prepared for. I could feel it every time I used my magic. My energy depleted so much faster in Shadowhurst without the coven's power to back me up. Though, that could have been the lack of resources I had to pull from. The Crystal Cauldron, Shadowhurst's only occult shop, had an abundance of items for me to use, but the supplies were not nearly as strong as the ones in the High Coven's possession.

Maybe it was time for a visit to replenish.

"Wilhemina?" Sebyl asked, concern coating her words.

I shook my thoughts away and dropped to the edge of my bed, pressing the phone tighter to my ear. "Yeah, sorry. I'm here. All is good on my end. Nothing to report yet."

"Hmm..." Sebyl sighed. "I would think after all these weeks, you would have gotten some lead on the hunters."

"Me too," I lied, "but they're keeping it low key. I'm pretty sure the incident with Evanora didn't go unnoticed. I need more time."

"Not too much time, I hope."

"What's wrong, Sebyl?"

On the other end of the line, the high priestess breathed heavily. "Nothing to worry about, darling. Mira's daughter reached coven age last week, and we're initiating her tomorrow night at the new moon. Rhiamon was hoping you would be here for it."

My heart ached for the fierce high priestess. Rhiamon was always a favorite of mine, and I hated not being there to stand next to her during the initiation. When a young witch reached the age of nine, she was welcomed into the coven as a witch in training. It was a beautiful ceremony where every witch under the High Coven's ruling joined their magic to initiate the new member. I always loved the ritual, ever since my own took place and I insisted on being a part of every ceremony following. It was the only time I felt the full magic of my coven mates, and nothing compared to that sense of security. Being with River was a close second, but even his sexy abs couldn't take the place of that much power coursing through my veins.

"Me too," I whispered. "I'll be there for the next one, I promise."

The line grew silent, and I checked the screen to make sure Sebyl was still there. "Sebyl, can I ask you something?" I asked when I heard her breathing.

"What is it?"

"What happened to Evanora? After the coven took her."

Knots twisted in my stomach just asking, but I made a promise to River to find out whatever I could about his mother. He was still conflicted over her arrest. Not that I could blame him. I continued to love Beatrix long after she was imprisoned, so I understood his point of view here. No matter how much of an asshole his mother was, he had to love her just the same. She would always be his mom in the end.

"All you need to know is that the rogue witch is securely held in the prison. There is no reason for you to worry over it," Sebyl said. Her words had a finality to them, and I knew not to press further. The high priestesses made it very clear that there was information they refused to share with me, and it made no difference how many times I asked, I would undoubtedly hit a dead end. It pissed me the hell off.

"But you'll let me know if something happens with her, right?"

There was another lengthy pause on the line. "I must go now, Wilhemina. The coven requires my attention."

That's a hard 'no' then.

"Okay," I said, annoyed. "Tell Rhiamon I'll call her soon."

Sebyl did not bother saying good bye and the phone died in my hands. I tossed it to the side, letting out a frustrated groan before hanging my head in my hands. The high priestesses were aggravating me to no small extent, but that wasn't what was bothering me, and it wasn't what was twisting me up inside. Talking to Sebyl reminded me of my duty to the witches in Stamwick, the ones that stood by me for so many years. Yet here I was, considering betraying them by meeting the leaders of the resistance that gunned to have them dead. It wasn't right and I couldn't do it. I wouldn't. I had to tell Peyton it wasn't happening.

With determined steps, I made my way back to the living room where Silas still snored like a broken tractor.

"Anything?" River asked as soon as I walked in.

I knew what he was asking. He wanted to know if I had some information on Evanora and my chest hurt just thinking about letting him down. I shook my head and tried to give him a reassuring smile but failed miserably. I seriously needed to stop scowling so much. *Like, who are you?*

Without pause, I crossed the room to face Peyton. "Hey," I said, placing a hand on her shoulder and squeezing it lightly. "I don't think I can meet the leaders. It doesn't feel right."

Her face dropped and I could sense her disappointment as though it was my own. My best friend was not happy with my decision, but she'd have to deal with it. There was no logical reason why I should go through with it.

"Babe?" River coughed out.

I turned to him, noticing the uncomfortable glimmer of nerves in his eyes. "For the love of the fae, what is it now?"

"Nothing, calm down." He smiled and I was instantly at ease. My shoulders dropped and when he came to stand by me, I turned to liquid from his body heat. "We've been talking while you were on the call, and I think I changed my mind. You should go."

My eyes popped out of my head, and I took in a sharp breath. "Wait, what?"

"This resistance is nothing to scoff at. We think if you don't go, they might retaliate."

"Retaliate how?"

"I'm worried they might come after Peyton's family."

My eyes snapped to my best friend. "You think they'd do that? Hurt them?"

"I don't know what they could do," she answered as calmly as she could, but I could hear the sobs building in her voice. "I can't risk it. They would outnumber my parents, and what about Kai? He's only three! You gotta help me out here, B. Please!"

As if on cue, Silas mumbled something in his sleep, and we all jumped. I almost forgot he was there for a minute. Before I could move, River walked over to check on him, shooting me a quick thumbs up when he was certain the butler was fine. I breathed out and turned back to my best friend. Her eyes were dark and wet, and I wondered how she wasn't falling apart in front of me. Peyton was so much stronger than I gave her credit for, and she was holding it together way better than I would have in this situation. Granted, my only real family was locked away behind bars, but still.

"What about the High Coven?" I asked.

Peyton's hands reached for me, and she entwined her fingers in mine. "You don't have to tell them anything yet. Just meet the leaders and then we'll figure out what to do. If it doesn't work out, I promise I'll help you take them down, no matter what. I'll always have your back, B. You know that, but right now, I need you to have mine."

Well, damn me to next Thursday. How the heck was I supposed to say no to that?

A sturdy arm wrapped around me, and I sank into River's chest. His heartbeat fluttered at my back, and I closed my eyes, taking in his scent like the greedy bastard I was. "I'm coming too," he whispered. "You won't be going in alone. Ever."

As my resolve weakened, I found myself unable to speak. There were no words left at this point because no matter how much I didn't want to disappoint the High Coven, I couldn't put Peyton's family at risk. *Guess we're going into the lion's den...* I sighed. I could only hope that the leaders weren't lying, and we weren't about to walk into a trap, but if we were, I had to be prepared. And I had to make sure Peyton and River were too. It was time to power up my magic and strengthen the energy in my blood. If the resistance was up to something, I'd be ready for them. And I'd rip them to shreds if they so much as touched a hair on Peyton or River's heads. No one messed with my people.

Chapter Seven

Leaves of every color lined the sidewalk as I marched down Main Street toward the Crystal Cauldron. Fall in Shadowhurst took my breath away and despite my teeth chattering from the impending cold, I was smiling from ear to ear. Around me, patrons pushed past each other as they ducked in and out of shops, their eyes greedy for whatever it was they were looking to buy.

My feet skidded to a stop in front of the worn-out sign I've grown to love, and I zipped up my leather jacket before stepping in. As soon as the overhead bell rang out, Ms. Broussard's grey eyes were on me. Her lips spread into a smile and the twinkle in her eyes told me she was just as happy to see me as I was to be here. In the last few weeks, the Crystal Cauldron had become a second home to me, and I loved spending time in the small occult shop after school. Ms. Broussard's energy was always calm, and it balanced my manic self to perfection. I even brought River to meet her several times and was relieved with her honest approval of the hunter. For someone who aided witches that passed through the town, Ms. Broussard was fairly open-minded. Though, I was certain that she only liked him because he made me so damn happy and since she knew my mom as a child, her loyalties lay with our family. Besides, I was a walking ball of mush around River and there was no hiding it. I was pathetic.

"Billie!" Ms. Broussard yelled out and gestured me forward. "What brings you by?"

I crossed the shop, inhaling the rich scent of patchouli in the air as I walked. Each day, the Crystal Cauldron carried a unique smell, and I enjoyed the guesswork of what it could be before entering. The last time I was here, the air hung heavy with lavender and castor oil, an interesting combination that I couldn't wash off my clothes for days. I had to admit I was much happier with patchouli.

"Hi, Ms. Broussard," I said with a grin. "I need some more supplies. Something strong. I have to get a few protection shields going."

The shop owner raised an eyebrow my way and leaned in on the glass counter. "Oh? Something the matter?"

"That's one way of putting it."

Something was more than the matter. I still couldn't believe I let Peyton and River talk me into meeting the resistance leaders. It was a dumb move, but I couldn't very well back down now, not when Peyton's family might pay the price for my cowardice. Not that I was afraid of the leaders. If anything, I was eager to see who the bastards were. The problem was that based on what Peyton had told us, there were too many shadowers for me to take on alone. If things went sideways, which they almost always did in my world, I'd need the High Coven's help to get rid of them. Calling the witches was the right thing to do and I probably should have already done that but there was too much risk with getting them involved. It could put Peyton and River on their radar, which wasn't something I was willing to overlook. Until I knew how to hide them from the High Coven, I couldn't get the witches involved.

What was it the humans say about times like this? Caught between a rock and a hard place? Well, at this point, I could feel the rock press against my chest and the hard place was all but crushing me whole. Absolute damn disaster.

Across from me, Ms. Broussard jingled the rows of bracelets on her arm, drawing my attention back to the shop. "Billie, be a dear and flip the open sign," she instructed. "I have a feeling we'll need some tea for this conversation."

Fifteen minutes later and we were sprawled on Ms. Broussard's soft couch with steaming mugs of chamomile tea in our hands. I breathed in the scent, my shoulders dropping as its potent notes reached the rear of my throat.

"Thank you for this," I whispered and raised a glass. "I am in serious need of chill time."

"So, tell me what it is you feel you need protection from?"

I bit my lower lip, considering lying for a second. While I trusted Ms. Broussard wholeheartedly, there were still walls around me that would take time to knock down, walls that took me years to construct. No matter how much better I got at talking about my feelings or asking for help, I was still always one foot out the door. Which wasn't so bad, really. All that meant was that I'd be the first one out if shit hit the fan.

"I told Peyton I'd meet the shadower resistance," I finally bit out.

"Interesting..."

Ms. Broussard's face twisted, and a scowl formed on her face. I had already revealed to her what we knew of the shadower resistance as soon as we found out about it from Peyton, so it was no surprise to her to know I was toying with the idea of meeting them. In fact, the reason I was most worried about going was because of her warnings. The shadowers were a scary bunch and the shop owner feared I'd be unprepared with only Peyton as a backup. She wasn't wrong. My best friend was capable AF, but I doubted she could do much if the shadowers outnumbered us.

Taking another sip of tea, I leaned back into the sofa. "I don't think I have much of a choice."

"There is always a choice, Billie," the shop owner whispered.

"Not this time. If I don't go, they could hurt Peyton's family."

"If you go, they could hurt you both."

"Three of us, actually," I corrected her. "River's coming too."

A smile formed on the shop owner's lips. "I always liked that one. He seems to have taken quite a liking to you."

Blood rushed to my cheeks, and I glued my eyes to my waist to fight the embarrassment. Suddenly, the folds on my leggings were the most interesting thing in the world.

"I see the feeling is mutual," Ms. Broussard added. *Relentless.*

"For the love of fae, we're just dating. It's not a big deal."

"A witch and a hunter dating is an enormous deal, dear. You two must be careful. You never know what the High Coven will do if they found out. I'm certain you've come to understand that from what you learned of Evanora's past."

I really freaking did. The High Coven didn't think twice about making River's mom vanquish her shapeshifter lover when they found out she was pregnant with River. It was a brutal move and one that, a few months back, I would have no problem with. These days, my loyalties to the coven wavered almost hourly and I was no longer convinced that their viewpoints on the shadowers were the absolute truth. Not after meeting Peyton or finding out River was part shadower himself. The boy was the kindest person I've met and the thought of someone wanting to vanquish him made my blood boil. Even if it was the High Coven that deemed it so.

"That's one more reason I have to meet the leaders. I need to contain this situation before it gets back to the coven, and they make their way here. We can't have an all-out war in Shadowhurst, not when other people could get hurt."

"Not when River could get hurt, you mean?"

She smiled and the red spread across my cheeks. "Yep. I can't risk it. He..." I collected myself. "He's become important to me." *That's putting it mildly.*

The shop owner raised herself off the couch and reached for the small alabaster kettle on the coffee table. With a satisfied grin, she refilled her cup before lowering back down to face me. The creases in her brow deepened and they threw me for a loop. Ms. Broussard had a smooth, caramel exterior that was surprisingly young for someone her age, and if she was frowning enough for wrinkles to show, I had best be worried.

"The high priestesses can never find out about you two or else all hell will break loose," she said. "Just ask your mother."

No shit, I thought and fought the urge to roll my eyes. Beatrix managed to get herself locked up in the magical prison for using magic in front of a human, so I had no doubt my fate would be much worse if the coven found out about my extracurricular activities with a witch hunter. Although, I still wasn't sure that unlawful magic use was the reason they took her away in the first place. Something about what she said when I visited her in prison had been gnawing at the back of my mind for weeks. *Is that what they told you I did?* Her words rang through me each night when I closed my eyes, and I vowed to look into her arrest when I had some time to spare. The High Coven spun the truth whichever way they deemed fit to protect the witches, so there was a good chance they lied about Beatrix as well. I knew they did so to protect me, but I wasn't a child anymore, and if there was something to Beatrix's claims, I would find it. It was mine to know by right.

"So, this protection shield," Ms. Broussard said when I haven't spoken for a few solid minutes. "What are you thinking?"

"I'm thinking I'll need some black candles and a shit ton of burdock root. I'll need some malachite too."

The shop owner nodded and crossed her arms over her chest. "I can get those for you. I believe I have some malachite in the back, but the rest should be up front. Take what you need."

"You must let me pay you this time," I begged. "I can't keep taking stuff for free. I feel like a leech."

"Nonsense!" she exclaimed. "Trust me, the humans buy plenty enough for me to keep the shop going, and I'm happy to part with a few things to keep you safe."

"Well, at least let me come by here on the weekends and help out. I insist."

Her lips curled and she reached over to pat my shoulder. To my surprise, I didn't pull away from her. It was shocking how much a few weeks could do to change my outlook on people. Now, when someone tried to touch me, my first instinct was almost never to knock their teeth in. Almost.

"I'd like that," Ms. Broussard said. "You're welcome by any time, Billie."

Somehow, despite everything I've been through, I believed her. I was welcome here in the Crystal Cauldron, in Shadowhurst, amongst all my new friends. I've never felt welcome at Stamwick, not even in the coven. The witches had my back, this I was sure of, but there was always some invisible shield that prevented me from getting close to them and I could never understand it. Leave it to me to finally feel welcome in a witch burning town out of all places.

My phone buzzed and I snatched it up, eyes narrowing as I read the message that popped on the screen. Pressure built at my temples and even the strongest lavender tea could not relax me at that moment. I reread the text, hoping I made a mistake, but there was no error on my part. Company was on its way, and I dreaded the moment it would arrive.

Life couldn't just let me be happy for one freaking second, could it?

Chapter Eight

s soon as I got the message that Rhiamon and Luna were coming to visit, my insides twisted. I've always been jumpy around the high priestesses, even before all the secrets I collected, but now, my nerves amplified by a million. They had shown extra interest in Shadowhurst recently, and it only made me more anxious. Junior witches didn't keep things from the higher ranks and here I was, hiding away an entire world from them. This couldn't end well.

Hoping to alleviate the pressure, I convinced the high priestesses to meet me for lunch at the Handsome Devil, a local restaurant that was all the rage around these parts. Peyton told me the joint had the best steaks in the country and I couldn't wait to dig my teeth into a medium-rare bite of Heaven. If the high priestesses insisted on keeping a close eye on me while I was here, they may as well front for the bill.

My mouth was salivating as I sat on the small patio in the restaurant's front and read over the menu. It was a surprisingly extensive selection and my greedy stomach teeter tottered between items, growling louder each time I read over the ingredients.

I was still fighting the urge to order a meal before my company arrived when the familiar tingle of magic alerted my senses.

There was no need to turn around, I could sense the high priestess with my back turned to the entrance, and my eyes glued shut.

Around me, people gawked and whispered as the two women walked in. Even without their ability to sense magic as I did, the humans in Shadowhurst knew strangers when they saw them, and Rhiamon and Luna stood out like sore thumbs in a quaint town such as this. I turned to follow the stares of the townspeople, my jaw hitting the floor at the sight of the women. As always, Rhiamon was decked out head to toe in leather with an exposed midriff showing off her smooth, dark skin unabashedly. The tightly woven braids of her long hair hung down her back, out of the way enough to showcase the thick, crystal-encrusted choker she wore daily. As I thought back, I realized I had never seen the high priestess without it, and I wondered if she slept with it on. I had the notion to ask Luna about it, but whatever relationship the two women had, it wasn't openly discussed, and I didn't want to overstep. Still, that choker was a nuisance, and I had no clue how Rhiamon managed not to topple over with it on. I'd have eaten pavement already from the hefty weight.

Beside her, Luna's flowing, red lace dress dragged the floor-boards, and the obnoxious jingle of the bells that adorned the hem filled the restaurant. The priestess loved her bells. Something to do with her role as a seer and the connection the sound had to the other world. I never understood it, so for the most part, I left it alone. To be honest, I left Luna alone too because her mystical mumbo jumbo annoyed the crap out of me. Unlike

Rhiamon, Luna was soft and not at all built for battle. Her limbs were thin and long and despite her short height, she looked like a gazelle as she floated to the patio. I noticed a few men turn their gazes toward her as she passed, their eyes locking on the intense stare of her violet eyes. Luna, of course, was oblivious to their stares. Instead, her face was blank and though I couldn't be sure, I had a pretty good feeling she was reading the patrons of the restaurant as she passed them. *Sly, little witch.*

The high priestesses approached me, and I squared my shoulders. "Rhi! Luna!" I yelled out, false excitement in my voice. "So glad you finally made it!"

They exchanged looks and hesitantly sat at the chairs opposite mine. The scent of the herbs tucked into their clothing invaded my senses, and I clutched the side of the table to keep steady. Goddess, how I missed the potent strength of the elements the coven wielded.

"This is an interesting choice," Rhiamon noted.

"You'll love it," I said. "Best steaks in town!"

In front of me, Luna winced, and I immediately felt like an idiot for not thinking of her restrictive dietary choices. Luna was a strict vegan and turned her nose at everyone who refused to take on the lifestyle. *Whatever, I want steak. Deal with it.*

"They have a plant-based selection too," I said, and Luna's shoulders relaxed. "It's good, trust me."

I could almost laugh at my own words. Trusting me was the last thing the high priestesses should be doing.

Before I could spew more nonsense, Rhiamon snatched a menu off the table and the two eyed the items before making their selections. "Excuse me?" Rhiamon said loud enough for a nearby waiter to hear. "We're ready to order."

I rolled my eyes and grinned apologetically at the young

man stuck waiting our table. The poor kid had no clue what he was getting into with these two.

A few tedious and awkward moments later and we placed our food and drinks order with the waiter. I waited a few seconds to give him time to leave before speaking. You never knew who was around these days, and I had no intention of discussing coven matters in front of humans.

"Not that I'm not glad to see you," I lied, "but why the surprise visit?"

Luna shifted her weight, burrowing her sharp eyes my way, and I swear I shrunk in size just a little. "Goddess, Wilhemina. Can we not simply have come to see you?"

"Yes, definitely." I blushed. "Sorry, I'm a little jumpy here. Eager to get it all over with and come home."

Man, I was turning into a skilled little actress. Even I believed the crap I was laying down.

"We miss you too, Billie," Rhiamon said sweetly. "And we think we have a way for that to happen sooner rather than later."

Here we go. I knew there was a reason for them being here. There always were ulterior motives with the high priestesses. I peeled my eyes from the table to look at her. "And how's that?"

"I have foreseen something of interest," Luna said, her attention still on me. "An uncertain future in your path. A dark future."

My face paled and I choked back a gasp. *Damn it! Can she feel the shadows that riled beneath my skin? Is that what she's seeing?* My throat burned and blood rushed to the surface of my skin as a panic set in. Deep inside, the shadows rocked in the base of my stomach, and I fought the need to let them loose. It was becoming increasingly difficult to control them, and I hated walking around like a ticking time bomb, ready to go off. No matter what I tried, they dug their way through me, altering the DNA of my magic to fit their form. It was uncomfortable, to say the least, and it drove me insane on most days. Today, it drove me absolutely bat shit crazy. Hiding the shadows from humans was one thing, but hiding them from the most powerful witches on Earth was quite another. It was a task I wasn't sure I would succeed in. I really needed to figure them out one of these days, though that was looking like an impossible task. The only thing I knew was that they were somehow connected to the ring my father left me and according to Beatrix, I was never to go looking for the man. My mother's words were worth about as much as a penny at auction, but it was all I had to go by. So basically, a dead end.

"What kind of dark future?" I finally choked out. "Something I should worry about?"

"That remains unknown," Luna cooed.

Excellent. More vagueness. Love it.

"But it worried you enough to come here?"

"Actually," Rhiamon interjected, "no. We're here on another matter. One that we believe will work well to get you out of this... situation faster."

I arched an eyebrow her way. "Oh?"

A cool wind blew past us, tousling my hair in its embrace. The high priestesses grimaced as though it burnt their skin before looking to each other again. I was tired of the silent conversations they seemed to have and had no doubt I was about to get slapped in the face with another set of news I was unprepared to hear.

"The coven has learned of a shadower resistance here in Shadowhurst. One we need you to handle immediately."

Shit, shit, SHIT!

"Huh..." I said as calmly as I could manage. "How?"

Rhiamon reached over the table and took hold of my unsteady hands. She smelled of old leather and I couldn't help but suck her in, my senses going into overdrive. Something about the scent jogged a memory, but no matter how hard I tried, I couldn't bring it into focus. *Interesting.* I'd need to look into that later.

The high priestess's hold intensified, and I tried to pull away, but she was much too strong for my feeble attempts. "The High Coven requires you to narrow down the location of the resistance and eliminate the threat. Taking out the leaders should suffice, and we do not believe it will be a hard task to accomplish."

"It sounds like a damn well impossible task to me." I shook and while on the outside, my behavior could have read as anger, I was all nerves and fear at this point. Did they know that I had already planned to meet the resistance leaders and was this just a ploy to see how far I can burrow into my own lying mess? How much have they found out already?

Luna's hand dragged over the plaid tablecloth and she pressed it to my shoulder. The touch, though seemingly innocent, send shivers down my spine and I willed my body to stay in place. Every instinct told me to run, but I forced myself to breathe, pushing the shadows that loomed at the surface further down.

"If you cannot take on the task, we are more than happy to send some head witches here in your place..."

"NO!" I yelped, shaking my head. "No need for that. I can do it."

Rhiamon forced a smile and let go of my hands. "Wonderful, Billie. I must say, I am impressed with the skill you've been showing lately. You are well on your way to your next initiation. I couldn't be prouder."

Next to her, Luna nodded, though there was not one hint of a smile on her face. "Very proud, indeed."

It took everything I had in me not to gag. Not that long ago, being this close to initiation into the head witch circle would have been my greatest joy. Which was no surprise. Every junior witch wanted to be elevated to that status, and some even fought tooth and nail for it. Becoming a head witch was the next step after training as a witch and most did not live up to the task. It required a lot of magic, the type that could undo you if you wielded it too often. Head witches were the strongest witches in the coven, with the exception of the high priestesses, of course. Though, most did not make it far up enough the chain to be considered for the pristine position. A high priestess was chosen by a full coven vote, and only the most powerful were awarded the title. Being a head witch was honorary enough. It was something I dreamed of ever since Beatrix disappeared and the High Coven took me under its wing.

Today, however, it was far from what I wanted. Not until I got my hands on the secrets the coven was keeping from me and the other junior witches. I would not follow them blindly any longer, even if they *were* my kind. Inside, I could feel the shadows squirm. They agreed.

The rest of the meal passed in a blur ,and I couldn't remember anything else discussed. Something about the new witches in the coven and Luna's moon cycle readings. In earnest, I had no interest in anything the priestesses said after they dropped their request on me. The High Coven knew of the resistance, which only meant one thing for me and my friends. We were running out of time.

It also meant something else, something that tore me apart as I lamely chewed on the perfect cut of steak on my plate. They expected me to kill the leaders of the resistance. The coven wanted me to betray my best friend's wishes to keep the peace, and I could not think of a single way to get out of it.

Chapter Nine

"I don't understand why they keep pushing you into this? Aren't they powerful witches? Why do they keep dumping things on you like you're some sort of solider for their army?"

River's face was red, and his anger filled the guesthouse to the brim. His green eyes were darker than wilted leaves, and his pristine jaw jutted out as he ground his teeth against each other. As much as I loved his concern, even agreed with him a little, getting pissed right now was not helping one bit. Disobeying the High Coven would only raise eyebrows, and I was determined to keep them out of my business for as long as possible.

"Babe," I said in the softest voice I could manage, but the words burst through me in a growl. "I don't have a choice here. We both know why."

River scooted over on the couch to lean into me. "If you're doing this to keep the coven out of my face, you can forget about it. I'm not putting you in danger to save my own ass."

Fool. Hot, adorable fool.

"It's not just to save your ass so you can get over yourself, hunter." I smiled. "It's Peyton's ass too, if you have forgotten. Not to mention her family and our other friends. They're all in trouble if the priestesses get wind of what's going on in Shadowhurst. And we still don't know what their reasons are for anything. I want to trust their judgment here."

"Well, I don't trust them one bit."

His words cut me like a knife, and I shifted my weight to put some distance between us. It was hard to get mad at River when he was like this, but I wasn't about to cave just because some hot guy flashed his pearly whites my way. Even if that hot guy was my boyfriend. Or whatever he was. We never discussed the terms of our relationship and though I knew River had no intention of dating anyone else, I assumed something like this had to be talked about. Sealed in a blood ritual, or whatever. What the hell did I know? My experience with men had been limited to make out sessions in dark parking lots and the occasional coffee date. As Peyton put it so eloquently, I was an emotional virgin. I hated that she had a point.

"Can you at least trust *me* then?" I demanded.

The icy air between us disappeared and I was in his arms in seconds. My chin rested on his wide shoulder and the heat rolling off his chest suffocated me as I breathed him in. An overpowering aroma of musk filled my nostrils and I relaxed under his hold; the hunter was many things, but it was his innate ability to disarm me that bothered me most. I was weak around him. A puddle at his stupid feet and it confused me to no small extent.

River's lips brushed against my ear, and I argued the urge to groan into his neck. "You're the only one I trust anymore," he whispered. "And the only one I worry about constantly."

"That's not fair," I bit out and pushed away from him. "I can't do what I'm expected to do if I'm trying to play it safe."

"You're not expected to do anything. I wish you'd see that."

I grimaced. "They're my people. Nothing there has changed."

Darkness spread over his features and my heart jumped into my throat. Not long ago, I thought the shade that often coated River's eyes was some mysterious sexy move he played to get a rise out of me. These days, I knew better. His shadower blood was crawling to the surface, more so each day, and it terrified me. Not because I was a witch and raised to rid the world of his kind, but because he had shapeshifter blood coursing through his veins. Shifters were unpredictable and prone to letting their animal instincts take over their logic. They were hard and arrogant and the opposite of everything River was to me. As a fun little bonus, they mated for life and not by choice. A shifter's mate was determined solely by their energies, and once it kicked in, there was no escape. What if River's shadower side overtook him and he found his true mate in someone that wasn't me? Was I prepared to let him go? The thought of him holding a slutty shifter like he was holding me right now was enough to make me want to retch right there on the couch, and I fought the bile that rose in my throat as I pictured it. I'd vanquish anyone that laid hands on him, no questions asked.

"You there, babe?" he asked, and I jerked my attention back to him.

"Yeah, sorry. You were saying?"

He brushed a hair off my face, letting the tip of his finger trail along my collarbone. "I said that I'm your people now. Me, Peyton, and the hunters. No matter what the coven decides, we have your back."

"HA!" I cackled. "Can't picture Savannah having my back."

"She will if I ask her too."

Just like that, my guard was up again. Savannah has been

getting annoyingly close to River ever since we told the group about us, and it drove me wild. That chick had to learn to keep her hands to herself before she got them magically removed. Not that I could do that, but still, it didn't hurt to dream. *You're acting like a child, get a hold of yourself.* I pressed my palm to his chest and nudged him back. "What's going on with her? She's all over you all the time."

"You jealous?" He winked.

"You wish."

"I kinda do. You're hot when you're pissed."

"No one is hot when they're jealous," I sniped. "It's stupid."

A powerful hand gripped my neck and River pulled me in. His lips were on me before I could object, not that I would, and I moaned against them, sending his desire into overdrive. His hands squeezed my hips, and I wriggled under his body to press us closer together. River's lips left mine and I missed their softness, relieved only when they landed on the slight curve on my neck. His teeth grazed my skin and shivers spread down my thighs as my need for him exploded. I pulled back the soft curls of his hair, bringing his lips back to mine, my tongue brushing against his.

River let out a low growl and I let myself melt into him. My legs weakened and when he flipped us over to lay between them, I was nothing but a marionette, moved and rearranged by invisible strings only he had hold of. River moved against me, and I threw my head back, eyes rolling to the back of my skull as I struggled with myself to not rip his shorts off. Every inch of my body screamed his name, and I could feel the shadows respond to my excitement. They wanted him as much as I did, and I was powerless to stop it. It was as though some primal part of me got unlocked whenever we were together, and it made my head spin to think about the loss of control I allowed this guy to have over me. No one deterred me from my missions, and yet, here I was, oblivious to the rest of the world and panting like a dog on a hot summer day. River undid me, and I wondered if this is what all teenagers went through when they found someone they liked this much. Somehow, I doubted that. River and me? We were something different. Something special.

Magic pressed against my skin, reaching for him as I found his lips again and nibbled. Blood rushed to my face, and I panted as our bodies continued to rile against one another, the friction driving me insane. I took a deep breath and I tried to control the shadows that pushed to be free of the confinement my skin provided, but it was useless. They spread over my arms and legs, wrapping themselves in a cocoon that encased us both.

Above me, River pulled back, his gaze drifting over my body so slowly, I thought I might implode. His hand traveled down my chest, over the bump of my breasts, and to the edge of my tank top. As his fingers traveled under the silky fabric, my brain screamed for release. I pulled him into me but before I could bite down on those beautiful, full lips of his, something flashed in River's eyes, and I froze. His emerald eyes burned into me, and I let out a gasp as my brain registered the glow behind them. It wasn't the usual sparkle River's eyes had. This was different. Animalistic. Shifter eyes.

I pushed myself back, but River was oblivious to whatever change was rolling through his body. He pinned me down, harder and more defiant than before. I knew River would never hurt me, but my flight instinct kicked in before I could talk myself out of it. The shadows around me darkened, spreading away from my body and rushing to his. I called them back in, begged them to return, but they refused to listen. Cursing under my breath, I tried to push River off me before I accidentally hurt him, but he was too heavy, and I was too flustered to think. Before I could warn him, the shadows shot out of my hands and into his chest, pummeling him away from me with so much force, he cleared half the room and collided with the wall opposite us in a loud thud.

"What the hell, babe?" he yelled out, rubbing his neck and rolling his shoulders to straighten.

From where I was, I could see a charred mark on his white shirt where my shadows attacked him, and it broke my heart into pieces. Sticky, hot tears formed behind my lids, and I blinked them away with little success. They fell down my face, streaking my mascara until I looked like a scary clown in a horror film. All I was missing was a red balloon and a catchphrase.

I wanted to run to him. To tell him I'm sorry and that I didn't understand what had gotten into me, but my body was solid on the couch. Something in River scared the crap out of my magic, and it scared me too. "I don't know what that was," I finally choked out. "But something is wrong. With us."

"What? What are you talking about, Billie?"

I didn't answer, mostly because I did not understand how to. Our hope that River's shifter side would stay dormant was crashing all around me, and I didn't know what it would mean if he let it loose. He had no more control of his shadower side than I did of my own demons, but for the first time, I doubted I'd be strong enough to survive him if the change took hold.

Great, I thought, my eyes still trained on a dumbfounded River in front of me. *Like I don't have enough to worry about already.*

Chapter Ten

"You ready for this?"

The three of us stood before an old, beaten down house in the middle of a wooded area on the far side of town. Peyton's eyes burrowed into me as I looked over the spot that housed the shadower resistance while River clutched my hand like I was a flight risk. In a way, I supposed I was.

For a resistance, the shadowers picked an odd location to gather. Looking at the house—which was a deathtrap—it resembled more of a place a serial killer might hide bodies than a location for a growing army. The shingles on the roof were decrepit, and I was pretty certain that the lightest touch of rain might knock the entire place down. Beneath them, broken windows lined the two stories of the Victorian structure and my eyes traveled along them, trying to spot some movement behind cracked shutters. There was a wraparound porch that had seen better days, and it stretched the length of the house's rugged exterior. Even the foliage that spanned the small clearing in front had overgrown after years of abandonment.

I gave another glance to the house and turned to Peyton. "You sure this is it?"

"Yep." She sighed. "Looks like a pile of crap, huh?"

"Perfect place to hide a body," River growled.

My eyes snapped to his and I smiled. "My thoughts exactly."

I was already starting to spiral when Peyton grabbed my arm and pulled me forward. Her eyes shined with excitement, and I had to bite down my annoying huffs as we made our way to the front door. Unlike me, Peyton did not grow up with others of her kind, and I could read her eagerness to be around them clearly. In the end, she would always side with River and me, but for now, my best friend longed for others, and I wouldn't take that away.

A few shaky steps later and we faced the creepy wooden door that held the place together.

"Yo! Open up!" Peyton shouted, obviously familiar with the place. "Our awesome selves are getting bit to shit by bugs out here!"

My laugh was cut short by the opening of the door, and I fought back a gasp when I turned to see the welcoming committee. Before us, towering over the doorframe, stood two very large, very angry looking men. Their eyes were glowing in the dim fog that swallowed the porch, and they trained both sets on me. Next to me, River stepped forward, shielding me with his body, and I heard the men grumble something under their breath. One of them inched closer to River, inhaling the surrounding air before snorting back a laugh. *Shit! Are they shifters? Can they sense it on him?*

Oblivious to my panic, River squeezed my hand and shot a half-smile my way. His shoulders squared and he switched his attention to the shifters. Not letting that arrogant confidence

I've learned to love drop away. "We're here to see the leaders of your little group," he scoffed. "They're expecting us."

"They're expecting her," the first shifter retorted with a grin. One of his front teeth was missing and I noticed fresh scars along the side of his lips. Someone messed this sucker up real good, and I was certain he deserved it.

"Guys," Peyton chirped and crossed the threshold. "Meet Ashley. He's an asshole and he knows it."

The shifter she pointed to, Ashley, growled, but surprisingly did not clock Peyton in the mouth. Something about their exchange was familiar, and I wondered if my best friend had been to see these people more often than she let on. *Interesting.*

Before I could press it, Peyton gestured to the other man in the doorway. "The pasty one is Griffin. He's all right. For a shifter."

"Oh, good," Griffin bit out. "The comedian is back. Outstanding."

Despite their glares, the shifters parted way to let us pass and I swallowed audibly before following my friends inside. We walked behind Ashley and Griffin down the hallway, and it shocked me to see that the inside of the house was a much more pleasant experience than what the initial view offered. It wasn't the high-class abode of the Chandlers, nowhere close, but it certainly wasn't some rundown shack. The resistance hideaway was closer to what I was used to. Classic architecture and wide wood beams lining the walls and ceilings. As we walked, I noticed rooms span out from the hallway, each one with enormous sliding doors to hide them from view. One room was wide open, and I slowed my steps to peer inside.

Fear rushed through me when I saw a dozen shadowers huddled together over a round, mahogany table. I couldn't tell what species they were, but I knew it was a healthy mix. Shadowers didn't mix amongst each other, at least not from what I knew of them, and it blew my mind to see so many in one location. An older man whispered something to the group and the rest broke out in laughter, banging on the table to empathize their glee. *Holy crap! They're friends! This is insane.*

As though she could read my mind, Peyton nuzzled her face close to mine. "Everyone is friends here. Like a club or something," she whispered. "It's out of this world."

I didn't know how out of this world it was, but as a witch, it sure as hell was way out of my world. I peeled my eyes from the shadowers and turned back to our cocky tour guides, who had out paced us by a good ten feet.

"Better catch up," River hissed. "I don't want to be stuck here longer than we have to."

He wasn't wrong. I didn't want to be stuck here at all.

We sped up, catching up with Ashley and Griffin before they noticed us hanging back to scout. The shifters led us past a few more closed doors and rounded the corner. Their backs straightened as they paused in front of an extensive set of stairs, and I prayed to the Goddess our deaths weren't waiting at the top landing. My eyes jerked to the side where another doorway lurched in the shadows, this one differed from the rest. For starters, it was solid metal and looked like it could withstand a punch or two. It was also shut with what looked to be more than one set of locks, and the mystery behind it drew me in.

"What's in there?"

It was Griffin's turn to lay down the attitude. "Nothing for witches," he sniped and turned back to the stairs. "You can go up now."

My eyes trailed up the stairs, then landed back on River. Going up was not something either of us wanted to do. He pulled me back, wrapping his arms around me while keeping his gaze trained on the shifters.

"What's up there?" he asked.

"Relax, kid," Ashley retorted. "We don't bite our own kind."

River's shoulders tensed and I could see the remark hit him deep. Being a shadower was new to him and it was not something he wished to revisit. We barely spoke of it since his mother revealed her sordid past, and when we did, I could tell he hated thinking he might be a part of this world. I couldn't blame him, I hated it just as much.

In front of us, the shifters parted like liquid, and I wondered if they choreographed the move to intimidate those that came through this place. Joke's on them, I wasn't scared of Tweedledee and Tweedledum one bit. If anything, I was waiting for them to step out of line so I could vanquish their sorry asses.

"Cool story, bro," Peyton bit out. "Now step aside and let the grown-ups take the lead here."

My best friend's balls were literally made of stone, and I loved it.

To her left, Ashley mumbled something nasty under his breath, but one look from Peyton shut him up for good. Young as she was, Peyton was a soul sucker and the most powerful shadower species known. He was right to keep his mouth shut and his distance far. One touch and she could have him begging for his mommy and pissing his pants. Peyton seemed to know this too as she had no trouble pushing her way past the large shifter to run up the stairs.

When she reached the top, she turned to River and me and waved. "Come on! Let's get it over with."

She did not have to tell us twice.

Our bodies huddled together in an upstairs bedroom of the resistance house that left much to be desired. Even Peyton stayed close to me, and I was sure it had something to do with the powerful shadowers that crowded the space alongside us.

No one spoke and it annoyed the heck out of me.

I eyed them suspiciously, trying to decipher what their thoughts might be, but drew a blank. Unlike the other shadowers I'd encountered in my lifetime, the leaders were impossible to read, and it made me all the more wary of them. There were four of them in total. Two shifters, a mind reaper, and a soul sucker, and I didn't know which riled more fear in my gut.

The shifters, Mel and Raiden, were warriors through and through. The only parts harder on them than their muscle-stacked bodies were the glares they were throwing my way; something between fury and disappointment. Of the two of them, Mel seemed more accepting of my presence in the resistance and every so often, rubbed her partner's back to ease the tension between us. Her short purple hair was spiked into a million points that jutted out from the top of her head in a shield, and the unfair curves of her body made her seem both scary and hot at the same time. If I was a guy, I'd be confused as hell right about now. My eyes narrowed on her as she shifted her dark, golden body, revealing more of it to me as though she was on display in a storefront. Her sleeve tattoos covered most of her arms, but even with the ink, she was barely covered in the thin tank and high-cut shorts she wore.

Beside her, Raiden towered over the room and his almost seven feet tall body obliterated the small couch they sat in. He was a complete opposite to his partner, with skin as pale as moonlight and a bald head that reflected the shine from the small bulb dangling over our heads. As far as I could tell, he was an alpha male in whatever pack he ran in. Built like a fridge with glowing blue eyes. I wasn't sure what animal he was, but if I had to guess, I'd say something pretty damn big. Like, really big.

Someone cleared their throat and I turned to face Lorelei, the mind reaper that hid in the darkness of the corner next to an old writing desk. Her long auburn braid fell over her shoulder and reached down to her knee, and I calculated how long it must take her to wash it. My own hair only reached as far as my lower back and a good shampooing was the bane of my existence. I could only imagine the ritual this chick had to go through when it was time for a bath. Why even bother? I rolled my shoulders, squaring them as I looked her over. Unlike the shifters, Lorelei was tall and thinner than the models one would see on magazine covers, the unrealistic kind. She had a sharp nose and thin lips that crashed into a line, making her look perpetually upset, an attitude that was only further accentuated by her sharp, golden eyes.

As if made uncomfortable by my slack-jawed glares, Lorelei cleared her throat again and flipped the long skirts of her flowing dress to cross the room to the last resistance leader in the room. She moved like air, floating over the old parquet flooring.

When she stepped next to the soul sucker, my eyes focused on his and I nearly doubled back from their intensity. Marcus' narrow, hooded eyes bore into me, and I cringed at his attention. *Is this dude trying to figure out how fast he can kill me?* I wouldn't blame him. I've been pondering the same since I walked into the room.

He ran a large hand through his curly, long hair and patted the thick beard that adorned his aged face. Something about Marcus screamed wisdom and made him seem like the unspoken overlord of the resistance leaders. It would make sense. Anyone that wore a full piece suit on a casual afternoon meant business, and I was convinced the others saw him as someone to look up to.

"We're glad you could make it," Marcus said. He spoke softly and in such a low tone, I had to lean in to hear him. As I moved, River pulled me back, worried I'd step too close to danger. I didn't bother shaking him off. He had a point.

Marcus' dark eyes glanced at our entwined fingers, but he said nothing of the gesture. Instead, he ran his thumb over the long scar that ran down the right side of his face and raised his chin my way. "I'm sure you're as uncomfortable with this as we are."

"Doubt it," I said with a sneer. "I'm not the one who threatened you in the first place."

"Let us not forget who we are," Marcus replied. "Your kind has been threatening us for years."

I breathed out a fiery breath and ran my gaze over the other leaders. "All with reason, I'm sure."

Energy riled within me, and I felt Peyton's body lean into mine.

"You asked to see her and here she is," my best friend said with more strength than I've seen from her yet. Something about being in the resistance house changed her, made her more aware of her own power, and it frightened me to no small extent. "Why are you gunning for Billie?"

"We are not," Lorelei said. Behind her, Mel and Raiden exchanged knowing looks and I knew they were hiding something.

I pointed their way and scoffed. "Your shifters seem to disagree. From what I hear, they want me dead."

"They do not," Marcus offered. "I can vouch for it. Though, I believe others in our group do and I called you here to reassure you we do not stand by them."

"Cool story. Can we go now?"

A silent chuckle escaped Marcus and he crossed the room in seconds. His face was so close to me, I could reach out and touch it without stretching my arm at all. "The shifters in our group are uneasy with your presence in Shadowhurst. Especially considering what we're trying to do here."

"Which is what, exactly?" River asked, and I didn't fail to notice the protective stance he took when facing Marcus.

"Eliminate what I believe to be a common enemy of ours."

I must have looked baffled. Correction, I was utterly confused. The only enemy my kind had was tucked away in this house, and I couldn't think of anyone else they might be targeting that I'd want gone as well. I glanced from River to Peyton and shrugged. "And who's that?"

"The High Coven."

Laughing was likely not the best idea, but I couldn't help it. I was almost doubled over from what I assumed to be a joke when Mel left her partner's side to join Marcus next to me. "You still trust those bastards," she hissed, her animal side making an appearance. She turned to Marcus, not bothering to give me another look. "This was a mistake. She is blind to their evil and won't help us. I told you this would happen."

"Please, Mel," Marcus breathed out. "No theatrics. This is a lot to take in and we need to give her time to adjust."

My blood boiled and I could feel the shadows rile under my skin.

"If you think I will help you kill my kind, you're insane!" I yelled out. "Why the hell would I do that?"

Marcus looked down at mine and River's clutched hands. "Because I'm quite certain your latest choices would not be ones they approve of. Or do you mean to tell me the High Coven is jolly fine with your relationship with the hunter?"

Knots formed in my stomach. *The bastard has a point.*

"So what? You want me to help you kill people I care for

because they might not like who I date? You're crazy, you know that?"

I was not about to let this guy intimidate me, and I sure would not let him use River as an excuse to switch me to their pathetic side. They were the bad guys here, not me. Still, something about what he said struck a chord and I grimaced, thinking how much we truly had in common. If the High Coven found out about River and me, I'd be facing the same choice Evanora had when she had to kill his father. Would I be strong enough to fight against it or would River one day end up on the wrong side of my dagger? It wasn't something I wanted to think about, so I shook the thought of, frowning as it left my mind.

Sensing my turmoil, River rubbed circles on the inside of my palm, and I let myself relax into him. I was sick and tired of people twisting me in the direction they wanted me to go. The High Coven has done enough of that for most of my life, and it would be a frosty day in Hell when I let some filthy shadowers do the same.

"Your precious coven lies," Lorelei hissed.

"Nothing new there," Raiden added, his voice booming over the others.

A very big beast, indeed.

"So do you," I bit out, refusing to back down.

A light wind blew through the half-open shutters of the only window in the room, rattling the lightbulb over our heads. Its light shimmered across the faces of the leaders, and their menacing glares seemed to relax before me. Something glistened on Marcus' chest, and I tore my gaze from the shifter male to look at it. It wasn't anything special, a gold crescent moon pendant that hung from a ratted leather cord around his neck, but something about it gave me pause. I fought against my racing thoughts as they tried to form a connection. The pendant meant something to me, something I tried to remember but couldn't. *For the love of fae, what is happening here?*

"We understand this isn't standard behavior," Marcus said, forcing me to look at him. "But we believe you will come to see our side in this, and I can personally guarantee those who do not agree will not be a problem for you. We can handle our own people."

I didn't doubt that, not in the slightest. The resistance leaders held some power over the remainder of the shadowers in the house, and I noticed it as soon as we walked in. No one stepped out of line here without answering to them, that I was sure of. And somehow, they held that power over me too. Ever since we walked through the front door, my first instinct had not been to run. It was almost as though I felt I belonged here. Maybe it was because of the secrets I had kept from the coven, or perhaps the shadows I had growing inside me. Whatever it was, I felt a connection to the resistance that I didn't like.

There wasn't much time for me to dissect the issue when a loud bang sounded downstairs.

Before I could ask what happened, Ashley burst through the doors, a panic over his features. In an instant, River filled the space between me and the shifter, his wide shoulders hiding me from view.

"What the hell was that?" he asked. "What happened?"

The shifter didn't acknowledge his question. Instead, he moved around him, clocking his shoulder as he passed to get close to Marcus and the other leaders. "There is a disturbance in the ranks. The shifters got wind that the witch is here. They're not happy about it."

"Idiots," Peyton mumbled under her breath.

"Second that," I whispered.

I reached for the dagger in my boot when Marcus' hand

gripped my arm. His eyes told me to pause, and I pulled my hand back against my better judgment.

"Leave," he said coolly, "now. Go through the window. There's a small landing on the other side. You should be able to jump without injuring yourself."

He stepped aside to let us through, but my body stayed still. I wasn't about to back out of a fight, and if there was a chance to teach the shifters that wanted me dead a lesson. I would take it.

"If you want her to live," Raiden hissed at River, "get her out of here."

I didn't have time to object. My arm jerked as River tugged me to the window, Peyton on his heels. I tried to fight against him, but he was too strong, and his grip was unyielding. His eyes met mine and I saw the green in them darken as his shifter blood came out to play. River wasn't budging and I knew better than to argue when I had no leg to stand on.

He gave me another tug and gritted his teeth. "This is not the time for a fight. Let's go."

One more tug and I was being pulled through the window. Frigid air hit my face and my hair flew behind me as we piled onto the wide sill to jump down. Just as Marcus instructed, there was a landing a few feet below us, breaking our fall as we landed. My knee hit the rotten wood, crashing through it with a bang. Pain rushed up my leg, but it didn't pause me. I had little time to register the sharp needles that climbed up my body when I was pulled forward again, jumping the rest of the way down.

Screams echoed in the house as we beelined for the darkened trees that surrounded the resistance house. There were growls and yelps and what sounded an awful like fists colliding with flesh. I grimaced, speeding up to keep pace with River and Peyton as we put more distance between us and the resistance. It was beginning to look that my presence was a nuisance to everyone around me and as much as I hated the shadowers, I didn't like that the simple act of me being around them caused them grief.

Am I turning into a resistance supporter? The thought dug into me, and I looked back on the house, glimpsing it once more as River dragged me away into the woods and into the darkness I knew I belonged in.

Chapter Eleven

*P*eyton's heavy breathing was impossible to ignore, and I gave her side-eye glances every few minutes as we flipped through the books on our laps. We had come to her place straight after our feeble escape from the resistance, and I called the Chandlers to let them know I'm staying for the night. Looking at Peyton crouched on her side of the bed with one of the hunter books from the library and me lying on my stomach with my grimoire spread open, I had to laugh a little. This was the weirdest girls' night I could imagine.

My best friend let out another annoyed huff and slammed the book shut.

"Still nothing?" I asked.

She shook her head. "These are even more useless than an internet search. I mean, come on! These hunters know nothing about shadowers. Like, do me and my people not register on their radar or something?"

"You're upset there's a group out there that *doesn't* want to kill you?" I asked, one eyebrow arched.

"Well, kinda. Feels rude is all I'm saying." She rummaged

through the other books on the nightstand before picking up a different volume. "This one feels lucky... Come to mama!"

There was a knock on the door and we both jumped up, tossing the books under the covers.

"Come in!" Peyton yelled out.

The door creaked open with hesitation, and Peyton's dad poked his head through the sliver of space. His thick glasses slid down his small nose and he narrowed his eyes our way, scanning the room as though making sure we didn't sneak boys in. To my disappointment, we didn't. River went home to shower and get a good night's rest and I was already missing him like crazy. I was a freaking sap, and it was disgusting. But I couldn't help it. River made me feel things no other boy had done before, not that many have tried. Every time we were together, I could tell how much he cared for me and that he would do anything to keep me safe. I never had someone on my side that way before, at least not someone that wasn't another witch. Beatrix did one hell of a number on me, and for River to be able to pull my defenses down meant a lot. More than I cared to think about.

Mr. Ling looked from me to Peyton, seemingly satisfied with our lame night in. "You girls doing all right in here?" he asked. "Your mother wanted me to check to see if you're hungry."

"Rock solid, Dad," Peyton bit out. She gestured to the untouched cold cuts on her nightstand. "We got snacks covered."

"Those are not snacks," Mr. Ling said. "Those are an early heart attack waiting to happen."

My best friend rolled a slice of chicken and tossed it in her mouth, shooting me a wink as she chewed. "Delicious... Heart... Attack..." she mumbled and swallowed.

"Just promise me you'll at least have a vegetable of some

sort. For your mom." Mr. Ling flashed us a smile and shut the door, his footsteps receding down the stairs.

"Girl," Peyton said in annoyance, "he is all over me these days. Can you say stalker?"

I laughed and punched her shoulder. "I think it's nice. At least you have parents that care."

"Sorry, B. I'm an idiot."

"It's fine. I'm used to not having Beatrix around. And the Chandlers have been awesome, I really like them."

Peyton's features brightened and she flashed her teeth at me. "That's great! More reason for you to stay!"

Dread overwhelmed me as I thought about one day leaving Shadowhurst. My place was with the coven but the idea of leaving her, River, and the Chandlers made my skin crawl. I'd even miss the hunters when I left. Well, maybe not Savannah, but the rest of them for sure. Lately, I've been thinking about it so often that I woke up in the night, sweat covering my PJs and tears staining the pillow. It wasn't something I was looking forward to and every time I pictured the day that would surely come soon enough, I broke down. Shadowhurst had become a home for me, somewhere I felt at peace, and I couldn't imagine living anywhere else. *Maybe I can visit?* I pushed away the tears that threatened to blind me, refocusing my gaze on the grimoire.

Next to me, Peyton shifted under the covers and scooted closer, her eyes following mine. "What are you looking for in that thing again?"

No clue, girl. No clue. I sighed. "I'm not sure. Something keeps dragging me back to it, but I can't make sense of it. It's like there's some memory I'm trying to pull on but every time I do, I draw a blank. Been happening for days and I was hoping the grimoire would help, but I got nada so far."

"What's River say about it?"

"...I haven't told him yet."

My best friend's eyes grew two sizes, and she dug her nails into my arm. "Trouble in paradise?"

"What? No!" I exclaimed. "I don't want to worry him. He's always so intense when it comes to me, and this will only drive him crazy."

"That's hot."

"Not if it means his shifter side kicks into gear and he tears me to pieces," I scoffed. "He's been different lately, darker somehow, and I'm scared he'll shift any day."

"He could also never shift at all and you're overreacting," Peyton offered.

I tugged my arm from her grip and forced a smile. "Let's hope you're right."

We sat in silence for a while, each one of us keeping our eyes on whatever words caught our attention in our respective books, and I let the stillness of the evening take me in. There weren't many chances where we could hang out without something popping up that needed our attention, and it was pure bliss to spend time with Peyton. Something I've never had back in Stamwick, and I was more than eager for our girls' night.

Peyton cleared her throat and I looked up to see an annoyed look on her face.

"What?"

"Nothing," she said. "We gonna talk about what happened at the resistance, or is it reading time for the rest of the night?"

I closed the grimoire, sliding it across the skull-printed cover of her bed. "What's there to talk about? They want to kill me."

"Not all of them."

"Maybe, but it's still a huge risk. And I don't enjoy going against the coven. I definitely don't want to keep lying to them. It's driving me crazy."

"'Kay, that's fair. But maybe there's a way you can get the best of both worlds here?"

My ears perked up. "Meaning what?"

"What if we found out who the shifters are that are causing all the chaos and took care of them? I got the feeling from Marcus that the leaders want them dealt with just as much as you do. So if we do this, they'd owe us."

"You seriously think someone as powerful as Marcus and the other leaders could side with us? I'm a witch, Peyton. They want all of my kind dead."

"I don't think that's what they want."

My lungs tightened in my chest, and I barely coughed out the next words. "You got that from meeting them a handful of times? They're dangerous. I don't like you going over there."

"Girl, please. First of all, it's more than a handful of times," she said. *I freaking knew it!* "Second, whatever the High Coven told you about shadowers hasn't been all that on point so far. I'm a good example of that. So are my parents. There are many who do not want it to be us against them. We just want the chance to live our lives in peace. It's not a lot to ask."

"Sounds like you agree with their plans," I bit out.

She smiled, though the gesture did nothing to placate my worries. "It's not what you're thinking. I agree with them, to an extent. But mostly, I just want to not be afraid of your coven anymore. Is that unfair?"

I shook my head and looked past her. It wasn't unfair at all. In fact, it was her damn right not to live her life in fear. Since meeting Peyton, I've come to realize that shadowers are people the same as witches are, and for my kind to vanquish them without question makes us no better than the hunters that burnt us at the stake all those years ago. Perhaps Peyton had a point, and I could separate the good from the bad within the resistance. Take out the rotten apples and help the High Coven while eliminating any danger the resistance poses to Peyton and her family. If I would be leaving Shadowhurst, I might as well make sure my friend was safe when I've gone. And I had to admit, having the leaders owe me something could prove useful if they stepped out of line in the future. Worst case scenario, if it didn't work, I could tell the High Coven where their decrepit hideaway was and call it a day.

"You might have a po—" I started to say when my phone vibrated somewhere under the covers. My hands searched blindly, pulling it out to read the text that popped on the screen.

"Who's that?"

"River," I answered.

Her eyebrows danced and she made a rude gesture with her mouth. "What's lover boy want at this hour? Let me guess, he's after your—"

I held my hand up to stop her. Whatever was about to lunge from Peyton's mouth would likely make me blush until tomorrow.

"The hunters are training tomorrow. He wants me to come with."

"Oooooooh!" Peyton jumped up on the bed, unable to hide her excitement. "I'm totally coming too. We're a package deal, B!"

A chuckle burst from me, and I slapped her thigh, knocking her back down to the mattress. *Such a little weirdo.* Somehow, I had the distinct feeling that a soul sucker and a witch were not a package anyone wanted to receive in the mail.

Chapter Twelve

The longbow kicked to the right and I stumbled over my boots, staggering to follow it. My eyes scanned the target in the distance, but, of course, the arrow was nowhere in sight. For someone who had spent almost her entire life training for battle, I sucked monkey balls with archery. Frustrated, I knocked another arrow and took my stance. This one was an even worse attempt, and the arrow flew past the target and impaled itself in a nearby tree.

Behind me, Savannah howled, her laughter echoing across the field.

I shot her a death glare and passed the bow to Jayden. "This is hopeless."

"No worries, my witchy friend," Jayden said with a smile. "You'll get it."

I somehow seriously doubted that.

Rolling my shoulders, I stomped back to the shaded spot under the trees Peyton lounged at and dropped beside her. We'd been at Savannah's family farm all morning, her parents were out of town, as usual, and my best friend was yet to join in training. She seemed content to watch, so I let her be. Far be it from me to judge anyone's lack of participation. It wasn't as though I was Miss Popular.

"Still no luck with the bow?" she asked, handing me a bottle of water.

I shook my head. "I suck at it."

"Looks like River's getting the hang of it, more or less."

She pointed down the field and my eyes snapped to River's rigid back as he let an arrow loose. It hit the target spot on, and I couldn't help but roll my eyes. *Stupid jock.* With unease, I looked to Savannah, who was already creeping toward him, a jungle cat ready to strike. Her curls bounced over her shoulders as she walked, and I grimaced with each step she neared River. My teeth chattered in anger as she reached a hand over his shoulder, twirling her fingers across the exposed skin of his arm. Savannah leaned in to whisper something in his ear and my insides exploded. Before I could stop myself, my fingers tightened over the amethyst pendant on my neck, and I reached for my magic. Glittery lights exploded in my vision as I solidified the connection and pushed my palm forward, throwing a gust of wind Savannah's way. The pressure pushed her back, knocking her away from River and straight on her ass.

Keep your hands to yourself, asshole. I shook my head and shoved my hands in my pockets before I did more damage. *Who are you even right now?*

Savannah growled, brushing off the dirt from her tennis skirt. Her eyes snapped to me, and she sneered, her glossy lips parting in anger. "Jealous much, witch?" she fumed.

"Sorry, I was aiming for the target. Missed my mark," I said. *Not really, though.*

Back on the field, River shook his head and walked over to help Savannah up, his eyes meeting mine. I could sense his disappointment from where I sat, and it did enough to make me feel like an even bigger fool. River and Savanah had been friends since childhood, so I understood the camaraderie. My behavior was uncalled for, and I needed to get my selfish feelings in check before I became *that* girl. You know, the one that doesn't trust anyone. Unfortunately, that was exactly the kind of girl I already was, Beatrix made sure of it. Still, I didn't want River to think I was some freak with a possessive streak, and if that meant making nice with Savannah, then that's what I would have to do. Even if she did make that nearly impossible. I closed my eyes and counted to ten. *Be the bigger person, be the bigger person, be the bigger person.*

When I opened them, Savannah was towering over Peyton and me, her eyes glistening in the sunlight. "No magic in training," she hissed. "I thought we made that clear?"

"Should have made it clearer," Peyton snapped.

I let out a low laugh, which only seemed to anger Savannah more.

"Someone who doesn't bother getting off her ass to train doesn't get to be snappy," she said to Peyton. "If you wanna talk a big game, you better show you're worth something."

Ladies and gentlemen, I present to you the Queen of the freaking Underworld...

I was about to lash out at her for talking to my friend that way, but to my surprise, Peyton had her own back covered. She jumped up, rising on her tiptoes to level Savannah's eyes. Her hands stretched out until her fingers were an inch away from the bimbo's throat. "We both know I could kill you before you blink, Barbie," she breathed out. "Don't mess with someone unless you're ready to bring it."

The heat of the blazing sun spread over us as Peyton's power left her body. Her slight frame vibrated, and I held back a gasp, ready to stop my friend from doing something we'd all regret later. I was on my feet in record time, inching closer to Peyton in a feeble attempt to keep her calm. It wasn't necessary. My best friend had her powers in check and from where I stood, I could see she was pushing out just enough of it to scare Savannah but not enough to hurt her. *Sly bitch.* Peyton had so much control, it was breathtaking. None of the hunters knew that she was a soul sucker, but her outburst gave Savannah pause enough to back down a little. She might not have known what Peyton truly was, but there was enough confidence in my best friend to scare her and she was right to be scared. Peyton wasn't bluffing.

In a flash, River and Jayden were at our side, their faces grim and worried.

"Sweet!" Jayden exclaimed, "Girl fight!"

All three of us turned to him, our eyes shooting daggers. He looked from one girl to the next, gaze landing on me at last. With a toothy smile, Jayden straightened his varsity jacket and took a step back, hands raised in defeat. "Easy, tiger," he purred my way. "Don't hex me or something. It's just a joke."

"You're on my list," I said teasingly.

Jayden's eyebrows arched and he licked his lips, a grin spreading over his face. "I like the sound of that..."

Ew, gross. I reached out to smack him, but River beat me to it, his hand slapping the back of Jayden's head and making him topple over. Despite the hit, Jayden continued to grin like a fool, which sent me into a whirlwind of laughter. I was still in stitches when my eyes caught River's and I swallowed hard as I registered the darkness in them. His shifter side was not happy with someone else flirting with me, and for the first time, I didn't hate seeing him this way. It balanced out the playing field and made me feel less uncomfortable about my earlier reaction to Savannah.

As if he could sense my relief, River relaxed his shoulders, the darkness in his eyes disappearing from view. They were once more the stunning green I was used to, and I could sense them drawing me in with their intensity. Ignoring Savannah, I closed the distance between us and cuddled into his side, my lips brushing against his cheek. "Truce?" I whispered out of earshot of the others.

He nodded and shot a wink my way, pressing his hand to the back of my neck to pull me closer.

Footsteps sounded behind us, and everyone turned to see Morgan emerge from the cornstalks. She bounced our way in a bubbly cloud, her frilly, floral skirt whipping in the wind behind her. Today, Morgan's hair was up in a simple ponytail with a few loose strands framing her heart-shaped face. She looked stunning and I immediately turned to Peyton, relieved when I recognized a glimmer of longing in her eyes. I'd been rooting for these two to hook up since I found out Morgan played for the other side and was glad to see Peyton take notice. Not that I was desperate to set my best friend up with someone, but I liked Morgan. More so, I liked her for Peyton, and it looked like Peyton might have liked her for Peyton too.

"How goes it?" Morgan sang when she reached us.

We all shrugged in unison.

"Billie thought it was a good idea to use magic on me 'cause she's a freaking child," Savannah growled. "Other than that, dandy."

There were no words for how desperately I wanted to knock Savannah on her ass again, but I stayed quiet. No point for more unnecessary tension, and with River's hand still on my neck, I was far from worried about the idiot. I turned to Morgan, flashing my teeth. "Glad you made it. Where's Abigail and Tyler?"

"You really need to ask?" The redhead raised one eyebrow and laughed. "So, what are we working on today?"

"Archery," Jayden said. "But personally, I'm working on getting a girl fight going."

Three hands shot out to punch his shoulder.

"Ouch!" Jayden exclaimed. "Touchy much? Hands off, ladies." He stalked off down the field without a second glance back.

Several curses followed him, plus a rock Morgan chucked his way before turning back to us. "Fun! I love the arrows. Let's play doubles. I got dibs on Peyton!"

Beside me, my best friend stiffened but didn't object. She followed Morgan to the target, glancing my way for support, and I threw her a thumbs up when no one was looking. Peyton deserved to have a little fun to get her mind off the resistance, and I swore to make it my mission to make sure she got it, whether it was with Morgan or not. Though I had to admit, it relieved me to have it be the gorgeous redhead and not some random shadower.

I started to follow them, but River's hand pulled me back. His fingers laced in mine, and he spun me around to face him, his wide chest pressing against my own. My breath quickened from the heat his body gave off and I swallowed the puddling spit in my mouth to avoid drooling. Drool was not attractive, I learned that the hard way when I first met him.

River glanced at Savannah and gestured his head to the field, urging for her to move her butt and leave us alone. She grumbled under her breath, tossed an annoyed look my way, and stomped out of sight.

That's right. Keep it moving, loser.

As I turned back to River, my magic jumped to attention. His chest rose and fell, and I could feel his heartbeat under the thin tee he wore. Bump, bump, bump. The most beautiful sound in the world as far as I was concerned. His eyes met mine and a blush spread over my neck and cheeks; I was useless when he looked at me that way, and I loved every second.

"I wanted to ask you something," he whispered.

"Uh-huh," I managed to choke out.

He pulled on my lower back, eliminating any distance left between us. "Probably should have asked before, but it's been crazy around here. I was hoping you'd be up for coming by for dinner. To meet my dad."

"...Uh-huh."

Dude! Use your words, you weirdo!

"Is that a yes?" he asked, leaning into me.

It should have been a 'no', but I couldn't do anything except nod like an idiot. River's dad was not someone I was eager to meet and considering his off-kilter view on River's extracurricular activities with the hunters, I very much doubted he'd like me one bit. But this was what normal people did when they dated, and though nothing about River and I was normal, I had to give him this. Since Evanora's imprisonment, his father was his last hope of safety, and I didn't want to be the reason for bad blood between them. I would meet his dad and I would play the part of a perfect, human girlfriend. Or friend, whatever we were. *Ugh.*

River's lips brushed against mine in a kiss that was much too quick for my liking, and we walked back to the rest of our group. I'd have to worry about meeting his dad later. Right now, all I had to concern myself with was not sending an arrow into Savannah's enormous mouth. No matter how much I wanted to hit that particular target.

Chapter Thirteen

"So, Billie," Otis said with enough bite to his words it stopped me cold. "River tells me you're new to Shadowhurst. From Stamwick."

Thus far, the dinner with River's father had been one awkward exchange after another, and I couldn't wait to get out of there. As I searched for something the two of us might have in common, a realization hit me in the face, and I gritted my teeth. I did not like Otis Hunting one bit. Unlike River or even Evanora, Otis did not speak what was on his mind, choosing instead to tiptoe around topics in some lame attempt to catch me in a lie. The joke was on him, I'd been lying long enough now to know how to cover my tracks in a conversation.

Beside me, River inched his fingers under the table to rest on my thigh and I relaxed into his touch. It didn't do much to distract me from the glare Otis had trained on me, but I took solace in the gesture, nonetheless. Still annoyed, I chewed the last piece of apple pie on my plate quicker than a starved animal and turned back to Otis.

This dinner could not be over soon enough.

"Yep," I said, swallowing the warm remnants of apple in my mouth. "I'm really enjoying my stay here so far."

Otis turned his head between River and me and scowled. "I can see that."

Seriously, what was it with this family and their obsession with their son's love life? It was frustrating the crap out of me. No one in the coven overstepped their boundaries in this manner, and for the most part, I was free to see whoever I pleased. Although that was likely because I never actually dated. Still, as far as Otis knew, I was a plain old human that his son met in school, so what was his deal?

Can he smell the witch on me?

It was a crazy thought and I pushed it off. Otis never knew Evanora was a witch, so what were the chances my cover would be blown by this obviously clueless creature? None whatsoever.

"I hear you've had some trouble back in the city?" Otis asked.

So that's why you hate me? Cool.

I cleared my throat and put my fork down. It clanked on the plate so loud, I felt River jump at my side. "Nothing major. Just your usual teen angst."

"Is that usual, you would say?"

I shrugged. "It's all settled now and I'm doing much better here. The Chandlers are great, and I love staying with them."

"Hmm."

"Are you happy to be back?" I asked, knowing full well the intention behind the question. It was a loaded one at best, considering that the only reason River's dad returned to Shadowhurst was because of the unfortunate disappearance of Evanora. Something the High Coven did an outstanding job of covering up with false police reports and a shit-ton of magic. As far as everyone in town was concerned, Evanora had a mental breakdown and left Shadowhurst to find herself, or whatever. It was a decent enough story, and River's insistence that she'd been on the verge of insanity for years helped seal the deal. No one was the wiser to what truly went down. No one except myself, River, and our friends, and we all promised to keep it that way. Maybe we let something slip without our knowledge and Otis was catching on?

I looked him over, trying to find some hints in his expression, but he was cool as stone. *Tricky bastard.*

River's father's eyes landed on me, and I shrank into the wooden back of the dining room chair. His hands fumbled with the napkin on the dinner table, and he tossed it aside before speaking. "I am glad to be back," he responded with zero affection. "I would have returned sooner if I knew Evanora was not in her right mind."

His eyes snapped to River, and he frowned.

"Sorry, Dad," River whispered. "I didn't want to worry you."

"All good, kid." Otis plastered on a fake smile that reminded me of the slimy salespeople I saw on late night infomercials. "Your mom was always a problem. I'm just glad she's finally out of our lives for good."

The anger that flashed over River's face was so strong, I almost buckled back. Sure, Evanora was an evil witch that used her son to get what she wanted, but that didn't give his dad the right to bad mouth her like that. A decent father would have been more diplomatic when speaking of this, and I was starting to realize that there was nothing decent about Otis. He didn't care for River, not one bit, and I wanted to rip his face off.

Inside, the shadows growled against my blood, mirroring my rage for the self-centered man across the table. I breathed into them, begging them to stay put. The last thing I wanted was to hurt River's dad in his own home, but I couldn't help myself. River's pain was palpable, and it made me want to destroy everything in my path.

As if on cue, River's fingers found mine under the table and he looped a circle with his thumb over the soft part of my palm. My teeth chattered as I compelled myself to think of something else other than growing resentment. This dinner was more bullshit than I was willing to swallow, and I was over it. Like, really over.

I reached across the table, picking up the tiny handle of the espresso cup with shaky fingers, and downed the last gulp. It burnt going down, but I urged myself to deal, hoping to end this charade sooner.

I could tell River wanted the same as he noisily chewed on the last bites of his pie, avoiding his father's eyes.

Judging by Otis' annoyed face, he wasn't about to warm up to me any time soon and it suited me just fine. I already decided I couldn't stand the man and the less time I spent around him, the more chance there was I would not do something I'd regret.

There goes my plan to be normal.

Wind howled through the thin crack in the window as we drove up to the Chandlers' house and River parked his Porsche in the driveway. His hands were clutching the steering wheel so tight that I could see his knuckles turn white from the pressure. Jaw hardened, he turned to me, and I narrowed my eyes in return.

"...Soooo," I whispered, "that went well."

River let out a chuckle and shook his head. "Sorry about my dad. He takes a little getting used to."

"I don't think he'll ever get used to me. He hates me."

"No," River said, but I could sense the tremble in his words. "And even if he does, who cares? I like you, so he'll have to get on board."

I smiled and dropped my shoulders. River had a point, but it still didn't make me feel any better. Our relationship was already confusing as hell, and I wished we had at least someone on our side. Sure, the Chandlers adored River and so did my best friend, but somehow, it wasn't enough. All it did was draw my attention back to all the people that didn't want us together. Evanora, Savannah, the High Coven, and now Otis. It felt like everyone in the world was rooting against us and it made my stomach turn.

"What if he doesn't?" I asked.

"Then he's an idiot. You're the kindest, most caring person I know, and he'd be a tool not to see that."

The leather seats grunted under my weight as I turned to face him. "I think there's a lot of people who don't see that. Maybe because it's not actually true."

"Babe, are you nuts?" River smiled, tucking a loose strand of her behind my ear. "I wish you could see what I see when I look at you."

"And what's that?"

"Someone that tries to do what's right no matter the risks. Although, I do wish you'd consider those risks a little more from time to time."

"I want to," I said. "I really, really do. But it's not that easy sometimes. I feel like the whole world is against us and it's scary as hell."

His hand reached for mine, wrapping over the fists in my lap and obliterating them from view. "Whatever comes our way, we'll deal with it. Together."

"What if it gets to be too much? I wouldn't blame you for

wanting nothing to do with me. I'm a mess, and it's not cute. I mean, you can have any other girl in the school, and I'm pretty sure none of them would put your life in danger just by being around." It was official, I was freaking out again.

River sighed and leaned over the emergency brake. His arm looped around my shoulder, and he pulled me in, stretching the seatbelt over my chest until it burnt into me. In one quick move, he unbuckled it and dragged me across the seat, his lips landing on mine in desperation. His kiss was feral, and it shot blazing heat across my skin as his lips commanded my own. I groaned into his open mouth, tilting my head back to deepen our kiss. River's tongue brushed against mine and something snapped in me. A release I've been waiting for all night. I pressed into him, ignoring the discomfort of the emergency brake as it burrowed into my leg.

He pulled away, looking me over once more. "I'll take you any way I can get you, witch. Danger and all."

My fingers pulled on his hair, and I inhaled his scent hungrily and with more need than I had in days. River was as starved as me, it seemed because before I could pull away, his grip tightened and he let his lips travel down my neck, biting and kissing at the same time.

Within me, the shadows stirred, and the staggering lights of my magic rose to the surface. I blinked them away, closing my eyes and arching my back to give River more space to explore my skin. His lips covered me in flames as he kissed every inch of my neck and collarbone until I was ready to combust. My thighs shook and I stifled the urge to climb onto his lap and rip his clothes off. My hand fisted around his shirt, and I dragged him to me, meeting his gaze and gasping for air. River was just as breathless, his eyes bloodshot and his skin reddened with excitement.

If we didn't stop now, I'd be hauling him to the guest house behind me.

I blushed, running my thumb across his full bottom lip, a playful smile spreading across my face.

"You're killing me here," River whispered.

So far, we have done nothing other than kiss and as hot as that was, I wanted more. But I had to hold back despite myself. We promised we would take things slow, get to know each other before rushing into anything and considering everything else going on it was a fantastic plan. At least, it was, until a few seconds ago when River's lips found that ticklish spot at the base of my neck. I shivered thinking about it and uncurled my fingers from his shirt. "We should stop," I said and cursed under my breath. "Right?"

River arched an eyebrow but didn't lean in. "Have a good night, Goldilocks," he purred. "I'll see you tomorrow."

With a sigh, I pulled myself away from him and climbed out of the car. My legs were liquid and I surprised myself by not dropping like a sack of potatoes as I stepped outside. Cold air wrapped around me, and I turned to flash River a quick smile before hurrying up the driveway and ducking into the house. My mind was clouded with thoughts of him as I trekked through the dark hallways of the main house, past the backyard, and into the guest house. *That boy will be the death of me.*

Why did I not invite him in again? I had no clue, and I was already reaching for my phone to call him when a low groan sounded in the darkness of the living room.

My eyes squinted, adjusting to the dimness, and landed on the shadowy figure that lounged on the couch.

"About time," Ashley growled.

I stumbled back, hitting the door with my butt, and flicked a switch. The light blinded me, and it took a second to focus my eyes back on the shifter. When I did, the icy fingers of hatred grasped my heart. "What are you doing here?"

Ashley's sneer spread and I could tell he was about as happy to be here as I was to have him.

"Marcus wants you back in the house," he said. "You have to come with me. Now."

Chapter Fourteen

The only way I agreed to go anywhere with Ashley was if we picked Peyton up on the way. Walking through the nightly trees to the resistance house made me realize it was the right choice. My best friend hopped around the shifter with her power on her fingertips as we marched, threatening to smoke his ass if he got out of line every ten minutes. Each time she said something else nasty, Ashley growled under his breath and his annoyance made me laugh. If I was going to be uncomfortable with this meeting, he should be too.

"You know," Peyton said smugly, "you're kinda slow for a shifter. Been hitting the donut shop a little too often lately?"

She turned back to wink at me, and I doubled over laughing.

Not far ahead, Ashley swiped a tree branch out of the path and let it go fast enough to hit Peyton in the shoulder. It didn't bother her one bit.

"Sticks and stones, my furry friend!" she yelled his way and ran to catch up.

I sped up before I lost them to the darkness, scowling as the decrepit view of the resistance house as it appeared through the trees. The moon hid behind clouds tonight and cast an eerie fog over the house, making it an even less welcoming sight. Hesitantly, I climbed the rotten steps to the front door and crossed the threshold. As soon as I stepped through, knots twisted in my gut, and I grabbed Peyton's hand as we walked into the house. This time, I didn't bother to look around and marched straight for the stairs. My legs shook as I took the first step up and I pulled myself together, squaring my shoulders to prepare for what lay ahead.

"Not there," Ashley snapped.

His hand moved to stop me, but Peyton smacked it out of the way. "Use it and lose it, furball!"

"They're in here. Follow me."

Ashley walked past the stairs, and it shocked me to see him close in on the locked metal door I saw the first day we were here. Tonight, it was slightly ajar, and he kicked it open, stepping aside to let us pass. Something about this felt off, and I didn't like being forced into a secret room with that many locks on it. For all I knew, the damn shadowers would lock us in there. I spun to Peyton, but there was little worry in her eyes, and I wondered if my best friend's blind trust in the resistance would be the end of us.

"Any time tonight would be great," Ashley scoffed, winning himself a punch to the ribs from Peyton. "Just get in there. Marcus doesn't like to wait."

"Yeah, well, I don't like to go into dark rooms that feel like a prison, so..."

Ashley sneered and stuck his arm through the door, waving it around confidently as though that was supposed to bring me comfort. *Idiot. It's not like I'm scared the air will kill me.*

Before Peyton could smack him again, I shook my head and stepped around his arm and into the darkness ahead. The air felt thicker here, hotter and more intrusive, and I wondered how many shifters waited on the other side. Although, this could have been Mel and Raiden's doing. The shapeshifter leaders were strong, and I felt their power heat the room the last time we were here.

Peyton's body grew rigid beside me, and I smiled her way before leading us down the unlit corridor. It seemed we were walking forever before another doorway appeared, this one with light streaming through the edges. *Goddess, how big is this house?* I breathed in until my lungs felt like they would burst and let the air out in a gasp while reaching for the handle. Still shaking, I twisted the knob and pushed my way inside.

My body froze.

This room was nothing like the one I met the leaders in. It had no embellishments or furniture, only gray concrete flooring, and padded walls. If I didn't know better, I'd think we were in one of the cells in the magical prison in Stamwick. There was another door at the far end of the room, and it was ajar enough for me to sneak a glance. My blood hardened as my eyes took in the stacks of weapons inside. Knives, bows, guns, and a lot of other weaponry that looked medieval in make lined the metal shelves that spanned across the interior of the storage space. It reminded me of my walk-in closet back in the guest house, except this closet was all kill and no fashion.

Next to me, Peyton's jaw slacked as she followed my gaze.

"Welcome to our training room," Marcus said, and I jumped back from the sound. I was so enthralled with the potential danger we were in, I didn't notice the four resistance leaders that leaned against one of the padded walls.

As always, Marcus took the lead in speaking and the other

three stayed silent, throwing untrusting glares our way. *Feelings mutual,* I all but hissed at them. Uncurling my back, I faced the soul sucker, my eyes darting between the scar on his face and that crescent moon pendant. I still couldn't place why it resonated with me so much and decided to leave it for another time. *You can over-analyze your memories when you're not in a kill room surrounded by shadower leaders.*

My gaze turned from Marcus to the storage space. "Training, huh?"

"What can I say?" the soul sucker said. "We like to be prepared."

"So, don't try anything," Raiden bit out.

His attempt to intimidate me was laughable and I kicked back my boot, pulling out the trusted dagger I carried and pointed it his way. "Right back at ya!"

I was still holding up the dagger when Marcus came around the side and placed his palm on my outstretched arm. Slowly, he pushed down, urging me to lower my defenses. Everything in my body screamed, yet I obeyed, eyes still trained on the massive shifter in my sightline.

"Give it a rest, babe," Mel said to her partner. "We'll get nowhere if we don't trust each other."

"That little room of horrors says otherwise," Peyton sneered.

"You will not think so when the coven has you in their sights," Lorelei retorted. Her long hair fell in luscious waves over her shoulders and a pinch of jealousy hiked through me. I've never seen a pure-bred fae before, but something about Lorelei made me think she might be a close resemblance. *Get a grip, she's a mind reaper. The fae wouldn't be caught dead with her kind in their midst.* Then again, what the hell did I know? The fae were nothing but a fairy tale these days.

Next to me, Peyton shrugged and turned to Marcus. "So

why are we here? It has to be important for you to pull our asses out of bed this late at night."

Marcus chuckled and the sound of his voice soothed me for some unknown reason.

"Girl," I laughed out. "It's like nine-thirty. No one's sleeping right now."

"Not the point," my best friend said between clenched teeth.

Not far from us, Raiden opened his mouth to speak, but one look from Mel shut him up for good. I was starting to get a better idea of the dynamics of their relationship, and a sense of relief drifted over me as I looked them over. Mel seemed to be on my side here and it relaxed me to no small extent. Girl power or whatever.

Tearing my eyes from the shifter couple, I turned back to Marcus. "Seriously though, why are we here?"

"I thought—" he paused. "I believe it might be time we were honest with each other. Us with you, more like it. I think it might help you see our side of things."

Not this again. How many more secrets would I have to uncover before I decided enough was enough? I wished there was a manual somewhere that outlined everything the people in my life kept hidden from me so I could just get it over with in one go. But no, I had to find out one piece at a time. It was the equivalent of dying by a thousand cuts, which at this point was looking like a preferable alternative.

"Honest in what way?" I asked.

"In the way your High Coven isn't," Lorelei barked out.

Marcus shot her a disgruntled look and the mind reaper faded into the wall behind her. Her eyes darkened as she backed off, though I could still see the hatred in them clear as day. There goes girl power. *Asshole.*

"Look, I know the coven isn't your favorite, but they only keep things from the junior witches to protect them."

"Protect them from us?" Marcus raised an eyebrow and frowned.

"Well, yeah. I mean, no offense, but shadowers have no regard for humans and your thoughtless rampage on them will get us all killed. The witches burnt once. We aren't about to let it happen again." Peyton's shrug was audible, but I refused to look at my best friend for fear of the disapproval I might find in her. I hoped she knew by now that when I spoke of shadowers, I never lumped her in with them. Peyton wasn't a shadower to me, she was something else. Something more.

Marcus' eyes brightened and his lips curled into a half-smile. "Ah. I see there are a lot more untruths we have to cover tonight than we anticipated."

"What in the fae are you talking about?"

"Your High Coven lies, Billie. We are not what they make us out to be. Let me take a guess here and assume you know nothing of how our kind came into existence?"

"Of course, I do!" I bit out. "It was our fault. The witches. Our magic messed with human DNA and now you're here. A pain in all our asses."

One glance at the weapons room and I realized I should have been more careful with my choice of words. Didn't matter now, it was already said, so I squared my shoulders and breathed in deeply. *I am not afraid of you!*

"That is not the case, I'm afraid," Marcus said, dropping the smile on his face. "While it is true that witch magic created the first of our kind, it was not by accident we came into existence. There was no mistake. No spreading of magic and no unintentional turning of human DNA."

My eyes widened and I took a step toward the soul sucker, close enough to smell the iron on his breath. "What?"

"Huh?" Peyton asked a second behind me.

"The shadowers exist simply for the fact that your High Coven willed it. We were an experiment gone awry. A faulty spell that spread like a disease while the witches probed and prodded human blood to create a supernatural army to do their bidding. Your coven is the reason we are all here."

My throat closed up and I tried to take a breath in, but the air came in jagged pieces. Knees buckling, I turned away from Marcus and reached a trembling hand into the back pocket of my jeans. Tears threatened to blur my vision and I fumbled with the keys on the phone, typing as quickly as I could.

Babe? Are you up? Call me.

I waited until I saw the message went through before tucking the phone back in my pocket and forcing myself to turn around. "You're telling me the coven made you? All of you?" My head twisted to Peyton, but she seemed as shocked as I was. However, the leaders found this information out, it wasn't widespread news among the shadowers. Then again, it could all be a lie to get me on their side. "I don't believe that."

"We can prove it," Marcus said. He gestured for Mel and the shifter crossed the room to stand by us.

There was no time for me to object when Marcus snaked his arm over mine and grabbed the dagger from my hand. His eyes flashed and he whispered a quick, "I'm sorry," before slicing Mel's outstretched palm with the blade. Blood pooled over her skin, and I winced as empathy pains took over. I didn't normally feel sorry for shadowers, but this chick was nice to me, and I didn't appreciate having to watch her suffer in this. I wasn't sure what Marcus had in mind, but hurting his own people seemed like a disgusting way to prove anything.

He stretched a hand my way. "Your turn," he said, and held the dagger's hilt in my direction.

"I'm sorry, what?" I asked, baffled.

"Mix your blood with hers. You will see the truth."

Oh, hell to the no! Weren't there some rules against this somewhere? I didn't know much about the effect of shadower blood on a witch's system, but I was pretty certain that nothing about this was a good idea. It was unsanitary, to say the least.

"Trust me," Marcus urged.

Somehow, I did.

Unable to stop myself, I took the dagger from him and pressed the blade to my palm. The pain was sharp and quick, blood rushing to the surface of the cut before my brain could register the wound. I battled the need to pass out and took a few steps toward Mel. My hand shook as I reached for her and she pressed her red-stained palm to mine, encircling her fingers around me in a vice lock. A dull ache spread over my body, and I peeled my gaze from our clasped fingers to meet her eyes. My magic swirled, bouncing off the edges of my skin in a panic. Mel's eyes snapped wide open, and she grimaced as magic pulled on her blood, drinking her energy in.

This was madness.

What I felt when Mel's energy rolled through me was unlike anything I've ever experienced. Her blood called to me, and acid lumped in my throat as I let my body drink her in. Horror sank in when I understood that it wasn't shadower energy I was sensing. There was no thickness to the air, no remnants of shifter blood to hold on to. As Mel's blood mixed with mine, I could only sense one thing. Witch magic.

I yanked my hand back, shaking it like I could shake off whatever it was that spread through me, but it was too late. The truth hung heavy in the air, and I let the tears drop from my eyes and run down my cheeks. Beside me, Peyton whispered something, but her words never struck me. I stood there with my jaw on the ground and my wet eyes unblinking. Wiping the blood on my jeans, I reached for the phone, disappointed to find no answer from River.

"What does this mean?" I choked out through sobs.

It was Marcus' turn to fall apart, and he gritted his teeth against each so loud, the sound echoed through the padded room. "It means that we are not so different after all," he said, and my world imploded.

Chapter Fifteen

Black circles lined my eyes as I leaned back on the wood frame of the canopied bed and tried to pretend I was home alone. After we left the resistance house, I barely remembered getting back and spent the entire night pacing around and unable to sleep. Somewhere in the early hours of the morning, I dozed off, only to be woken by the incessant ringing of the phone I forgot to put on silent and a million texts from Peyton. It seemed my best friend worried about me all night, and her idea of a good remedy was a girls' day with the hunters.

Watching her and Morgan sprawl out on the floor of my bedroom next to Abigail, I was wondering how much of that plan had been intended for me.

Despite my tired bones, I wasn't the least bit weary, though my head was not in the room with the rest of our friends. My thoughts were still in the resistance house, with Marcus and the shadower leaders and the horrifying truth I found out last night.

I wasn't sure why it hit me so hard. I knew the High Coven

for its secrets, but something about this one struck close to home. Finding out that the witches created shadowers in some feeble attempt to amplify their power in the supernatural world was unnerving, and it made me hate my own kind. All the lies, all the stories about why we hunted the shadowers, were nothing but a cover up for something much darker. It was only a story told to unsuspecting and blind witches like me to get us to do the coven's bidding and help the high priestesses cover up their own mess. It was pathetic.

Someone yelled something and my attention jumped back to the bedroom.

"Huh?" I asked, eyes blinking as though I came through a fog. In a way, I supposed I did.

"I said," Savannah hissed in annoyance, "did you invite us over here to watch you stare at the wall, or are we going to do something fun for a change?"

I didn't invite you over at all. "Yeah, sorry. Just thinking."

"That's a first," she mumbled under her breath.

I let it go, but Peyton had other ideas. Her head snapped to Savannah and an ominous shadow passed over her eyes. "You're only here because unlike you, Billie's not a tool. Door's that way. You can leave at any time."

Savannah rolled her eyes and rearranged her seat on the rim of the window. "Whatever. What's your deal, anyway?"

She didn't look at me, but I doubted she was asking anyone else.

"Oh, I don't know," I said. "Could be that my entire life has been a lie. But you're right, let's just paint our nails and watch a movie. That makes everything better."

Savannah sneaked a glimpse my way, then trained her gaze out the window again. Her long, bronze legs stretched out in front of her, and she faked a yawn. "We should have gone shopping."

"Oh! I second that!" Abigail yelled out. "I need a fresh dress for dinner with Ty Friday! Something easy to rip off."

"Ew," Morgan sniped and slapped her friend's bare thigh. "When are you going to give it a rest? It's been ages. Aren't you tired by now?"

Abigail wiggled her eyebrows. "Have you seen my man's abs? Honey, you don't tire of that washboard unless there's something wrong with you."

"I don't get it," Peyton whispered. "They're just abs."

There was a loud cackle from the window. "That's 'cause you're too busy checking out Morgan's assets!"

The room grew still, and I could see the blush spread over Peyton's face. Anger roared in me, and I wanted to march over to Savannah and shove the jackass out the window. I don't care how long she and Morgan have been friends. It wasn't her right to embarrass Peyton like that. I hopped to the edge of the bed, ready to leap when Morgan whispered something to Peyton and the two giggled under their breath.

My best friend looked at me and a wide, genuine smile spread over her face, making my anger crawl back to the hole it came from.

Something vibrated under the pillow, and I jumped to pull my phone out from underneath. Disappointment rolled over me when I saw an email from Sebyl pop up and I swiped it off-screen. There had still been no word from River after my text last night, and it was unlike him not to respond. Worry banged against my chest as I thought of all the horrible things that could have happened to him when another laugh from Savannah tore my gaze from the phone.

"Not River, I take it?" she asked, a sneer on her lips.

"Nope," I responded. "I haven't heard from him all morning. Something must be wrong."

"I'm sure he's fine," Abigail breathed. "Don't spiral. Boys are stupid sometimes."

"That's why I don't dabble." Morgan grinned and high fived Peyton. The redhead sat up and looked around my room. "You got any cards or something? We can play a game. I'll kick all y'all asses in poker, hands down."

"Oh, you're on!" Peyton screeched and jumped up to rummage through my bedside table.

Books went flying in every direction while she pulled out each item on the table before giving up and going back to her spot on the floor. The only cards I had on me were a few tarot decks I picked up at the Crystal Cauldron, and I very much doubted the girls wanted to spend the rest of the day getting their sordid futures told. Besides, my tarot game was weak. I was no Luna in readings, and I was totally okay with it. Who had time for that nonsense when there were so many lies to uncover? I seriously hated my life these days.

I checked the phone again and let out a sigh.

"Stalker much?" Savannah sniped. "Calm your shit, Billie. He's fine. I talked to him this morning."

That did *not* make me feel any better. Why was River talking to her and not to me? There had to be a good explanation for it, but that thought did not make me feel any better. Between Savannah's flirting and him not answering texts, my mind was racing. I knew I had better things to think about—like the fact that the High Coven lied to me again—but I couldn't help myself. River was one of the most important parts of my life here in Shadowhurst and the primary reason I stayed behind. If he wasn't into me, he should have the guts to tell me himself instead of leading me on. *Okay, let's just get over ourselves for a second, cool?* I was a hot mess, and it wasn't helping the current situation we had on our hands. *Deal with the shadowers then worry about your own damn feelings.*

Ignoring the self-assured grin Savannah had over her stupid face, I swiped on my phone to write him another text when I noticed a missed call from the High Coven. My stomach tightened and I white-knuckled the phone case, dread filling my gut. My finger bounced between the message icon and my email, where that annoying red notification bubble still hovered. Aggravated, I typed out a quick text to River for the twentieth time, then signed into my email.

The room fell away as I read the long-winded message Sebyl sent, and the knots in my stomach intensified. Word after word, my body weakened, and I leaned on the bed frame to ease the pressure. My eyes glassed over when I reached the end, and I tossed the phone on the bed with so much force, it slid off the side and fell to the floor with an agonizing thud. A scream burst from my lips, and I fisted my hand, driving a punch to the pillow next to me.

"B? What's wrong?" Peyton asked.

I didn't answer. How did you tell your best friend that everything was wrong? Where would I even start?

Chapter Sixteen

"Read it again," Peyton demanded.

My friend's pale face taunted me, and I knew how difficult it was for her not to react after hearing what the High Coven revealed in the email Sebyl sent. The hunters did not know of her shadower blood and while I agreed to keep it a secret from them, having the girls in the room when she found out the news must have been torturous.

Dark-lined eyes stared at me under the red streaks of her hair, and she bit her bottom lip, choosing her words carefully. "What are the chances the spell will work?"

I really had no clue. The High Coven didn't exactly disclose the intricacies of the spell they've been working on in the email, and I was sure it was well above my pay grade. All Sebyl said was that for the past few weeks, they had been working on a way to uncover the exact location of all the soul suckers in the world. Something about their blood being most potent, though deep down, I knew that wasn't the reason they wanted to flush out Peyton's kind. The soul suckers were the most difficult to track down since they did such an excellent job at hiding amongst humans. Their energy was almost untraceable, and it made it impossible to take them out. If you wanted to vanquish a soul sucker, you basically had to wait for it to come to you. Or be lucky enough to be present when they attacked a human which usually meant a whole lot of death for everyone involved.

In my brief life, I've only vanquished a handful of them and now that I knew Peyton, I didn't think I'd ever have the stomach to take on more.

"Probably damn good chances," Savannah answered before I could. "They're powerful witches, right? I'm going out on a limb here, but I'm assuming whatever spell they perform has like zero chance of failing."

Peyton looked to me, and I sighed. "She's right."

"So what? They want to find every soul sucker out there, and then what? Kill them all?" Morgan asked.

I wish it was that simple.

"They want me to follow the soul suckers once they figure out who they are. The ones in Shadowhurst," I said, refusing to look at Peyton. "They think they can track them to the resistance."

"How the hell would they even track them? A magical GPS or some shit?" Savannah asked.

I nodded. "Kind of. Sebyl didn't share much, no shock there, but from what she said, the spell will target soul sucker energy in their blood. Kind of like a beacon. If the elements they use to bind the spell are potent enough, every soul sucker in the immediate radius will give off a signal of sorts. An energy magnet that will draw them to any witch around. I don't know how it would work exactly, but I have the feeling that if the spell succeeds, being near a soul sucker will give off an alarm somehow. I'd be able to sense them with my magic."

From the corner of my eye, I saw Peyton shift in her seat on the floor. We were both thinking the same thing. This was freaking bad.

"Uhm, 'kay..." Abigail said. "So, they're expecting to blast off this spell and then have you hop around town looking for soul suckers until you find the resistance. Cool."

"Not cool," I snapped. "We already know where the resistance is, remember? When they came for me?"

River, Peyton, and me agreed to tell the hunters only what they needed to know about the shadower resistance. That meant no mention of Peyton, and if anyone asked, the resistance came for me out of the blue to ask for my help. It was close enough to the truth that we didn't feel bad about lying, but right now, I wished we were honest with the hunters. I grew to trust them in the last little while, even Savannah, and I knew they would do the right thing in the end.

I opened my mouth to speak, then closed it again.

One warning look from Peyton told me to keep my mouth shut, so instead, I pretended to read over the email again as though I didn't already have it memorized.

"I still don't get why the resistance needs you," Morgan said. "I mean, if they want to go against the High Coven, have at it. Why bring you in?"

I grimaced, weighing the options of how much I can divulge. "Because if they get me on board, they have an inside man for the job. I think they want to use me to infiltrate the High Coven from within and then strike. It's actually a brilliant plan, if you think about it." *I had the same one for them.*

"Yeah." Savannah scoffed, "And I'm sure having witch hunters on your side is a good little bonus."

It sure as shit is, isn't it? I haven't considered it before, but Savannah hit the nail on the head. This entire time I thought they let River come with me to their hideaway because of his shifter side, but maybe that wasn't it at all. Maybe they let him in because they needed the hunters for their plan to overtake the High Coven just as much as they needed me. These kids were good at what they did, and without a magical signature, they were invisible to the witches. No wonder the high priestesses were so adamant for me to track their group down. They posed a problem for the coven and one the witches didn't want to let stand. Just freaking great.

Savannah's features tensed and she trained her eyes on me. "I still don't see why this is such a big deal? You said it yourself. The shadowers are evil bastards who prey on humans. Why not just tell the High Coven how to find the resistance and get it over with? Have them solve that problem and call it a day?"

"Are you kidding me right now?" Peyton hollered and jumped to her feet. She crossed the room, barreling to Savannah in seconds. "You haven't met these people, Barbie. They're not all bad. I know it's hard for you to grasp but think of someone else for a second!"

The room grew quiet, and everyone stared at Peyton as her outburst took hold of us. If I didn't know better, I'd be pretty damn scared of my best friend right now. She was fierce as hell and I had to admit, I enjoyed seeing Savannah squirm for a few moments. It didn't last long, and Savannah was on her feet and towering over Peyton before anyone could blink. Her hair bounced over her face and the snarl that left her lips made Morgan and Abigail freeze in their spots.

"Anyone that kills innocent people is a monster," she bit out. "Get your facts straight."

"Correct me if I'm wrong," Peyton said, not missing a beat, "but didn't you want all witches dead not that long ago? Don't be an idiot. You're human and possibly the worst person any of us have ever met, so don't go throwing stones in your glass house."

On their spot near my bed, Morgan and Abigail exchanged

looks, but no one came to Savannah's defense. *Good going, you tool. Even your best friends think you're garbage. Well played.*

Despite wanting to see how this played out, I jumped off the bed to step between Savannah and Peyton. "Let's take it down a notch, guys."

Savannah narrowed her eyes at me but backed up and I led Peyton to the bed, sitting her down before she could out herself to the girls. We had enough problems on our hands to worry about their reaction at the moment.

"Whatever the High Coven wants with the resistance," I said as calmly as I could manage, "we can't let them go through with it. Peyton is right. From what I've seen at the resistance house, not all the shadowers are as evil as the coven made them out to be. We can't let innocent lives pay the price for the High Coven's misdirected anger and I don't know about you, but I couldn't live with myself if that happened."

The look the girls gave me told me they agreed.

"So, what do we do?"

"I think—"

There was a knock on the front door and all five of us gasped. I turned on my heels, rushing to check who it was and leaving my friends' questioning eyes behind. As soon as I turned the handle and slid the door open, the smell of wood invaded my senses and I buckled back. In front of me, River's green eyes twinkled in the sunlight, and I squinted against the light to take him in. It had only been a short while since I've seen him, but it felt like lifetimes. I craved him near me the same way I craved air to breathe, and it repulsed me. Repulsed and excited me at the same time, which only made me more confused. *How can one person have so much power over me?*

"Hey," he said and smiled. "Got your text."

Seriously? I took a step back, unwilling to let him persuade me to not be mad. "I sent that last night. You just got it?"

"Had some stuff to take care of. Are you okay?"

"I guess," I choked out. "Not really, actually. You missed a lot. And why didn't you return my text?" *Welcome, stage one clinger, we've been waiting for you.*

"Babe, come on. I didn't see it until this morning and my dad was on me to spend time with him, but I came here right after. Are you mad?"

"A little." I shrugged. "But I'll get over it. We have more important things to think about right now."

River stepped through the threshold, eliminating any protective space I was holding between us. His arms wrapped around my waist, and he dragged me into him, his lips brushing against my ear. "Anything to worry about?"

I tried to look upset, but my dumb face gave me away and I smiled instead.

"Something we should all worry about."

He arched a perfect eyebrow my way. "Oh?"

Un-freaking-believable. How is this guy just casually going on after everything we've found out? Oh right, he has no clue. Ugh.

The smile dropped from my face, and I laced my fingers in his, tugging him into the bedroom. "Come on, the girls and I will fill you in." I didn't have time to register the confused look on his face when I pulled him behind me and into the lioness lair of my bedroom. Whatever River's problem was, a few hours with these chicks would be enough to teach him a lesson. As we stepped into the bedroom, the girls exploded in chatter, and I could see him try to back out. I grasped his shoulders and pushed him into the center, winking before hopping on the plush mattress. *Have at him, ladies.*

I grinned and leaned back on the bed as the hunters filled River in on everything we've discovered. His jaw slacked with each piece of fresh information until it hit the floor and he looked back at me, astonished from the news. His face was serious, and I sensed he wanted to speak with me in private, but the girls were circling him like sharks in the water. Satisfied, I shot him a thumbs up and chuckled. Next time, maybe he'll think twice before ignoring my texts.

Chapter Seventeen

Filling River in took longer than I expected and by the time the girls were done talking his ear off, it was already midday and my stomach was growling from hunger. We decided to break for lunch and after twenty more minutes of arguing over where to get takeout, and about fifty eye rolls from Savannah on everything I suggested, we settled on sandwiches from the vegan spot on Main Street. Personally, I hated vegetables or any food that didn't come slathered in grease but kept that to myself. Pick your battles and whatever.

Since Abigail and Morgan were knee-deep in painting their toes and Savannah refused to do anything to help, we left them behind to pick up the order. I couldn't be happier to be out of the guest house. The fresh air nipped at my face as we sped through town to our destination, and I laughed each time Peyton slammed the brakes and sent us flying into the dashboard of her Jeep. Behind me in the backseat, River wasn't quite as amused, which only made me laugh harder.

"You are a hazard," he growled as the car's wheels smoked on a sharp right turn. "A serious damn hazard."

Peyton laughed and turned the radio to the max, blasting the latest Taylor Swift tune out the window. She bobbed her head, singing along at the top of her lungs, ignoring him entirely.

"Is she always like this?" he asked, leaning in.

I grinned and nodded. "Yep. Every damn time. You gotta love it!"

"You really don't."

He grimaced and my smile widened.

"Hey, speed racer!" I yelled out over the bridge of the song, inching my fingers to the volume button to turn it down. "You got some steam to let off, or what?"

At the wheel, Peyton's face paled, but she kept her eyes on the road. Thank the Goddess for small miracles. "I'm not feeling your coven right about now," she said. "This spell is crap and you know it."

"Have to side with her there," River backed up my friend from the back of the car. "Sorry, babe."

Trees blurred in my vision as the car picked up speed and I tugged at the seatbelt to make sure it was still in place. Though, at this point, I doubted anything could save me if Peyton went wilder than she already was. Her power drowned out every other element around, and I could feel it in my bones as we raced down the hills of Shadowhurst. My best friend wasn't just pissed, she was terrified, and I could sense it drip off her like molasses.

We passed a small grouping of local shops, bringing us closer to our final destination, which, by the way Peyton was driving, could have been the literal interpretation of the words. The car drove past the familiar sign of the Crystal Cauldron and a pang of guilt bubbled inside me. I was yet to come by and help Ms. Broussard at the shop as I promised, and it should have been the least of my worries with everything going on, but the guilt still festered at the back of my mind. Ms. Broussard was one of the kindest people I've met in Shadowhurst and I considered her a true friend, someone that deserved my undivided attention and I hated that I couldn't give her that. At least not right now.

"We'll figure it out," I said. "I won't let them go through with it. But..."

"But what?" Peyton snapped and I instantly regretted saying anything.

I looked back at River and frowned. "But maybe we should tell the hunters about, you know, who you are."

"Nope. Uh-uh! No freaking way!"

"Why? They can help us and if you're worried about them treating you any different, take it from someone who's been through this, they're pretty accepting if you give them a chance."

"No one will bat a lash about it," River reassured her, but Peyton did not seem to hear it.

The Jeep's engine roared and before we could prepare, she slammed on the brakes, and my body yanked forward. The seatbelt burnt into my chest, and I rubbed the red mark spreading on my skin. "A little warning next time, girl."

"We're here," Peyton said and looked away.

Behind us, River tensed, and I could see him trying to figure out what the best play here was. I had no idea. I've never seen Peyton like this. The girl was fire and for her to be this bent out of shape over a threat was not normal. Glancing back to River, I nudged my head to the door.

"Ah, right..." he said. "I'll get the food. You guys wait here."

Sometimes, I loved that he could read my silent gestures.

When River was out of the car and away from earshot, I turned to my best friend. "Talk to me, what's up? Is it Morgan? Are you scared of what she'll think?"

"What? No! I'm not scared that some chick's not going to like me. Geez."

"Then what?"

Her lips tightened into a line, and she drew in a deep breath. "I'm scared for my family. Again. And I'm sick of it. It's like every time we get a break, something else comes up that threatens them, and I hate that I can't protect them. You know, the other day, my dad actually suggested moving us out of here? Like that could solve something! I don't want to run, and I don't want to hide, but I gotta tell you, B, your coven is making that impossible."

The wind picked up outside, howling through the crack in the window and tossing fallen leaves all around the car. My eyes studied Peyton as I tried to think of something comforting to say, but words refused to form. What could I possibly say to make her feel better? She wasn't wrong. The High Coven was out for blood, and I was powerless to stop them. We all took turns reading over the email Sebyl sent and no one could come with anything that would be helpful. How were we supposed to stop the witches from outing all the soul suckers and destroying the resistance if we didn't know what this spell was they would perform? Besides, I wasn't even sure I wanted to stop them from getting rid of the resistance. They were just another problem on our radar and another threat to Peyton and her family. It was as though we walked face-first into a spiderweb and were now biding our time until the unavoidable end.

My pulse quickened and a dull ache formed behind my eyelids as I considered what my best friend was going through. I never had a proper family growing up but if anyone consistently threatened the people in my life now, I'd be utterly broken.

"Peyton," I whispered and placed a hand on her shoulder.

"I will help you. We have each other's backs, you know that, right? I don't know how, but I will figure it out."

"And if you can't?"

"Then someone else will. We're a team. All of us. Is it a totally effed up team? Sure! But everyone wants to help you here, you just have to let them."

She rolled her shoulders and finally turned to face me. "Okay. I'll think about it. But don't say anything yet."

I nodded.

"So, about Morgan..."

Peyton's eyes shot daggers my way and she smacked my hand off her shoulder. "One more word and I'll lose it. I swear, B, I'll freaking scream and call the cops on your ass for harassment."

It seemed the universe was trying to get a kick out of me because just as she spoke, a cruiser pulled up in the parking spot next to us. A stocky officer crawled out of the passenger side and looked us over before stumbling inside the coffee shop next to the restaurant we picked for lunch. When he ducked inside, Peyton's fingers wrapped around my arm, and she squeezed. "Perfect timing."

A laugh burst from me, and I doubled over, slapping my thighs. Next to me, Peyton joined in and before I knew it, we were nearly in tears from the uncontrollable giggles that escaped us. After everything that's happened recently, it felt damn good to laugh with her again and I cherished this moment above all else. We were in the middle of a monumental mess, but I meant what I said to Peyton; no matter what happens, I had her back. Always.

"You know," Peyton said when we stopped laughing, "we're going to have to tell the leaders about this spell crap. There are soul suckers in the resistance, Marcus including, and they have a right to know."

"I know," I agreed. "But let's hold off until we know more about it so we don't cause a panic."

She sighed and looked past me to the street. "Agreed. Although I wouldn't mind scaring the crap out of Ashley, I'll tell you that much."

I smiled and followed her gaze to a hotter-than-hell River crossing the parking lot with three bags of deliciousness in his grasp. I wasn't sure what excited me more, the tight button-up he wore that did all the right things for his body or the carbs he was hauling my way. Whatever it was, I welcomed it whole-heartedly.

When he reached us, I rolled down the window to snatch the bags from him, but the look on his face gave me pause.

"You good, babe?"

"Better than good," he answered and tossed the bags in my lap. "Savannah has something on the spell. The girls called Tyler and Jayden, and they're all meeting us at my place. Let's roll."

With that, we were back on the road, tossing and sliding as Peyton veered the car, carrying us to the first glimpse of hope we've had in days. And this time, I didn't mind her reckless driving one bit. The faster we got some answers, the better.

Chapter Eighteen

The others were already piled up on River's front lawn when we arrived, and one look at the hunters told me they were just as eager to hear what Savannah had to say. Jayden was jumping from foot to foot, and the dumb grin on his face did little to hide his excitement. Near him, sitting on the steps of the front porch, Morgan swatted at his legs to get him to calm down with little success. Abigail and Tyler were entwined in yet another disgusting display of public affection, but it was Savannah's reaction that startled me the most. The hunter's eyes were questioning as we approached, and she stared me down like a snake spotting a mouse in the field.

We neared them and I held up the sandwich bags, waving them around as one would wave a white flag on the battlefield. "We got lunch! Who's hungry?"

Hands shot up, but Savannah's eyes never left me.

"Why don't we go in?" River said, turning to Savannah.

She grumbled something under her breath and spun on her heels to follow him inside. We walked through the house in silence with only the occasional chirp from Jayden about the pictures of River on the wall. There were fewer of them now than I remembered, and I wondered if his dad had something to do with it. I wouldn't put it past Otis to get rid of anything that reminded him of Evanora, and I made a mental note to ask River about it later.

Rounding the corner, we piled into the French-style kitchen, and everyone grabbed a seat around the island. I looked around, scanning the room, and hesitantly climbed onto a stool.

"He's not home," River whispered in my ear as he passed.

Stop reading my mind, hunter!

My hand reached out to brush against his and the jolt of energy was enough to keep me going until River came back with the stack of books he hid in his bedroom. By the time he returned, we were already halfway through the sandwiches, and I scrambled to wipe mustard off my face before he noticed.

"Missed a spot," Savannah said loud enough for everyone to hear.

Ears burning, I swiped a napkin to wipe my face, keeping my head down. When I finished, I looked up at her and waved myself over dramatically. "Better? Didn't realize we were in a beauty pageant here."

"Like they'd let you in."

Everyone froze.

"Ouch!" Jayden yelped. "Shots fired!"

My hands tightened into fists, and I slammed them on the marble counter, rising from the stool. I could feel magic tensing in my stomach, using anger as an excuse to lash out. The moonstone ring on my finger glowed faintly, and inky shadows crept up around it as I focused my energy on Savannah. The idiot wasn't even phased. Instead, she raised an eyebrow and glared like she was begging me to make the first move.

Before I could let the shadows loose, a hand curled around my fist, and I turned to see River's concerned face in my peripheral. He shook his head, and it was enough to get me to back off. *Head in the game, Billie. She's not worth it.*

River slammed a stack of books on the counter, and everyone leaned in, happy to be busying themselves with something other than my unbalanced emotions. They each reached for a book, but I stayed still, waiting to see what Savannah will do next. To my relief, she peeled her gaze from me and snatched the book Abigail was gunning for. "This is it. That's where I remember reading it."

"Reading what, exactly?" Tyler asked.

Barbie doll flipped through the pages, scanning the words until she found what she was looking for. "There," she pointed to a section and turned the book to face us. "Right here."

Every single person in the kitchen held their breath as we read in silence. I couldn't be sure what my friends were thinking, but if it was anything close to my own thoughts, the words 'holy shit' must have made several appearances. I read over the page again, tilting the book to see the spine. I must have gone over these texts a million times with River, but I couldn't remember this particular book. Why is this the first time we were seeing this?

"This book is new," I said. "Where did it come from?"

River's shoulders rose up and down, and he took a while to answer. "After—" he took a breath in before continuing, "—after Evanora left, I went through her bedroom, in case there was some stuff there that might be too weird for my dad to see when he moved back in."

"Witch stuff?" Abigail asked.

"Yep."

"And?"

"Didn't find much. But this book was hidden in her closet,

so I figured it was important. I kind of forgot about it, to be honest."

My eyes narrowed and I looked between him and Savannah. Something was off here, and I couldn't place my finger on it. If River's mom had this book in her possession, it must be an enormous deal. There was something here she didn't want anyone to see, something that aided her somehow in her misguided attempt to take down the High Coven. More importantly, if River hadn't looked at it since he found it, how did Savannah know to find what we needed inside?

"Wait, how do you know about it then?" Peyton asked, eyebrows kissing.

My thoughts exactly.

"I, uh," River fought for words. "I let her come by to check it out when I found it. Figured she's always the best with this kind of stuff, so what's the harm?"

Discomfort clouded my vision and I struggled to think of anything but the annoyance that threatened to overtake me. River finding this book belonging to his mom so soon after her capture could not have been easy and out of all people, he called Savannah. Not me. Her. I urged myself not to worry, but no matter how hard I tried to spin it, it was abundantly clear that Savannah and her bitchy attitude were part of River's life no matter how much it bothered me. Sure, they were childhood friends, but shouldn't I be the one he called about this stuff? If anything, I was the freaking witch in this group, so if anyone should get to see Evanora's things, it should be me.

Are you seriously worrying about this right now? GROW UP! I hissed at myself, pushing the rage into a dark corner in the back of my mind. *Who cares who read it first? It's here now. Deal with it.*

I filled my lungs and breathed out before turning my attention back to the book and away from River. One look at him would send me into a frenzy again and I couldn't afford that at the moment.

"Does this say what I think it says?" I asked.

"If you think it says that there's a book out there that belonged to one of the first witches in Shadowhurst, then yes," Savannah answered.

This couldn't be real, could it? I've never heard of such a book before. Not just a book, a grimoire from the sounds of it. One written by an original witch. If this existed, it could hold every spell known to the coven today. It would be priceless. Every witch in the High Coven had a grimoire, me including, and in it, we collected every piece of knowledge on anything related to our craft. It was a culmination of one's life work and some older head witches in the coven had grimoires the size of encyclopedias. I looked at Sebyl's grimoire once—stole it was more like it—and it was the most amazing thing I've ever read. She had spells in there that I never even knew existed, so I could only imagine the information that laid hidden inside the grimoire of an original witch. After all, the witches didn't just manifest from thin air like freaking fruit flies. As the story goes, the first witches were taught by the fae, and their power and abilities were far greater than those of the modern witch. While it was true that they were much more human than the witches today, their ability to use fae magic must have made them unstoppable. That is, of course, if you believed in fae in the first place. I still wasn't sure where I stood on that, but that wasn't the point. The point was that if this grimoire existed, it held spells that paved the way for the ones witches used today. Spells like the one the High Coven was working on to draw out the soul suckers.

"The Book of Darkness," I read to no one in particular. "Amazing."

"Creepy name for a book," Jayden teased.

I looked at him, hiding the pity behind a smile. *Poor, clueless human.* "Not just any book," I said. "A grimoire. One of the first ones ever written. If we can get our hands on this, I'm sure we can find the spell Sebyl and the high priestesses are working on!"

"So where is this thing now?" Peyton asked, and the hope in her voice spread over the rest of us. "B?"

"I, uh, I don't know. I've never heard of this thing before." My mind clouded as I raked my memory for anything that could lead closer to the book's location, but I drew a blank. There was no way I'd forget something like this, I was adamant with notes and my own grimoire was filled to the brim with every bit of information I could soak up in my lifetime of training as a witch. Foggily, an idea crept into my brain, and I was on my feet in seconds.

"That's it!" I yelled out, shocking those around me. "I have an idea!"

A million questions flew my way, but I ignored them all. My mind was on one thing and one thing only. I swallowed the last bite of the soggy sandwich on the plate—because who said no to food—and darted from the kitchen. Behind me, River shouted my name ,and I could hear him run after me but I didn't bother looking back. I was on a mission.

This Book of Darkness was written by one of the most powerful witches of our time, but I had something she didn't. I was an OCD level note-taker and if there was anything I came across that even remotely pointed to this book, I knew I wrote it down. Nothing got by my Sherlock Holmes level of research.

I raced through the house, barely registering River's insistence to drive me to wherever it was I so desperately needed to get to. As I climbed into the passenger side of his car and directed him back to my house, anticipation spread over my chest. There was a chance I could find the book and get us out of this mess and to do that, I had to tear apart my grimoire until I found what I was looking for.

Chapter Nineteen

The next hour went by in a blur. River barely had time to park before I bolted out of the car and took off in a dead sprint to the guest house. My heart raced the entire time I was packing up the grimoire and supplies to take with us to the hiking trail on the edge of town. Something about being as close to solitude as I could manage seemed appropriate at the moment, so I convinced River to wait in the car while I gathered my things so we could hightail it out of there immediately. I promised him the woods would be a more romantic setting to dig through my grimoire notes, and he had no objections, but the truth was I wanted to be near an abundance of elements in case I had to work a spell and my measly collection of herbs and crystals didn't do the trick.

With a bag in tow, I all but leaped into River's Porsche and tapped my foot the entire time we drove to the trails. It was likely annoying as hell, but River didn't seem to notice and only rubbed the back of my neck as we zoomed past the sleepy streets of Shadowhurst. The gesture did not go unnoticed and despite the hiccups our relationship had been having lately, I was more than glad to have him with me right now.

This was it. I could feel it.

We parked in the furthest spot in the lot and marched into the wooded area that spread across the outskirts of town. Trees towered over us, and I looked up as we walked, taking in the shifting colors of the slowly setting sun above. Energy poured from every element around us and I drank it in. Like a hungry fish in a pool of power.

When we found a spot I was comfortable with, one —far enough away from any of the popular trails, and —River spread the blanket I packed and I tossed my bag down, rummaging through its contents to find the grimoire.

The soft leather felt like butter under my fingers, and I ran them over the sigils sewn into the binding before flipping the hefty book open.

Magic hummed under my skin as I traced the pages with my thumb, speed-reading the words I had all but memorized in my years of referencing the book. I was twenty pages in when frustration reared its ugly head and spun my insides like an overzealous clothes dryer.

"AGH!" I groaned, pushing the grimoire out of the way and leaning back on my elbows. "What if I'm wrong and this is a lost cause?"

River's hand reached for mine, and he drew a squiggly line over my skin with his index finger. "Don't give up yet, you only started looking. Take your time."

"Time is not something we have," I growled. "The High Coven could be working on the spell as we speak."

He frowned but forced his lips upward when he saw me staring.

Smooth move, soldier.

"They're not," he assured me. "Sebyl said they're

performing the spell at the next full moon. That's not for another five days. We have time. Don't spiral."

The fists I hadn't realized I was clenching relaxed, and I looked him over. "Right. You're right. Don't freak out, everything will be fine. I mean, it's not like these are the same witches that tried to build an army of shadowers to do their bidding and screwed up so royally they had to lie to the rest of us to fix their mistake. Totally fine."

Okay, so I was definitely freaking out, but could you blame me? The High Coven that I trusted with all my heart, the same coven I risked my life for, was built on nothing but lies. Sure, having the high priestesses keep information from me sucked, but at least I could convince myself they were doing it for the safety of the coven, but this? This was something else entirely. Not only did they create the shadowers by torturing innocent humans to twist them into something so dark and evil, but they brainwashed the entire coven to think these people had to be hunted and vanquished for their own good. Deep down, I knew it wasn't the same witches that were alive today responsible for the mess. The shadowers have been around for generations and the witches that created them were long gone by now, yet that meant nothing to me. What hurt the most was the betrayal of the high priestesses, the women I admired since I was a little girl. The same women I thought were my family when Beatrix was dragged away. They held all the secrets, and I had no doubt they knew exactly how the shadowers came into this world. Still, they chose to lie to every witch in the coven to keep up the pathetic charade. They chose to lie to me.

"Babe?" River asked, his eyes full of worry.

"Yeah, sorry. Not freaking out."

He chuckled. "Since when do we lie to each other?"

My skin burnt as I tried to say anything other than what I was thinking. Unfortunately, my brain and my mouth were not on the best terms these days, and I blurted out the worst thing I could say at that moment without stopping myself.

"Why didn't you tell me about the book? Why Savannah?"

Excellent job, princess. Now he'll think you're an obsessed girlfriend. Female friend. UGH, whatever!

River didn't seem to notice the shiftiness in my eyes or the way my neck dripped with sweat. His fingers tightened around my palm, obliterating it from view. "Billie, come on. I had no idea this would bother you this much. It's just a book."

"It's not just a book. It was Evanora's book and it's important. If not for any other reason than the fact that it was important to her."

"I guess that's part of the reason I didn't tell you."

My brow furrowed and I spun around to face him. "Say what now?"

The sun was dipped below the tree line and a deep shadow crossed River's face. His eyes looked over the horizon, narrowing as the green in them reflected the low rays of light streaming through the branches. For a second, I thought I broke him, but before I could say anything else, River turned to me and smiled.

"If I told you about this book, you'd want to rip through it. I know you, Billie, information is like a freaking chocolate cake to you. And normally, I think that's great. But this was different. Evanora was just imprisoned, and despite how awful she was, she was still my mom."

"And you didn't want to spend hours talking about her or anything else she might have found to be important," I whispered, cluing in. Finally.

"Yeah." River's eyes darkened and a sheepish smile formed on his face. That damn dimple making me forget that I was supposed to be mad at him. "I'm really sorry. If I knew it would upset you, I would have shoved that book in your face and put my own bullshit aside."

My heart shattered. Even during his darkest time, he was still willing to put himself in the corner and let me have my way. I was an idiot not to overreact and a bigger idiot for thinking Savannah was any kind of competition. They may have been friends their entire lives, but he was mine now and I loved the thought of that.

The weight of the grimoire spread a dull ache over my thighs, and I turned back to the book with a sudden renewed interest.

"Let's agree that from now on, we tell each other everything."

"Shake on it?" River asked.

I reached my hand over to shake his and he yanked it forward, pulling me into him. Placing the lightest of kisses on my lips, River erased all my worries. His lips parted into a wide grin, and I pulled away, taking in the sight of him. A happy River was my favorite kind. When he let me go, I had to remind myself why we were in the woods in the first place. *Grimoire. Say it with me, Billie. Read the damn book and get some answers!*

Flipping back to where I left off, I scanned the next few pages. Something gnawed at the back of my mind, but I couldn't quite place my finger on it. Which was ironic because my fingers were literally on the very thing I thought could help us. Frustrated, I pulled out the amethyst pendant from under my sweater and turned the pages until I found a spell to help me focus. As I read over the incantation, a memory flashed before my eyes.

I was in the High Coven library back in Stamwick, huddled around the small circular table in its center. My hand was moving faster than a motor as I took notes while Luna force-fed me information on tarot readings. The memory was so clear, I could practically feel how much my head hurt from having to listen to her. I closed my eyes, forcing myself deeper into that moment. My fingers moved across the grimoire as I relived the memory again. Luna was off on one of her tangents, her eyes looking past me as she recited every card in the deck and its meaning. Sometimes, I wished I was as passionate as her about prophecy, but all I cared for in those days was hunting down shadowers and smoking their asses. I was an idiot. As Luna droned on and on, my gaze flicked around the room, reading the spines of the surrounding books. There were so many I wanted to read, each one full of spells and history that drew me in but there would not be enough time in the day to get through all of them, and since I only got a few hours a week to spend here, I made do with whatever teachings the high priestesses deemed necessary. My eyes traveled across the bookshelves, landing on one in particular. I had been dying to get my hands on this book since I was a kid, but the priestesses never let me touch it. It was older than any of the others in the library, but that wasn't what drew my greedy eyes to it. What I loved most about this book were the crescent moons etched into its side. All upside down and all calling me forward. Wet moons. Horned little bastards.

"OH, MY GODDESS!" I shouted as I emerged from my trance. Next to me, River shifted in his seat to kneel across me.

"What?"

My lashes fluttered and I smiled so wide I could all but feel my lips tickle my ears. "I know where the Book of Darkness is!"

River's eyebrows raised and his eyes widened. "Where?"

"The High Coven library. It was there the entire time! Of course, it was! That's how they got that spell, I'm sure of it. It's the only thing that makes sense."

"So, what does that mean?"

Loaded question, hunter. "It means we need to get that book. Immediately. It's our only way to get the spell the witches will use and block it before they ruin everything. I have to do this for Peyton and the other soul suckers. I can't let them get hurt, not like this and not on my watch." Tears burnt behind my lids as I thought about betraying the High Coven, but I pushed them out. "I have to go back to Stamwick. I have to steal that book."

"Not any time soon," a low voice rumbled from behind us.

I turned to face the intruder and acid rose in my throat.

Our romantic research date was officially over.

Chapter Twenty

"What the hell do you want?" River roared.

The three shifters that closed in on us didn't slow down. Their heavy footsteps pounded the grass, tearing it apart as they marched toward us. I narrowed my eyes on them and tried to recall if I met them at the resistance but drew a blank. Whoever these muscled giants were, I've never seen them before.

River, however, seemed oddly familiar with them.

Rage filled his eyes as he stepped around me, shielding me from the shifters' fiery gazes. My stomach did jumping jacks and I struggled to push my way past him, but each time I took a step, he mirrored the motion to keep me hidden. I peeked over his shoulder at the shifters and worry set in. They weren't just big, they were absolutely massive. The two on the right could have been linebackers with their broad shoulders and chests the size of mountains. Their eyes glowed a brilliant orange, and the wide shapes of their noses paired with matching army cuts made me think they were likely brothers. Even twins maybe. As scary as these two were, and they were scary AF, the one in the middle was my biggest worry. There was no comparing him to the others, and his height alone made him one of the biggest shifters I've seen. Something about his pale skin and glowing blue eyes reminded me of Raiden, and I wondered if they were related. He stomped his feet into the ground and pulled back on his toes like a bull ready to charge. Muscles tensed under the gray shirt that clung to his ripped body, and I could see steam rising from his thin lips as he breathed.

"Step aside, cub," Raiden-lookalike growled. "We have no business with you."

River did not budge. "Whatever business you think you have here, rethink it."

The linebackers exchanged looks and grinned. Their massive arms stretched over their chests, and they ripped their sports tanks off in unison. My eyes grew as their bulging chests glistened in the low light of the setting sun. *This is the weirdest strip show I've ever seen. Not that there were many.*

Frigid air blew past me, and I breathed in relief, inhaling the fresh scent of the trees that offered a welcomed opposition to the heated steam the shifters gave off. I veered my body and withdrew the dagger from my boot, one hand already clutching the amber I always carried with me. The crystal vibrated in my palm and its magic rode me in waves. I shivered as shimmering lights danced in my peripheral before sending my own magic to meet the amber. A bright flame burst in my palm and I growled, forcing my way from behind River to face our attackers.

"Getting your mate to do the dirty work, cub? Pathetic," Raiden-lookalike bellowed.

The two on his side chuckled. "She's not his mate. Gotta be a shifter to mate to this loser."

Sickness overpowered me but I didn't let it stop my resolve. If these morons thought they could intimidate me, they had another thing coming.

I flipped the dagger and buried my heels into the grass. My mouth dried and I forced myself to breathe despite having very little lung capacity left. Beside me, River tensed, and his eyes found mine. He nodded and I took it as a sign to move my ass. Without flinching, I charged for the shifters with River at my side. We tore through the distance, running headfirst for the twins. Wind whipped around me, and my hair flew across my face, blurring my vision. I didn't need to see them. Not really. I could feel the slimy bastards and the rage they had for me. It drew me in like a magnet. Leaping in the air, I sent myself flying at one twin, my boot outstretched and aiming for his stomach.

The shifter was caught off guard it seemed because when the sole of my shoe hit his chest, his eyes widened, and he toppled back from the impact. Teeth grinding, I charged again, this time landing in a crouch on the other side of him. In a flash, I sliced my dagger across the back of his thigh, hitting an artery. Blood burst from his legs, splashing over my face, and I spit it out on the grass. "Disgusting."

I glanced back to River and saw him dig his knee into the other twin's neck as he pinned him to the ground. These bastards may be big, but they were also stupid and slow. Something I hoped would give us an advantage. Before I lost my moment, I jumped to my feet and bolted for the twin I attacked as he fumbled on the ground, holding his bleeding leg. His feral eyes locked on me, and I raised my boot, kicking him square in the jaw. The shifter's neck cracked, and his head spun to the left. Blood and spit flew from his mouth, and he landed on the grass with a loud thud. He let out an angry growl, but it did little to dissuade me. I was on him in seconds, my fired-up hand digging the amber into his temple while I sunk the dagger into his chest. A horrifying scream left his lips, and I tore the dagger out, jumping away to put space between us as his body disintegrated into ash.

To my right, another scream echoed, and I snapped my gaze to River. So much blood covered him I could barely recognize his features and when his eyes found me, I stumbled back. They were glowing so brightly, I couldn't see the rest of his face. Not the emeralds I was so fond of, more like peridots. Beautiful and bright. River snarled and clenched his chiseled jaw, snapping his teeth like a freaking baby turtle. His entire mouth was covered in blood and when I looked down, a gasp escaped me.

Beneath River lay the shifter twin, his face unrecognizable. There was a large gash on his throat and blood spewed from it in every direction.

Did River just freaking bite the guy? What in the actual hell was happening right now?

I had no time to think on it as enormous hands gripped my shoulders, spinning me around. A scream rose in me, but no sound came out, and I was tossed onto my back as Raiden-lookalike pounced on top of me. Though it wasn't really him anymore. Instead, I was being pummeled down by a black panther the size of a mid-sized truck.

My feet kicked out from under me as I pushed myself back. The ground tore into my skin, ripping my sweater to shreds, and the pain of stone ripping flesh sent icy shivers through my body. I trained the dagger at the panther's chest, but it slammed a massive paw over my arm, pinning me in place. Tears streamed down my face, and I shut my eyes as the panther threw its open jaw at my neck.

"Get the hell off her!" River roared and lunged for the panther.

My eyes snapped opened, and I watched in horror as he shoved the shifter off me with his shoulder. They rolled away in a mess of limbs, and I worked to make out which part was River and which was the panther with no success. All I saw was dark fur and flesh and teeth. All I heard was growling.

"River!"

The shock of what was happening wore off and I was on my feet, running toward them. Before I could reach them, an animalistic yelp filled the air and I saw the panther drag itself away. Crimson red stained its fur, and the sound of bones breaking and reforming echoed over me. My legs pumped as I ran faster, closing the distance between me and River and dropping to my knees at his side. My hands traveled over his body, inspecting for any major wounds, but aside from a few scratches, he looked to be unharmed. Our eyes met and the residual glow I saw before still lingered in them. I threw my arms around him, pressing him to my chest as my breath returned to me.

Near to us, the panther was finishing his shift and when I peeled my eyes from River, I was staring at Raiden-lookalike again. A very naked Raiden-lookalike. I averted my eyes, hoping I wouldn't see a part of the panther that would scar me for life.

"Get the hell out of here," River hissed between breaths. "Now."

The shifter snarled but stayed in his place. His hand clamped around his waist where River's bite was still visible on his skin. He winced and his eyes darted between the two of us as he climbed to stand. "This isn't over, witch. Whatever spell you got on Marcus and the others won't help you. I'm coming for you. We all are."

He began to speak again when a rock hit the side of his head and pushed him back. River was standing next to me, his fingers wrapped around another boulder. *When the hell did he get up?* My eyes swelled as I looked up, registering the anger building in him again. Shakily, I climbed to stand and placed a hand on his shoulder, easing him off the ledge.

I looked at the shifter. "Take this as a warning and go."

"YOUR warning," the shifter bit out and took off running into the line of trees behind him.

"Babe," River breathed out, but I held my hand up to stop him.

Without another word, I spun on my heels and stomped back to the blanket behind us. My hands dug through the bag, pulling out my cell phone. I dialed a number and pressed the phone to my ear as the ring tone blared on the other end. "Peyton," I said when my best friend picked up the line. "Get a hold of Marcus and tell him we're coming to the house. I've had just about enough of this bullshit."

Chapter Twenty-one

*B*eing back in the resistance house was in the top ten of my list of things I preferred not to do, and somehow, I was there for the third time this week. Whatever joke the universe was playing on me, I didn't appreciate it one bit.

This time, we gathered in a room on the first floor, and I was starting to wonder if shoving me into a different location each time was the shadowers' twisted way of giving a house tour. *They're definitely not getting a good Yelp review from me.* I rearranged my legs and leaned into the ebony wood table we huddled over, pressing my side into River. He shifted uncomfortably but let me use him as a pillow without objection. Somehow, I knew he needed the closeness just as much as I did. To my left, Peyton stared down the shadower leaders with a poker face worthy of an award. Her lip curled into an ominous snarl and her arms crossed over her chest said she meant business. What business it was, I had no idea, but I was glad to have the feisty rocket on my side.

"You are not harmed?" Marcus asked and I shook my head.

"We took down two. I think they were twins."

Raiden and Mel exchanged knowing glances.

"You know them?"

"The Powell twins," Raiden grumbled. "They're a problem."

River growled. "Not anymore."

The discomfort in the room grew by a million degrees and I had to look away from the table. I scanned the area, noticing the array of pictures on the walls for the first time. The frames were mismatched and there were people in them I haven't seen around the house. There were so many photos, I couldn't count them all, and they filled every inch of the space. Something about the display was ominous and sad, and I found myself unable to look away.

"Everyone we lost to your coven," Lorelei said when she noticed me staring. "To remember why we fight."

I swallowed the spit collecting in my mouth and peeled my eyes from the photos. "I'm sorry for your loss."

And I wasn't lying. I was sorry that so many people got hurt because of something the High Coven did. Though, I was mostly afraid that some people in those photos were there because of me. How many of the shadowers ended up on that wall because I vanquished them? I hoped not many, but at this point, hope was a currency I couldn't trade in.

"What about the other one?" River asked. "The panther?"

With a sigh, Marcus turned to Raiden and narrowed his eyes. "Raiden will deal with his cousin. He has fallen in with the wrong crowd, but he's a good kid, we'll make sure he doesn't bother you anymore."

Cousins? I knew it!

"He didn't seem like he would budge," River said, his eyes darkening. "Actually, he seemed like he wanted to kill her. What are you gonna do about him?"

"I'll deal with Damen. This doesn't concern you."

River's lips crashed into a line, and he rose off his chair to lean into the table. "It concerned me when he almost killed Billie and it will continue concerning me until he's handled. Leash the guy or I'll take care of him myself!"

"Calm your shit, cub," Raiden warned.

"Stop calling me that! I'm a damn hunter and I'm not your freaking cub!"

His face was beet red, and I could sense his energy reach across the table. Whether River wanted to admit it, his shifter side was on the verge of breaking through and I shuttered to think what that would mean for us. No shifter had ever turned this late in life, and I didn't know how his body would react. Every day, a piece of River disappeared and was replaced by something else. Something feral. I didn't want to see it before, but after the fight on the trails, there was no unseeing it. River was powerful as a hunter, but as a shifter, he'd be dangerous. Too dangerous to reign in, perhaps.

Looking at Raiden and Mel, I could see their thoughts mirrored mine. Their backs were rigid as they watched River like they were trying to figure out if he was about to rip their throats out. I wondered if he could. The shifter leaders were impressive, but River? He was something else altogether. An anomaly, and one I hated to admit I was beginning to fear.

"Let's all cool down," Lorelei interrupted and for once, I was grateful for the mind reaper's obnoxious attitude. "Tell us more about this book."

Oh, yeah. Peyton spilled the beans on that. Wonderful.

I shot a side-eye at my best friend, but she only shrugged. "The Book of Darkness. It's the oldest grimoire in the High Coven's possession. I've never read it, but I'm willing to bet that whatever this spell is they're working on, it's in there."

"And you're certain they can complete the spell at the full moon and identify the soul suckers?"

"Hundo P," Peyton answered.

The mind reaper's face grew ashen, if that was even possible for her pasty complexion, and she immediately looked to Marcus. Her eyes wetted and my heart ached for the two leaders. They were friends, perhaps even more than that, and the possible threat to Marcus was tearing her apart. I could relate. I felt the same way about the danger Peyton would be in if the coven succeeded. Marcus crossed the room to stand next to Lorelei and she relaxed instantaneously. Her hand reached for his face, running a finger down the scar across it. The soul sucker closed his eyes, shifting his lips to kiss the inside of her wrist. *Interesting.*

At their exchange, River's eyes burnt at my side, and I turned away from the leaders to look at him. Even after all of this, andhis shifter blood and his hunter training, he was still the most beautiful creature I've seen. Pressure built up in my chest as I thought of one day losing him, and I pushed the thoughts aside, refusing to believe it. We were end game. We had to be.

"I can get the book," I blurted out. "I'm going back to Stamwick and I'll steal it from the coven before anyone can notice it's gone. It's a shot in the dark, but it's our only chance to block this spell from happening."

"It's too dangerous," Marcus said, surprising me. "If you go back, they might catch on to your plan and we won't be able to get you out. I can't allow you to risk yourself for us. Being under their roof is not safe. There are too many witches there. You won't stand a chance."

"She won't be alone," River said. "The hunters are going with her."

I frowned. We agreed that he would come with me to Stamwick, but I still didn't approve of the idea. I approved even less of Savannah and the other hunters joining, but after the shifter attack, he refused to budge. It was looking that I would have River stuck to me like glue whether I liked it or not. I mostly liked it.

Fighting the urge to punch him, I focused on Marcus. "And I won't be staying with the coven. Savannah offered to cover a hotel for all of us."

"Wait, what? She's helping?" Peyton's ears perked. "Barbie?"

"Beats me," I whispered.

The door to the room burst open and Ashley crashed inside. Sweat beaded down his brow as if he'd just run a marathon. Though, considering the size of the resistance house, he may as well have. He opened his mouth to speak, but I stopped him. "Let me guess," I bit out, "we have a problem."

Ashley nodded and I tried not to laugh. At this point, I equated his interruption of these meetings as a warning sign. Wherever Ashley was, trouble followed.

"What is it?" Mel asked.

The shifter looked between River and me. "Your friends are here. They're refusing to leave and the rest of the house isn't too happy about it."

I rolled my eyes and let out an exasperated sigh. River groaned beside me.

"We'll talk to them," he said and stood up. "Come on."

As we piled out of the room, I ran after Mel and pulled her aside. The shifter leader slowed her pace but didn't stop, hanging back just enough that she was walking next to me.

"Can I ask you something?" I pressed and pulled her back from the group. "About you and Raiden?"

A genuine smile flashed over her face and she paused to face me. "Sure."

"I, uh..." I mumbled. "I was wondering about how you two... How..." *GEEZ! Use your words!*

"How our mating bond works?" Mel asked, helping me along. I nodded. "It's not rocket science. I can't really explain it, but when I met Raiden, it was like I knew he was mine. We fit somehow. Two pieces of a puzzle. I would do anything for him and he for me, and anyone that gets in the way is a goner. Then there's this."

She pulled down the edge of her top and my eyes popped out of my head when I saw the strange tattoo just above her heart. It looked like a spiral and stood out amidst the other ink on her body. Probably because this one was drawn with an ink unlike any I've seen before. It sparkled. Literally sparkled like diamonds in the sunlight.

"What the hell is that thing?" I asked, absolutely baffled.

Mel smiled and ran a finger across the spiral. At her touch, the ink wriggled and shone brighter, and my jaw hit the floor. "Our mate bond. Once you're mated, it kind of shows up on its own. A real nuisance at first but you get used to it."

"Oh, okay."

Not okay.

"Is this about River's shifter blood?"

I waved my head 'no'. "Yep."

Mel pressed her hand to my wrist and frowned. "Look, kid, I don't want to get your hopes up here. If your boyfriend turns, none of us know what will happen. Most of our kind go through the shift when we're kids, so it will be an adjustment for him, to say the least. And while I wish I could tell you that you could have what Raiden and I found in each other, I can't do that. There's never been an interspecies bond before."

"Awesome."

"But, hey," she said, "if it makes you feel better, there are very few shifters who find their true mate, so maybe River's one of those."

That did not make me feel better one bit.

In fact, it did quite the opposite. My stomach turned in knots and vomit filled my mouth. The possibility of losing River if he went through the shift was mortifying and my body ached just thinking about it. Inside me, the shadows swarmed my blood and my pulse beat louder than a drum. The ring on my finger pulsed with energy and I shut my eyes to control the unbearable power of my magic. I pried my lids apart, forcing myself to look ahead, but all I saw was darkness as the shadows crept out of me and into the room. They swirled around my face and hands, a spiraling tornado of energy and hurt.

"Billie!" Marcus' voice tore through me and I toppled back, my shoulder blades meeting the frames on the wall. "Breathe, Billie. Breathe."

I followed his voice, reigning in the shadows back into myself as my body shook uncontrollably. They fought me with everything they had, but I refused to budge. I had to show these suckers who's boss before they ate me alive. One by one, I pulled them back in until my vision was clear, and my skin didn't feel like a forest fire. In front of me, Marcus said words over and over, but I couldn't make them out. I tried to read his lips, but all I got was cursing and a few mentions of fae. *WHAT IS HAPPENING TO ME?*

There was no time to figure that out. When I came to, Savannah's cross face was in mine and her snarl made me forget anything else I was thinking. I glanced over her shoulder to see the hunters trapped in a confrontation with two mind reapers and four shifters. Between them, River and Peyton tried to run interference, but there was no stopping the fight that was about to break out. I've been in enough showdowns to know where this was heading.

A shifter, a mind reaper, and a hunter walk into a bar...

Rolling my shoulders, I pushed past Savannah and ran face-first into the line of fire.

Chapter Twenty-two

A hand smacked my face and I stumbled back into Peyton, trapping us between Tyler and one of the shifters. The hunter's face reddened, and he threw another punch. His knuckles flew past the shifter, hitting the back wall with a bang, and he winced from the pain. Anger flashed in his eyes, and he charged for the shifter again, screaming at the top of his lungs.

"Peyton! Out of the way!" I shouted to my best friend, who was smack dab in between the two.

Her slight frame ducked down, and she swerved on her heels to give them a wide birth. When Tyler and the shifter collided, punches and kicks ensued, and my eyes jumped from their tumble to Savannah and Abigail's screams close to me. The girls were out for blood, knives trained in each of their hands and their teeth grinding so loud, I could hear the sound over the chaos in the house. Behind me, someone shouted my name and I turned to see River pull Jayden away, kicking and screaming, from the two mind reapers that towered over him.

The jock refused to be led away and he cussed out River like a drunken sailor as my guy dragged him back in a headlock.

One down, four to go.

I scanned the room for Morgan and was surprised to see her stay out of the fight. The redhead leaned against a wall, away from the ensuing madness, with her leg propped up for support. I searched for her attention, but her eyes never found mine. Following her gaze, I landed on Peyton. My best friend fought with a fierceness I didn't expect and delivered blow after blow to the shifter cowering under her weight. It looked that Peyton's style of attack was to climb on her opponent's back and scratch and kick whenever the chance presented itself. An uncanny combination, but it seemed to the trick and the shifter spun in circles, trying to kick her off him. Peyton's black-painted nails dug into his neck, and he yelped out, throwing himself back and slamming Peyton into the wall behind them.

At that, Morgan was on her feet and running to the rescue.

I smiled. Because I was a serial killer who found moments of happiness in battle.

A roar sounded near me, and I spun around, expecting to see a shifter changing form. Instead, all I saw was Savannah barrel toward someone and I froze in my tracks when I realized who it was. Her battle cry alerted the other hunters, and they followed her lead, running with knives outstretched toward Mel and Raiden.

Ohshitohshitohshit! I bolted. Legs pumping, I jumped to get ahead of them and placed myself between the shifter leaders and my friends. "River..." I hissed between clenched teeth. "We... have... a... problem..."

At my back, I could feel Raiden's heated breath on my neck and my eyes found Mel's, urging her to back down. The leader nodded with pity coating her features. She understood the hunters were reacting to a threat and wanted nothing to do with hurting them. *Thank the Goddess.*

My shoulder blades tightened, and I straightened my back as I faced my friends.

"Back the hell up, Savannah," I bit out. "If you stop fighting, they will too."

She didn't. Obviously.

Before I could react, Savannah lunged for me, and I knew she was glad to have an excuse to attack. The asshole was gunning for me from the start, and it seemed she got exactly what she wanted. I stood my ground, but someone's arm wrapped over my waist and pulled me away. Kicking air, I struggled against the hold, but it was pointless. A woodsy smell drifted by me, and I let myself relax as River dragged me away from Savannah's wrath.

"We need to put some space between the groups," he said. "Where's Marcus?"

What an excellent freaking question.

I looked around but couldn't see the soul sucker anywhere. *Did this guy seriously run away?* Some leader.

Not far from River and I, Savannah had switched her attention back to Mel and Raiden, and horror flooded my system. If she dared go for them, she'd be dead before her stupid little knife made contact. I turned to River, waiting for him to make a move when the screams silenced and everyone stopped cold.

Looking through the crowd, I saw Marcus. He sauntered down the hallway, parting the crowd like he was Moses parting the seas. Beside him, Lorelei matched his stride with her hands outstretched and on either of her sides, two mind reapers followed her cue. Their powers filled the hallway and everyone in their vicinity dropped to their knees. Hunters and shadowers alike. Hands clutched temples as the mind reapers took hold of people's thoughts, forcing them lower. Teeth chattered and the sound made me wince as I watched the chaos die down, replaced only with the pain of everyone involved.

"That's enough, Marcus!" I yelled. "Make them stop! We get it!"

The soul sucker snapped his head to me and raised a hand above his head. "There will be no more fighting," he commanded. "When you are free of the pull, you will put down your weapons and step away from each other. I want the hunters on one side and the shadowers on the other. Do you understand?"

People struggled to nod through the pain, even Savannah. Her bronze skin was ashen, and her eyes shut tight, but she made no move to disagree.

Satisfied, Marcus dropped his hand and Lorelei and her mind reapers mimicked his movement. Sighs of relief sounded in the hallway, and I heard a few bodies drop to the floor. My eyes landed on Savannah, who cursed under her breath before tossing her knives to the side. *Finally, the idiot is listening to someone.* I filled my lungs with as much air as I could muster and breathed out slowly, making my way to Marcus.

"They didn't mean any harm. They're just scared."

"I know," the soul sucker replied. "We mean them no harm as well. They are welcome here."

He scanned the room and waited until the shadowers who started the altercation nodded in agreement. Shaking, they stood up, dusting themselves off before scurrying off into unfamiliar rooms in the house. When they dispersed, Savannah held a hand out to Abigail and pulled her up. Next to them, Jayden and Tyler struggled to stand.

"What the hell was that?" Savannah asked, eyeing me suspiciously. "And why didn't it work on her?"

She pointed to Peyton and my breath hitched in my throat. My best friend was crouching next to Morgan, helping her get her senses back. Her dark eyeliner was smeared, but other than that, she was cool as a cucumber. Whatever Peyton had been doing in the resistance for the last few weeks must have benefited her because Lorelei and the mind reapers did not target her in their attack. They valued Peyton somehow, and I wished I understood it more.

Breaking away from Marcus, Lorelei moved to Peyton's side and helped her get Morgan to her feet. The redhead was still in shock and her eyes blinked wildly as she looked from my best friend to the mind reaper.

"We cannot afford to injure a soul sucker," Marcus said. "They already have targets on their backs."

Gasps spread from the hunters and all eyes turned to Peyton. *Good job, Marcus. Way to out her. Not cool.* The hunters looked from Peyton to River and me, questions in their eyes. I wanted to reassure them somehow, but my attention was only on my best friend, who looked like she was about to pass out. I had half the mind to rush over and hold her, but with Lorelei at her side, she didn't need a bodyguard.

"ARE YOU KIDDING ME?" Savannah roared and we all turned to stare at her. "She's one of them? I knew I hated you for a reason. You're disgusting!"

Peyton's eyes wetted and she dropped Morgan's hand like it burnt her. Tears streamed down her cheeks and her quiet sobs filled the hallway. Her pain made something inside of me snap, and I ripped myself away from River to face Savannah. I've had enough of this chick. No one hurt my best friend, especially not someone as insignificant as Savannah Michaels.

Without pause, I threw my hands toward her, shadows shooting from my fingertips and straight for her neck. When they reached her body, I flicked my wrists and wrapped them over her skin in a noose. I yanked another fast flick, and the hunter was up in the air, her face turning blue from the lack of air as I strangled her with my magic. There were shouts all around us and everyone ran in my direction. I heard them plead with me to stop, heard River's hard voice in my ear, but I didn't care. Savannah was a nuisance and one I wanted to eliminate.

Inside me, the magic darkened as the shadows took hold and I could see the ring on my finger light up in a brilliant glow of white. It vibrated over my skin, and I rocked from side to side, carrying Savannah's choking body with me. Her legs dangled as she swayed, hitting the walls on either side of her as she struggled to get free. I could see her face get blue and it brought me so much joy I could hardly contain myself.

My lips curled up and I chuckled. *What is happening to me?* Hurting Savannah felt good, better than good, and I wanted to stop but something urged me forward.

I was just about to tighten my grip on Savannah's neck when a hand pressed against my chest. Looking down, I saw a glimpse of finger tattoos and then my world went black.

Chapter Twenty-three

By the time I came to, the sun had set, and moonlight streamed through the half-cracked window. Every inch of my body ached, and I struggled to rise, eager to take a shower to erase the memory of what happened. I reached for my nightstand and almost fell off the bed when my hand sliced through thin air. *What the hell?* Shocked, I looked around my room but couldn't recognize anything in sight. None of my furniture was there, and the wallpaper that stretched the barren walls had seen better days. My head snapped to the window, trailing the edges of the wide crack that ran along the glass. Beyond it, only trees loomed on the horizon and their shadows sent dread through my tired bones.

I jolted up and regretted the decision immediately. My head spun and my vision blurred from the motion, and I eased myself back onto the mattress with a groan.

"Easy, tiger," a familiar voice said from the shadows of the room.

I blinked rapidly, bringing Jayden's cocky smile into focus. "Where am I?"

"One of the spare rooms in the resistance house. Marcus said we can put you here until you came to." He smiled. "Took a while, if I may add."

"Where's—"

"River?" he cut me off. "I had to send him away. The boy was scary. He didn't leave your side all evening, but I finally kicked him out. Sent him over to your place with a cover-up to tell the Chandlers."

I frowned. "I'm sure he loved that."

"Yeah, that was not fun to watch. But it's cool, Sav went with him."

Of course, she flippin' did. Fists clenched at my side, and I snapped my jaw shut, grinding my teeth to keep from screaming. I was out for a few hours and this asshole was already digging her nails into River. Goddess, I wish they just let me kill her when I had the chance. The thought startled me, and I lifted on the bed, horrified at myself. I almost killed Savannah. Sure, she was a grade-A bitch, but she didn't deserve to die. At least not for some offhand remark toward Peyton. What was even wrong with me? *Oh, my Goddess! Peyton!*

"Where's Peyton? Is she okay?" I asked, throwing my legs to the floor.

Jayden jumped at the foot of the bed and leaned me back into the soft mattress. His muscled arms tensed as I tried to fight him, but in the end, I relaxed and let him ease me back down. "Chill, girl. She's fine. She's shaken up and wasn't too happy with Sav, but she'll live."

"She must be horrified. What Savannah said, it was rude and unnecessary."

"Well, that's Savannah for you. Always running her mouth."

My brow creased and I let out an exasperated sigh. "Why is

she always this way? We're all on the same side here. I don't get it."

"Savannah is tough, she always has been, but she means well. Well enough at least. And trust me, she's a good friend when she wants to be."

Somehow, I seriously doubted that. The idea that Savannah would ever be a good friend to me was laughable. She hated anyone that interfered with her group, and Peyton and I threw ourselves in like two bats out of Hell. I doubted someone as controlling as Savannah liked that at all. Actually, I one hundred percent knew it.

"How's Morgan handling the news about Peyton?"

Jayden's eyebrows arched. "Finally! Someone else gets the lady love that's happening there!" he exclaimed. "Okay, dish. You think they'll hook up, or what?"

I chuckled and pain shot up my side.

"Wait, did Peyton use her freaking powers on me?"

"Sure did. It was badass."

"But I'm not dead?"

Laughter burst from Jayden and he slapped the tops of my thighs. "That girl is loyal to a fault. No way she'd hurt you. She just needed to get you to calm down before you, you know..." He sliced his finger over his throat. "Killed Sav and shit."

"It was that bad?"

"Oh, yeah! I almost pissed myself. But you know, new slacks and whatever. Mom would kill me if I came home covered in urine."

It was my turn to laugh, and I winced from the tension it sent through my body. "I feel like a truck ran me over. Peyton's got some explaining to do."

"Not to freak you out, but you do too. River was pissed. Like crazy pissed. I think you really scared him back there."

And I scared a shifter. *Awesome. Well played.* I tossed the blanket over my face and groaned into it. This was not how I wanted to introduce the hunters to the shadowers. They were at each other's throats as soon as they met, and that wasn't even everyone at the resistance. I could only imagine how that meeting will play out. Instead of calming everyone down, I scared the crap out of them by not controlling my emotions. When was I going to learn already? I wasn't in Stamwick anymore and couldn't go around lashing out at people the way I did on shadower patrols. There was an intricate balance that needed to remain if we had any shot of stopping the High Coven from performing the spell, and everyone had to play nice. My flipping out on Savannah in front of everyone would not help keep that balance one bit. It was stupid and I felt like a complete idiot for how I behaved. More as a spoiled child than a witch. It was pathetic.

"He was that mad, huh?" I asked.

"Oh, yeah."

I scoffed. "Good thing Savannah's there to make him feel better."

Jayden slapped me again and this time, I felt the sting across my thigh.

"Ouch! Stop that!"

"I will when you stop being a tool," he retorted. "Look, I get how Savannah is all over him and that's gotta suck, but you can't let it get to you. River has no interest in her. That boy is so into you, it's actually sickening."

"Why? Why me when he can be with her? Savannah is a tool, but she's his best friend."

DING! DING! DING! Here comes the self-pity mobile!

"You know," Jayden said with a smile, "for a crazy intimidating witch, you're kind of an idiot. Savannah might not want to admit it, but you're awesome, Billie. We all think so."

"Even Abigail?"

"Even her. We might have all been friends most of our lives, but that doesn't mean there isn't space for someone new. And you and Peyton are part of the group now, so get used to it."

He was right. I had to get with the program here.

"It's weird you guys are friends with someone like her," I blurted out before I could stop myself. "Sorry. I just meant—"

"I know what you meant. Don't sweat it." Jayden's eyes lightened and he flipped his thick dark hair off his face. "I'm gonna tell you something, but if you repeat this, I swear I will murder you in your sleep."

Eyes narrowed, I sat up to lean closer to him. "Drama queen."

"You know it! Anyway, you should give Savannah a break. She might come off all high and mighty, but she's had a tough go at it. Her family sucks and her parents treat her like garbage. They're basically never around and when they are, she wishes they weren't."

"Why?"

"Let's just say the Michaels family are as screwed up as they come. I don't think they ever wanted kids and when Savannah was born, it ruined all their plans for a perfect, selfish life. So they take it out on her. Emotional warfare or whatever. Anyway, just cut her some slack, if you can. Okay?"

Hesitantly, I nodded. "You're kinda observant, huh?"

"Not just a pretty face." He grinned. "Although it sure is pretty."

I smacked Jayden's shoulder, pushing him back until he fell on the blanket at my legs. We both burst out laughing and the tension I felt before dissipated. As much as I wanted River here when I got up from the ass-kicking Peyton laid down, I was glad Jayden kept me company. It was nice to have a friend around when I needed one, and he really wasn't just a pretty face. I looked back to Jayden's widening grin. *What a cocky bastard.*

Wind howled outside and a tree branch banged against the glass, drawing my attention to the window. Unease settled at the base of my stomach, and I could feel eyes on me. There was no one else in the room and I couldn't hear anyone in the hallway outside, but the sense that we were being watched refused to leave me. I chalked it up to the remnants of Peyton's soul sucker powers coursing through my system and peeled my eyes from the window to lean into the pillow. The wind continued to howl, and I closed my eyes, letting sleep drown out Jayden's laughter.

Chapter Twenty-four

eeth were everywhere. A wily fox flew straight at my face with its jaw unhinging as it inched closer to my neck. I twisted out of its path just in time and it slammed into the padded wall behind me. Its head rolled to the side and its eyes snapped shut as the shift took it over. In moments, I towered over a totally naked slender brunette with a tree tattoo running down the side of her tanned body. I swiped a random sweater off the floor and tossed it over her form, hopeful she'd take the clue and cover up when she came to.

With the shifter out of the way, I focused my attention on the mind reaper at the opposite side of the room. Magic swirled in my hands, and I rubbed a large pearl between my fingers. With a quick sleight of hand, I blasted the mofo with enough wind to toss him into the wall and he bounced back, settling on his knees a few feet away from me. His silver eyes found mine and he snarled.

Not a chance in hell, buddy! I jerked my hand and willed the wind to knock him down. His face hit the floor and I heard a tooth crack. When he looked back up, blood dripped from the side of his lips and the snarl was gone. *Should've stayed down.*

"Low blow!" someone shouted, and I was met with a pair of hooded black eyes.

I didn't hesitate, running the blade of my dagger across my palm and slamming it to the floor. Power rolled through me, and I directed it into the blood smearing on the ground, pushing my hand around to draw the rune I needed. With my other hand, I pulled an amber crystal from my pocket and called for a flame. It burst from my skin, and I brought it to the rune, fueling the spell with my magic.

In seconds, flames rose all around me until I was standing behind a fiery wall of protection.

The black-eyed shifter's bones cracked as he attempted to switch form, but I was faster. Tossing the dagger aside, I pressed my palms to the flame and blew it outward. Flames barreled at the shifter and he jumped right. The ball of fire hit the back wall, charring the soft fabric that lined it. The shifter yelped and slapped his large, hairy hand over the fur that grew on his arm, and the smell of singed skin filled the room.

Marcus said he wanted me to train the shadowers to get them ready for any attack the High Coven might bring forth. He never said I couldn't have some fun while doing it.

My lips curled up and I turned to the fifteen shadowers cowering against the back wall. "Who's next?"

"I'll give it a go," a low, honey-soaked voice said. My eyes widened as River stepped into the center of the training room with a cocky grin plastered on his face. "But you better play fair, Goldilocks."

I snarled. "The coven won't."

His grin widened and before I could utter another smart-assed remark, a knife was flying at my face. *What is with these damn hunters and their knives?* My eyes darted to the dagger on the floor, and I dove for it, dropping my keep on the wall of fire. The flames extinguished and any chance I had to keep myself out of River's grasp disappeared with them. I rolled on my side, snatching the dagger with one hand while using the other to push myself up. Behind me, River's knife impaled the padded wall and my lips crashed into a thin line. That would have been my face if I didn't move. Did he know that?

Forcing myself to move, I bolted for River. I was almost on him when he pulled two more knives from his back pocket and tossed them in my direction. One after the other, they sliced the air toward me and I bolted, veering left and right to miss the blades.

"You said to play fair!" I shouted and skidded to a stop.

"And you said no," he hissed back.

Resolve flushed my system, and I narrowed my eyes at him. *That's it. Hotness is going down.* My legs pumped as I soared at River, flames bursting from both my hands while I ran. We agreed I was not to use my shadows until I had better control of them, but that didn't mean I couldn't use magic. The High Coven was a serious threat, and everyone in this room, shadowers and hunters alike, had to see firsthand what they were walking into. I knew the older shadowers in the resistance had plenty of run-ins with witches, but the younger kids I was to train had their jaws trailing the floor as they watched me work. If they thought *I* was bad, they had no chance against the coven. We were screwed.

Shaking my head in disgust, I continued to run for River until I was face to face with him.

I growled.

He grinned.

AGH! STOP THAT! My hands shot out on either side of him, and I sent the flames flying just past his ears. He winced but didn't back down, which was enough for me. I turned on my toes, swinging one leg to the side to hook over his shins. River's legs gave out from under him, and he fell back, landing on his butt. His sweet, adorable butt. He tried to stand, and I dropped on top of him, hips straddling his sides and burying my elbow into his neck.

"Here we go again," Jayden groaned from the wall. "Get a room!"

I shot a death glare at my friend and turned my attention back to River. His face was flushed, and I wasn't sure if it was because I overpowered him or from the way my hips were grinding against his body. Whatever it was, I would use it to my advantage. Raising my dagger, I swiped it for the elbow I had on his neck and pushed the blade down to keep him in place. His smile faltered when I reached for the amethyst pendant on my neck, ready to teach him a lesson. I was still tapping into my magic when the dagger flew from my hand and I was flipped on my stomach, one hand behind my back and one held down at the side. River leaned in and his warm breath tickled my ear. "Almost had me."

In my peripheral, I could see the peridot glow of his eyes and fear gripped me. His shifter side was crawling out and I was trapped.

"Get her, cub!" someone shouted.

Struggling to turn my head to the crowd, I fished out where the voice came from, noticing a group of young shifters howling at my guy. They fist-pumped the air and yodeled like morons as they cheered him on. *Since when does he have a fan club here? I* blinked them away. *Focus!*

River's hold on me was strong, but he made one colossal mistake. He left my legs unattended. I kicked back, slamming the sole of my boot into his back. *Thank you, yoga class.*

The hit knocked him forward and his hold on my arm lessened. I swiveled from under, ripping the amethyst pendant off and using the chain to wrap around his neck. I yanked on the silver, and he grimaced when the metal pressed into his skin. His shadower side did not like that. *GOOD!* My eyes twinkled and I spun him around so I could put him in the same delicate position he had me in. Slowly, I dropped and pressed my lips to his ear.

"My turn to be on top," I whispered, and his back grew stiff. "Ugh. Not like that. That came out wrong. Keep it in your pants, hunter."

River chuckled and I loosened my grip on the chain and the arm I pinned behind his back. He tapped the floor thrice and I threw my arms in the air to cheer. "Winner!" I shouted to no one in particular.

The room was not impressed. Shadowers moaned and complained, and someone mentioned cheating, but I didn't care. The High Coven would do anything in a fight. I should know, they trained me. These kids had to be ready for some sly shit if they wanted to survive the witches and Goddess knew, once I blocked this spell, they'd be coming for us.

Easing off River, I held out a hand and helped him up to stand beside me.

"Don't listen to them," he said, his voice low. "That was a fair fight. You did great."

"Maybe good enough for a mate," I muttered under my breath.

His eyes darkened and he caught my sleeve. "What's that?"

"Nothing. Come on, let's get the hunters. We should pair everyone off."

He looked puzzled but followed my lead. We grabbed a hunter each, pairing them off with shadowers, and despite everyone's objections, they did as they were told. It even surprised me to see Savannah saunter across the room to spar with an out-of-this-world gorgeous mind reaper. Not that I was checking him out because River was my everything, but man, this boy was hot with a capital H. Tall muscular build and long pale hair tied in a half-knot atop his head. His eyes were lavender, and his chiseled jaw gave River a run for his money. Savannah didn't seem to notice as she flashed him her best resting bitch face and crossed her arms over her face. That girl was hopeless.

As I looked around the room, I noticed Peyton wasn't anywhere in sight. In fact, there was not one soul sucker with us for training. Marcus said they were keeping them under close watch in case the spell set off early and they needed protection, but it wasn't like my best friend to not want to be in the heart of trouble. On second glance, I realized Morgan was also missing.

"Have you seen Peyton and Morgan?" I asked River.

He shrugged. "Not for a few hours. I think they went for coffee."

Actual freaking joy filled me to the brim. My best friend and I have not talked since the whole Marcus outing her incident, but I was excited for Peyton. Getting closer to Morgan was exactly what she needed right now. A distraction. And she was probably feeling guilty about having to use her powers on me, though truth be told, I didn't hold it against her. Peyton and I had each other's backs and sometimes that meant an ass-kicking when one of us was about to do something stupid like killing a team member. My actions asked for it and I got what I deserved. Peyton was not to blame for that.

"Let's get this over with so we can go home and pack," River said and nudged me forward.

Just like that, every happiness I felt evaporated, and nerves took its place. Tomorrow morning, we were catching the first bus into the city, and it wouldn't be long before I had to do the unthinkable. Stealing the Book of Darkness was necessary, but it didn't stop the guilt from eating me up. Despite their wrong-doings, betraying the High Coven did not sit well with me, and I hoped that when it came time to get the job done, I wouldn't let that guilt interfere.

I stalked to the focus of the room with River at my side and faked a smile. Fake it 'til you make it had never felt this real.

Chapter Twenty-five

*D*awn was breaking through when Peyton's Jeep rolled into the driveway and I held back a yawn, wishing I accepted Silas' offer of a coffee to go. We were determined to get to Stamwick as soon as possible, and though Peyton wasn't joining us on the trip, she insisted to drive to the bus station. Aside from my backpack and a small weekender full of magical supplies, I had nothing with me, and Peyton stared me down as I climbed into the passenger seat.

"Uh, is that *all* you're bringing?" she asked.

"I mean, yeah. It's like two days."

She eyed me up and down. "Girl, you know you're going to some fancy-assed hotel with River, right? You better have sexy dresses in that backpack or I'm not driving you."

I shook her off.

"I'm serious, missy!"

"Peyton," I huffed out, "it's not a weekend getaway. We're there to do a job and a dangerous one at that. There won't be time for sexy dresses or anything else. Besides, the rest of the hunters are coming too, so it's not some romantic trip for the two of us."

"Boooorrrrinnnggg..." Peyton sang but, to my relief, put the car in reverse.

We pulled out and I waved to Imala, who was watching us from the porch. Her ebony hair was tied into a messy bun, and she was still in her PJ's. This was the most casual I've seen her, and it made me smile. She was finally comfortable with me to look like a hot mess, though for Imala, that wasn't saying much. Even on her bad days, she looked ten times better than I did when I put some effort in. The woman was *that* stunning.

I shot a smile her way and turned back to Peyton. "You sure you don't want to come with?"

"Yeah, pretty sure," she said without pause. "Marcus said it's better if I'm close to the shadowers in case something goes wrong, and I agree with him. And I don't want to leave my parents and Kai alone."

"I get it. Thanks for driving me."

"Bitch, please! I haven't seen you for twenty-four full hours. I'm having withdrawal over here."

I chuckled and looked out the window, holding back another yawn. Rising this early had never been a strong suit of mine, and though I prided myself on never showing up late, mostly because being late to a vanquishing usually meant someone ended up dead, I wished we were catching an afternoon bus. I understood why everyone wanted to get to the city earlier to get situated, but the sun wasn't even up yet! Was this torture seriously necessary?

The bus station was a brief drive from my house and by the time we pulled up, the others were already waiting at the entrance. I hauled my bags from the backseat and leaned through the window to hug Peyton. "See you in a couple of days." I smiled.

"Try not to die."

She winked and peeled out of the parking lot with smoking tires. *Maniac.*

Turning back to my friends, I waddled with my bags dragging behind me. The lack of sleep made my arms feel like mush, and I was basically sleepwalking the entire way. River spotted me and ran to grab my bags, helping me carry them over. They weren't even heavy, but for the first time, I was not about to object to his macho crap. A girl had to pick her battles.

When we reached the others, I noticed most hunters had only a few bags each except for Abigail and Savannah. They had matching Louis Vuitton luggage cases with two carry-ons each. Savannah leaned against her suitcase, eyeing me suspiciously.

"You know I said to bring something fancy, right?" She scoffed. "This isn't some lame motel we're staying in. Dad set us up in the main suites and I already booked dinner at St. Thomas."

I stifled my need to lash out at her. After my conversation with Jayden, I was trying hard to be nicer to Savannah, but she made that extremely difficult. Not that I didn't appreciate her effort to give us the best of what Stamwick offered. In fact, dining at St. Thomas was kind of a big deal for most socialites, my problem was that she didn't seem to understand how important the trip was. If we failed this, the soul suckers were as good as dead and the same went for the resistance. We couldn't afford any mistakes or distractions, and I was pretty sure she had a ton of both packed in her over-the-top designer bags.

"I'll be fine," I said as nicely as I could manage. "Thanks for the tip."

"River, babe, tell her she can't wear leggings to dinner please." Her eyes looked past me like I didn't exist in her universe and blood rushed to my head.

I was way over her talking over me, and I stomped my foot to get her attention. "Maybe *you'd* prefer to be the one risking her life to get this book?" I asked. "I'm sure the High Coven would love to see your little outfit when you attempt it."

She looked away, leaving me free of her judgment. *Count to ten, don't try to kill her again.*

"Let me know if you're about to throw a punch," River whispered in my ear, reading my thoughts. "I'll get Peyton here real quick."

I nudged his side and yanked my backpack from his hands, storming toward the ticket booth.

"Where are you even going?" Savannah yelled out behind me.

Stopping in my tracks, I turned to face her. "To get the tickets. Where else would I go?"

"Ugh, you're honestly the worst." She blew a curl off her face. "We're not riding those human cesspools for hours. Dad's sending his company bus to pick us up."

Of course he is. "Oh, okay. When's it getting here?"

Princess didn't bother answering but as she turned around to whisper something to Abigail, I noticed the abomination that was to be our ride pull into the lot. Any hope I had of staying out of Savannah's way for the next few hours diminished when I saw our ride. This thing was loaded to the max and resembled a bus one used for bachelorette parties or sweet sixteens, not that I knew much about any of those. Either way, I could no longer count on a large crowd of strangers to keep me out of Savannah's path since it was just our group piling in.

River's fingers tugged at my waist, and I followed him to the souped up RV, dread filling my body. My heart raced with each step and sweat pooled under the hefty weight of my plaid overcoat. Four more hours and we'd be in Stamwick. I had the feeling they would be the worst four hours of my life.

To say that the hotel Savannah booked with her dad's connections was glorious would have been an understatement. Barbie doll somehow got us into one of the most exclusive boutique hotels in Stamwick and I felt like a roach on the carpet as soon as we walked in. While she fluttered her lashes at the check-in staff, I stood slack-jawed to the side, scanning the breathtaking decor of the lobby. It was a large, open area with the most exquisite modern design. A grand staircase led to an overhanging balcony that spanned the perimeter of the lobby and there was a freestanding fireplace in the center with lush, leather seating all around. On one wall, a gigantic aquarium took my breath away and I couldn't help but smile at the spools of fish that swam within it. Hotel guests were everywhere, and they all looked like movie stars.

I looked down at my ripped jeans and overcoat and frowned.

Maybe Peyton was right. I should have packed better.

Before I could bite my nails to the bone, Savannah called us all back and handed out the room keys. She pointed everyone toward the elevators and waved her dainty hand in the air for a bellboy. The flustered young man ran after her like a trained pup and acid rose in my throat as he gushed over her. Straining to haul all our bags on a cart, he somehow still managed to not take his eyes off Savannah. Instinctively, my gaze snapped to River, but when I turned, he was watching me with such intensity, I thought I would melt into the mosaic tiles under my boots.

"Ready to go?" he asked. "I got Sav to get us rooms on the same floor."

"That's great." I smiled, but deep inside, I hoped our rooms weren't too close together. I couldn't have any distractions and having River's body in the room next to mine at night, possibly undressed, would leave me sleepless.

We crammed into the mirrored elevator and made our way to the rooms. Floor by floor, each hunter stepped out, leaving only River and me in the elevator. When it kept riding, I checked the buttons as they flashed, landing on PH.

"We're in the penthouse suites?" I asked, baffled.

"Yep." He grinned. "Told you Sav could come through."

What in the actual hell? Savannah did this for us? *For me?* I was shocked. When River said she got us rooms on the same floor, I half expected us to be stuck in the basement somewhere. Yet, here we were, in the most expensive, gorgeous suites the hotel had to offer. My opinion on Savannah began to change, and I wondered if she was trying to make up for the way she'd been treating me. These suites seemed to be an olive branch, and as we stepped out into the wide corridor of the penthouse floor, I promised myself to give her a chance.

There were four suites on the floor, each one with a set of large, frosted glass doors leading to the rooms. River was two rooms away from mine, and I breathed in relief that we had some space between us. He didn't look as impressed, but I gave him a hotter than sin kiss before rushing off into my room to relax his tension. *Big baby.*

Opening the door to my room was like stepping through a wardrobe to Narnia. The penthouse suites were massive, with an open concept living area, a small kitchenette, and wide French doors blocking the bedroom from view. I dropped my bags at the entrance and inspected every single detail of the room. By the time I finished, I was standing in front of the floor to ceiling windows with a perfect view of the city with nothing left untouched in my path.

About to hop into a much-needed shower, I chucked my overcoat on the plum sectional and kicked off my boots. My hair hung heavy over my shoulders and I all but ran to the bathroom. I was already turning on faucets when a loud knock sounded, jolting me in surprise.

Frustrated at the interruption, I stomped to the door and swung it wide open. On the other side, River stood in only his jeans and his pale face made knots turn in my stomach.

"Marcus just called," he said.

Dread washed over me, and I clutched the door handle for support. "What happened?"

He didn't speak.

"River, what happened?"

"There was an incident at the house with some of the shifters." He swallowed hard. "They rounded on Peyton because of her connection to you. Marcus said they couldn't get to her in time. She's hurt, babe. Really hurt."

Chapter Twenty-six

"And we can't even talk to her?" Morgan asked.

The hunter's face was green and while the rest of us huddled in a tight circle in the living room of my hotel suite, she stayed off to the side. Her red hair clung to her face and from the redness of her eyes, I could tell she'd been crying. I wanted to comfort her somehow but drawing attention to whatever she and Peyton had going on would not win me any favors in the best friend department, so I kept my tongue leashed.

"Marcus said she's not conscious," River answered. "He said he'll call as soon as she wakes up."

"If she wakes up," Savannah muttered.

Tyler's gaze narrowed on her and he peeked out over Abigail's head, rearranging his girlfriend in his lap to have a better view. "Give it a damn rest, Savannah!" he snapped. "This is not the time for you to be a bitch."

The discomfort in the room went up a few notches and we all watched Savannah, waiting for some asshole retort.

"I'm not being anything," she said. "Those shifters were

top-notch douches and Marcus said they've been dealt with. He also said that he doesn't know if Peyton will wake up anytime soon. I'm simply stating the facts."

"Well, keep your facts to yourself, okay?"

Tears stung the rear of my eyes and I worked to focus on the conversation, but all I could think about was Peyton. I should have never let her stay there on her own. Savannah had one thing right, those shifters were awful, and I should have finished them all off when they dared attack us on the trails. Because of my stupidity, Peyton was lying somewhere in that damn resistance house and fighting for her life. My chest constricted and the sweatshirt I wore tightened against my skin like a straitjacket. I couldn't see, I couldn't speak, I couldn't even breathe.

Eyes burnt in my peripheral and I swung my head to River, shaking in my seat on the sectional.

"Billie?" he asked and everyone turned to me. "What are you thinking?"

"I... I..." I worked to speak but words made no sense. They sat in my mouth, suffocating me with their meaninglessness. "Why did he call *you*?" I finally choked out.

"Who? Marcus? I'm not sure. I think he worried about how you'll react."

WORRIED HOW I'LL REACT? I wanted to scream. To hop on the next bus back to Shadowhurst and cut the throats of every shifter that laid a hand on Peyton. *That's how I'll freaking react, Marcus!*

My thoughts jumbled and my vision blurred under the tears. Fingers laced in mine, and I looked up to see both River and Jayden holding one of my trembling hands. They squeezed tight and I forced myself to take a breath in, sobs escaping with every gasp of air. My best friend was in trouble, and I couldn't even make it better. The shifters beat her senseless, and by the time Marcus and the leaders got there, she was barely breathing. Whatever pain I felt now was nothing compared to what she went through, and the worst part was that it was all my fault. They targeted her because she was my friend. It was a message and I heard it loud and clear.

I would make sure they got a message in return.

"How are they handling the ones who hurt her?" Morgan asked.

River stiffened at my side and pulled his gaze from me. "They locked them up, for now."

"Not good enough," Jayden hissed.

"No kidding," Abigail said.

Blood rushed to my neck and my heart hammered in my chest. It sure as shit wasn't good enough at all. Locking those animals up would do nothing to make Peyton better, and Marcus' inability to right that wrong made me want to rip his face off. She was a soul sucker for fae's sake! One of his own kind! How could he simply lock those bastards up? He should torture them until they can't remember their names, giving them the slow deaths they deserved.

My entire body convulsed, and I ripped my hands from the worrying grip River and Jayden had on them. Unable to stop, I rose and yanked my overcoat on, tightening the belt with a growl.

"Babe?" River asked with worry. "Where are you going?"

"Out!" I yelled. *Why am I yelling at him? Oh, who cares! I need out!*

"Out where?"

"Just out. I need some air. Don't follow me." I glanced back at the group. "Any of you."

I slammed the door behind me and stormed down the hall to the elevator. When it opened, I threw myself inside, punching the button for the lobby with so much force, the damn thing cracked. The doors opened and I sneered at the couple waiting to get in. They stepped aside, giving me a wide birth as I stomped my way through the prissy lobby of the hotel.

One swing of the glass doors and I was free.

Frigid air hit my face and the tears running down my cheek froze on impact. Stamwick was a city surrounded by water, and I could smell the cold of the upcoming winter in the air. It was everywhere. Empty but for the ice that lingered in it, a perfect mirror to my heart.

I took off in a dead sprint, zigging and zagging down the streets I knew like the back of my hand. Every turn took me back to my time here, to the nights I spent on these very streets looking for a shadower to vanquish. As the sun set behind the skyscrapers, I let myself slow down. I knew this. This feeling of desperation and this need to fight. It was who I was deep down, and I wanted nothing more than to open up that Pandora's box and unleash my anger on the city.

Turning a corner, I swerved into a dark alley and the familiar smell of trash and urine invaded my senses.

Goddess, how I missed that disgusting combination!

There was an empty beer can close to me and I kicked it with full force, sending it straight into an overflowing trash bin. *That felt good.* I found another and did it again. Before long, I wasn't just kicking beer cans anymore, I was tearing the alley apart and destroying everything in my path.

"AAAAAAHHH!" I roared and kicked a loose bag of garbage in my way.

It ripped on my boot and trash flew everywhere, staining the concrete with liquids. I tried not to think about what they might be from. The alley reeked, but it didn't bother me one bit. This was only target practice for when we got back and I had my way with those damn shifters.

"You all right, kid?" a husky voice said behind me.

I spun around, breathless. My focus turned to the person and when he came into view, I noticed the way his skin reflected the moonlight above. For someone who liked to hang out in dirty alleyways, he was stunning. His flawless features stressed the pale green of his eyes, and I found myself unable to look away. He smiled and I let my guard down, stepping closer.

Before I could stop myself, I was inches away from the man, my hands reaching out to touch him. There was some pull between us, and I couldn't understand it one bit. I wasn't attracted to him, he was old enough to be my father, but something in his eyes beckoned me forward. Yanking my hand back, I shoved it into my coat pocket and plastered a false smile on my face. "I'm fine. Thanks."

"Why don't we get you out of here?" the man said and reached for me.

His cool fingers wrapped around the back of my neck and tugged me forward. My body went limp, and my eyes widened as fear set in. Magic fought within me. *Danger, Will Robinson! DANGER!*

My brain screamed at me to get free, but I could not move. The man's pale eyes burrowed into me, and a flush of energy entered my bloodstream. My magic roared and I opened my mouth to scream, but the man cupped his other hand over my mouth.

"Now what's a pretty little witch like you doing out by yourself?" he sneered and my arms dropped at my side.

A soul sucker. Goddess help me.

I struggled to reach for the dagger, but his power was overwhelming and every one of my limbs fell flat. This felt just like when Peyton hit me with her power, and I knew this bastard was using only enough of his abilities to render me useless, but not enough to kill me. Whatever he wanted to do with me, it was just beginning. Panic rose in my chest, suffocating every other thought I had. The man grinned, flashing two rows of perfect pearly whites, and I let out a sob against his palm.

"Come now," he whispered. "No need to cry. This will be over before you know it."

He dragged me back, pinning me against one of the dust-covered walls of the alley. My back hit brick and my head rolled back as his power rolled off me in waves. The man dropped his hand from my mouth and ran it down my collarbone. "So pretty..."

Bile rose in my throat, and I gagged on my spit. My head spun and I tried to focus but my vision swam uncontrollably. *No, no, NO! Think! Damn it, THINK!* Inside me, the faintest hint of my shadows emerged, and I breathed out in relief.

The man was so preoccupied with dragging his hungry gaze over my assets, he didn't notice when my eyes closed, and my body grew still. On my finger, the moonstone ring lit up like a beacon and shadows swarmed my hands. His attention snapped to the ring, and he let go of my hips and wrapped both his hands around my throat. My body shook from his power, and I was close to passing out, but I battled against it. Shadows wrapped around us, swirling and picking up speed as I beckoned them forward. A cry left my lips, and I slapped my hands to the soul sucker's chest, forcing him off me.

He flew back, hitting the wall opposite us with a bang.

Step by step, I walked to him, using the shadows as a shield. His eyes widened and his mouth dropped open when I reached my magic for his heart. Tears streamed down my face, and I was shaking so violently, I could barely stay upright. I let the anger building up lead the way and twisted the shadows over the soul sucker's heart. He cried out in agony, and I smiled.

"Hey!" another voice yelled in the distance.

I turned my head, dropping my shadows and letting them crawl back into my body.

At the end of the alley stood a young girl no older than me. Her hair was tied in a high ponytail and her gaze danced between me and the cowering soul sucker on the ground. Her eyes were saucers as she searched my face in recognition. "Billie?"

SHIT.

Chapter Twenty-seven

"Victoria?" I picked up my jaw from the ground and trained my eyes on the witch.

Her face was the same as I remembered. Round cheeks, a small pointed nose, and inky eyes the color of night. She was so small, I always wondered how she could be the same age as me, but her slight body was no indication of her power. Victoria was one badass witch, and I was proud to know her.

"Hey, what are you doing back?"

I swallowed. "I, uh, came for a visit."

"Missed me that much, huh?" she teased.

Victoria had been a part of the coven since birth, and when the high priestesses brought me in, we bonded immediately. Not the same way I had with Peyton, but for witches, we did pretty well in the friend department. We even patrolled together from time to time, and it always surprised me to see how she wielded her magic. While mine was forceful and loud, Victoria worked her patrols the same way she did her spells. With determination and control most other witches lacked. She was a force to be reckoned with, and her stubborn personality made her a brilliant match for someone like me. Out of all the young witches in the coven, Vic was the only one I would consider somewhat of a friend.

Which was exactly why running into her was such a problem. If anyone could see through the bullshit of why I came back, it was Vic.

"Um," I said and gestured to the soul sucker who hasn't moved an inch since I let him go. "A little help here?"

Vic's eyes narrowed at his cowering figure, and she curled one side of her thin lips. "Oh, yeah. No probs."

She was so fast, I had no time to register what happened. Before I knew it, I was being pushed to the side and Vic was crouching over the soul sucker, or what was left of him. Ashes spread in the blowing wind, and she ducked down to pick up a large, silver stake from the ground. She tossed it in the air, catching it in one hand and blowing on the tip like she had just fired a rifle. Her other hand pocketed an amber crystal, and she wiggled her eyebrows at me. "Done and done."

I looked between her and the stake. "Um, what's that?"

"My new toy. You like?"

She twirled the stake in my face and gestured over it dramatically.

"It's a little," I searched for the right word, "vampire slayer. Ish."

A cackle filled the alley and Vic flipped the stake again, tucking it into the waistband of her skintight leather leggings. She winked and wrapped an arm around my shoulder, rising on her tippy toes to reach my height.

"That's the point. Deadly with attitude. You know my style."

I really, really did.

Style was never something Vic lacked in. Out of all the

junior witches, she was the only one except me who even cared about fitting in with society. While the rest of them stayed close to the high priestesses and head witches, Vic spent her time in movie theaters and coffee shops getting to know the humans in the city. She loved everything Stamwick offered, and I was often jealous of her intense drive to fit in with the world around us. While I hated the spotlight, Vic cherished it like it was her precious. Taking every chance she could to make human friends. In the end, that was probably why she and I didn't form as strong a connection as I thought we could have. I was a loner and hated, well, everything, and Vic was someone that craved the attention of others. It was only on patrols that we bonded as witches and for a long time, that was good enough for me. Now that I had Peyton in my life, I realized how depressing our friendship was.

Shit! Peyton!

My chest tightened when I thought about my best friend, pulling me back to reality.

"Why haven't I seen you at the mansion?"

The mansion was what we called Sebyl's townhouse, where the coven did most of its gatherings. It was on the west side of the city, in one of the high-class neighborhoods, and the place I called home until they banished me to Shadowhurst. Getting sent away was the best thing that happened to me, but I'll never forget the pain I felt when the coven turned its back on me. No one called and no one asked how I was, not even Vic. It was a dismal time for me and one I wanted to forget, but I knew it would be a while before I was truly free of my demons. I mean, Beatrix got her ass locked up ages ago and I was still not over that rejection. As it would seem, my self-pity had no bounds.

"I'm staying in a hotel," I said. "Kinda awkward after every-thing, you know?"

She looked me up and down and my jaw tightened. *This is it. She's on to you.* Vic smiled and my shoulders eased up. "Totally get it. I'm sorry I haven't called, but you know how it is."

I didn't.

"Yeah, for sure."

"So, you gonna come by and see everyone? Wait, do the high priestesses know you're back?"

"Um..."

"You sick bastard!" she yelped and punched my shoulder. "Way to stick it to them. You know I wasn't on board with the whole sending you away thing, right?"

I nodded even though I didn't believe her. Vic hated not being liked, and I was pretty certain she did nothing to help me when the coven made their decision to get rid of me. If she did, I would have heard from her months ago.

"Anyway," she sang and snaked her arm under mine. "Let's get a coffee. I'm dying to hear about your life in suburbia! They told us how you helped find that Evanora bitch. Pretty awesome!"

"Um, yeah. Awesome."

"Come on! Let's hit up the coffee carts and go to the park like we used to. I'm so glad you're back!"

The sugar-coated words dripped off her lips and I wanted to believe her so badly, it actually hurt a little. Having this part of my life back was bittersweet and seeing Vic again pulled me right back into the High Coven's orbit. The guilt I've been fighting for days crept to the surface, and I choked back worry as I followed Vic out of the alley toward a coffee cart a few blocks down. I tried to convince myself that none of this mattered. Meeting her in that alley was just a coincidence and if I should have felt anything, it was relief that she didn't see me use my shadows on that soul sucker. Or did she? If she did, she didn't show it, which was well enough for me.

We ran up to the cart and Vic ordered our usual, one double-double and one black on ice. My hands wrapped around the warm cup, and I inhaled the delicious coffee smell with a sigh. I gulped the sugary sweetness as Vic droned on and on about all the gossip I missed in the coven. Who had the most kills, who was stepping out with a human, and other nonsense I didn't care much about. Having her by my side only dragged my thoughts back to Peyton and the situation in Shadowhurst. I wasn't in the city to run down memory lane with her. I was here to stop the witches from doing something that would hurt my best friend. It was unfortunate that Vic was one of them, but nothing I could do about it now.

My phone buzzed in my coat pocket, and I pulled it out.

Are you okay? River's text flashed across the screen.

I typed fast before Vic could notice me. *I'm good. Just needed some time to think.*

When you're done creeping around alleys, come to my room.

A wide smile spread over my face. Well played, hunter. Well. Freaking. Played. My cheeks burnt from the thought of being back with River and alone in his hotel room. So far, we've been fairly PG, but I had the feeling that plain old kissing was not what I needed tonight. No matter how hot our make out sessions were, what I needed was River. All of him. I couldn't spend another moment thinking about Peyton getting hurt, and if I didn't get my mind off things, I would blow our entire mission. I needed an escape, something that didn't have anything to do with the High Coven or the shadowers. Something normal.

I all but choked on the coffee as I inhaled it, hurrying Vic along. After almost a half-hour of listening to her chirp about the junior witches she hated, I managed to get her to stop talking and we parted ways, with a million false promises from me to hang out again soon. As Vic hopped away from me, I watched her back descend into the night and bolted for the hotel.

Tonight was about to turn around and I couldn't wait to drown out the world with River.

Chapter
Twenty-eight

walked the length of the hotel lobby then back again for the fiftieth time, trying to work up the courage to go upstairs. Nerves sky-high, I stopped in front of the aquarium and followed a crazed looking fish run circles over the others. He and I had something in common this evening, it seemed.

It'd been a good twenty minutes since I left Vic and got to the hotel, and yet, I still couldn't get my sorry ass into the elevator. *What am I so scared of?* I didn't understand why I was having this reaction. River and I have been on the path to this exact moment for a while now, and it wasn't as though I didn't want it to happen. I did. I really freaking did. So much so, I pictured it a thousand times in my head, but now that the moment was here, I was nothing but a sweaty, nervous mess. *Get a hold of yourself, loser.* I tightened my jaw and reached for my phone to dial a familiar number, and my back froze.

Heartache twisted me up when I realized Peyton would not be around to talk me off the ledge this time, and I broke down in the lobby when I thought about how much I missed her. She was an extra limb for me and having her fighting for her life was not something I took lightly. My best friend was stuck in limbo, and I was over here worrying about spending the night with a boy.

Pathetic.

My stomach did somersaults, and I turned back to the phone, dialing a different number.

"Hello?" Marcus's gruff voice sounded on the other end.

"Hey, Marcus. It's Billie."

The soul sucker cleared his throat. "Hi, hi, hi." He sounded like he wished he didn't answer the phone. "You're calling about Peyton?"

The sound of her name punched through me, and I crouched down, looking up at the weird little fish and battling incoming tears. My knees dug into the tile flooring, and I was sure that the other guests in the lobby averted their gazes. No one wanted to see a basket case explode. I squared my shoulders, pretending to tie my shoes, which seemed to put them at ease.

"How is she?"

Marcus took a deep breath and let it out. "A little better, but she's still non-responsive. We're doing everything we can. I have a few doctors here we can trust and they're keeping their eye on her. It's not looking good, though."

The matter-of-fact way he said it made me want to retch on the floor. I held my palm out, scraping my nails across the aquarium glass, and dispersing a spool of fish. *Sorry, guys, but you have no clue what I'm going through here.* The weirdo swimming in circles nudged up to my hand, ogled my fingers, then swam off with the others. *THANKS FOR NOTHING. I thought we were friends!*

Holding back tears, I sniffled and forced myself to stand. The grand lobby felt so much smaller now, I swore I could touch the walls if I stretched out my arms. Eyes watched me intently and I kept my gaze on the fish. *Just keep swimming.*

If Peyton was here, she'd know just what to say. She'd tell me to suck it up and keep my eyes on the prize. Of course, she'd also say it with a whole lot of attitude and even more cursing. Goddess, I missed that girl. I wished I could turn time around and be there for her when she needed me like she had been there for me all this time. No matter how hard I pushed her away, Peyton was always at my side, and when I needed to be at hers, I was nowhere to be found. Worse, it had been hours since she was hurt, and I still didn't deliver the punishment I vowed to bestow on those smug assholes that got to her.

Deep down, I knew I couldn't return to Shadowhurst without the book. Peyton would never forgive me if I did, and in truth, I wouldn't forgive myself. All of this was to keep her and her family safe, to keep others like her safe, and if I bailed now, I would fail her in more ways than one. I had to stay, and I had to complete the mission if I had any chance of doing right by Peyton.

"Billie?"

CRAP. How long was I quiet for? "Yeah, I'm here. Sorry."

"I know you're worried," Marcus said, but he did not understand how worried I actually was. "We will get her back. I have trust in the doctors, and everyone is on Peyton watch until she wakes up. We'll call you as soon as that happens so, please, try to relax."

"Easier said than done," I mumbled.

"I understand, but the best thing you can do for Peyton now is getting that book. Everything depends on it."

He was right. Of course, he was right, but I couldn't get myself to pay attention. All my thoughts were with Peyton, and all my fears were still ahead. Still nauseous as hell, I said good night and hung up the phone, determination building.

Peyton would wake up, she had to, and when she did, I would have so much to tell her.

Trembling, I pushed my insecurities to the base of my gut and focused my attention on the elevators. Thirty-seven floors lay between me and some semblance of escape, and for the love of fae, I needed that right now. I marched to the elevator, pressing the button repeatedly until the doors slid open. With an excited squeak, I hopped in and waited as they took me far from the lobby and the stupid weird fish that betrayed me at the first turn.

When the doors opened again, my hesitation returned, and it took everything I had to climb out. My knees shook and every step I took toward River's room was an explosion of nerves and eagerness. I had no clue which one would win the battle, and I wondered if he felt the same way while he waited for me to arrive.

Step after agonizing step I neared his door.

It was slightly ajar, and I looked around the corridor to see if he'd stepped out, but I was entirely alone in the hallway.

Is he waiting for me? *Oh, sweet Goddess, please, let him be waiting naked.*

I pushed the door open and stumbled in, cheeks blushing a deep red. His room was dark, but I could see a light on in the bedroom and followed it like a ship coming to shore. *Here we go...* My mind was still clouded but anticipation took form and by the time I reached the bedroom doors, I was a ball of giddiness and ache. I couldn't wait to talk to him, spend a night where it was just us and nothing else in the world to interrupt. Every part of my mind and body wanted River, and I felt stupid for making us wait this long to get here. He was mine and I was his and tonight, we'd be each other's in the best way possible.

Inside, my magic got the memo and was slamming against the edges of my skin to mimic my thoughts. *Great, even my magic wants him. This is going to be a shitshow.* I begged it to relax, but it didn't surrender and instead, I was met with the annoying blinding lights that meant I was about to explode. I had hoped that tonight, I would explode in a very different way.

Taking a deep breath, I wrapped my hands around the door handles and swung them open.

"Hey, babe, I'm her—"

My jaw unclenched as I walked in.

There, in the middle of River's bed, lay Savannah. Her long, bronze legs spanned down the bedsheets and my eyes trailed up her body and over the slutty ensemble she had glued on. Her boobs perked so high, they almost touched her chin, and I had to all but pick my jaw up off the floor to meet her eyes. The grin that spread across her face made me want to lunge at her, but I held myself back, trying to regain some composure.

"What..." I tried to talk, but words did not come together. "What are you doing here?"

"Hey, babe!" River's voice sounded from the opposite end of the room, and I jerked my head to face him. I was so shocked to see Savannah there that I completely missed him standing in the corner. "Sav wanted to go over our plan for breaking into the coven's library, so I figured we can do it here."

Savannah smiled and my cheeks turned a bright red. *I am an actual idiot.* Here I thought River was inviting me over for a date, but that was definitely not the case. Embarrassment flooded me and I worked not to puke on the soft carpet under my feet.

"You okay, babe?" River asked.

"Yep." *Not at all.* "All good."

"Cool, so I was thinking we should probably figure out where the hunters will be while you're inside."

I wanted to stay and work this out with them, I really did. But my insides were twisting and shouting, and as foolish as that was, I knew I couldn't simply hang out with them right now. Not when I thought about how differently I expected the night to play out. There was no doubt in my mind that I was behaving like a tool, but my head was not in the game at that moment. I didn't need a plan to break in, and I didn't need Savannah's boobs in my face all night. What I needed was a night of peace, and it looked like I would not be getting that here.

Peeling my eyes off Savannah's legs, I forced a smile to my face. "I'm actually kinda beat. Is it cool if we do this tomorrow with everyone?"

"Um, sure. You sure you're all right?"

River's eyes were full of worry, and I bit back the traitor inside me that wanted to stay just to be close to him. "Definitely. Just tired and need a night off. You guys can handle it, I'm sure."

I placed a gentle kiss on his cheek, ignoring Savannah's staring, and bid them good night. The two of them had things covered and if they wanted to come up with a plan, they could do that. I trusted River enough to know he'd never do anything to hurt me, and tonight, all I needed was for my racing thoughts to calm the hell down.

I turned on my heels and walked out of his room, not bothering to look back. As soon as I was out in the hallway, tears pooled behind my eyes and my heart raced, but I kept moving, pumping my legs harder until I reached my suite. My hands started to shake, and I couldn't slide the keycard through, and when I managed to do so, I burst through the door and kicked it closed behind me. Burning, aching sobs left my lips and I crumbled to the floor. I didn't know why I was reacting the way I was, but something in me needed a release. It was as though all the events that led me here built a dam in my soul and it took something as simple as not getting what I was expecting to break it. I was exhausted and beaten down. The thought of betraying the High Coven weighed heavily on my shoulders and as much as I tried not to think about it, it was all my mind reached for. That and Peyton.

My knees bounced off the tile, though I didn't register the pain as it shot through the rest of my body. My shoulder blades hit the door and I hugged my knees into my chest, burying my sorrow in them.

There was a loud knocking on the other side, and I heard River shout my name at the door.

Shadows swirled around me, and I closed my eyes, drowning them out before shakily rising to stand. When I finally opened the door, I looked like a hot mess.

"Babe?"

"I-I'm sorry. I don't know why I'm freaking out right now," I whispered, burying my face in his chest.

His arms wrapped tightly around me, and he ushered us into the room, closing the door behind him. "Come on," River said and led me to the couch. "Strategy can wait. We need a night off."

I stifled a sob like the weak loser I was. "You sure?"

"Positive. Let's see what's on TV. Take our mind off things for a while."

We huddled close in the center of the couch and while River looked for a movie, I practiced calming down my hysterics. This may not have been how I envisioned the night going, but it was still close to perfect. At least as perfect as someone like me could expect. *There is no one on our side in this world.* Beatrix's words tore at my memories, and I shoved them away. *Maybe not on your side, Mom, but I have someone in my corner. I am nothing like you.*

Chapter Twenty-nine

At a quarter past eight, we gathered in the hotel's restaurant to discuss the condition in Shadowhurst. My head still pounded from spending the entire night thinking about betraying the coven, and I kept my gaze down to avoid questions from the hunters. Somewhere during the night, River carried me to the bedroom, though sleep never came. I was a hollow mess and my friends' eyes on me only confirmed my suspicion that I looked like a steaming bag of dog shit.

Savannah sat a few chairs from me with a self-assured smirk on her face. As always.

I kept my eyes trained on my lap.

"Finally," Abigail huffed out, "he's here. I'm starving."

There was only one person missing from our group and as soon as my eyes met River's, he rushed to the empty chair beside me. A smile spread over my face and when I looked up at him, his expression mirroring my own.

"Hey, bruh," Jayden, and wiggled his brows. "Long night?"

River didn't answer. Instead, he leaned over to plant a kiss on my lips before sliding into the chair beside me. He smelled fresh from the shower, and I reveled in the comfort his body heat provided next to me. *Last night was just fine, Jayden.* I elbowed my friend in the ribs and turned back to the table.

"Morning, River," Savannah purred. His eyes snapped to her and the peridot colored glow in them intensified. In my peripheral, I noticed her sink lower in her seat, turning to the side to face Abigail. "Some people are just not good with mornings."

The intense eye roll that left me must have been more exaggerated than I expected because Morgan grabbed my hand under the table and forced me to look at her. Her blue-green eyes filled with worry, and she leaned in closer to my ear. "Don't stress, we have your back," she whispered.

I nodded her way. Savannah was dying to get under my skin, and I wasn't about to let her. With everything else running through my mind, her pathetic attempts to flirt with River were the last of my worries.

Squeezing Morgan's hand under the table, I flashed my teeth at her. "I'm good. Thanks."

An older server approached our table with a carafe of coffee, and everyone stretched out their cups for a second round. He went around the table, filling the cups until the smell of coffee drifted through the air and into my nostrils. I lunged for the jolt of caffeine this man offered, needing every ounce of perkiness this morning. The hunters were not going to like what I was about to say, but as far as I could tell, we had no other options.

When the server departed, I faced my friends. "All of you need to get back home. I spoke with Marcus this morning and he told me there is an influx of shifters who don't agree with how the leaders are choosing to run this whole thing. I'm worried about Peyton and the rest of the resistance."

"Girl, we're not leaving you here alone," Jayden said.

"You have to. There is a considerable number of shifters in the house, and I don't want Marcus and the others to deal with them alone. Having you guys there will help ease the situation. Maybe you can talk some sense into them."

"I'll go," Morgan offered.

I knew her going back had more to do with Peyton than the resistance, but it relieved me that at least someone was listening. "Guys, please," I begged. "I can get the book on my own and it's not like any of you were going in with me to grab it. It's better this way."

"No." River's words cut through me like knives.

I turned to face him, fighting everything in me that screamed to punch his teeth in. "Excuse me?"

"I said no."

"The resistance needs your help, all of you. I can handle the coven."

His face darkened, a lock of hair falling over his eyes he didn't bother brushing aside. "I know, but it's not up for debate. The others can go, but I'm staying. I'm not leaving you."

My heart was overcome with emotions, and I didn't know which part of me was which. On the one hand, River's need to stay by my side was the hottest thing ever, but on the other, the worry I felt for everyone back in the resistance house refused to subside. I uncurled my fingers and focused on the red crescent moon shapes my nails left behind on the soft flesh of my palms. The tiny indents drew me back to the Book of Darkness and Shadowhurst. They drew me back to Peyton. If River wanted to stay behind, I would not waste time arguing about it. We needed to secure that book and help the soul suckers before the High Coven did something I couldn't fix.

Squaring my shoulders, I leaned in close to him. "Okay. And thank you."

"I'll stay too," Savannah said.

"You should go back with the others. Billie's right, the resistance needs our help. We left friends behind in Shadowhurst and I don't feel right having them unprotected," River said calmly.

Savannah took another sip of her coffee and left a red-stained mark on the edges of the white porcelain. *Who the hell puts lipstick on for breakfast?* This girl was way too extra.

She swallowed and stared River down like she was about to eat him. "You don't get to boss me around, bud," she scoffed. "If the witches catch Billie in their library and attack, you'll need backup. They won't just let her walk out of there with the book after she betrays their trust, and no offense to both of you, but we all know I'm an excellent fighter. You'll need all the help you can get if she's caught."

"I won't get caught," I hissed.

"Let's hope so." She grinned. "I'm staying, anyway."

A throbbing ache formed at my temples, and I rubbed my forehead to relieve the pain that settled there. Visions of Sebyl's disappointed face clouded my mind and my vision blurred. I was moments away from losing it right there in the restaurant. Looking around at the well-dressed patrons near us, I very much doubted they wanted a helping of teenage drama with their breakfast. I breathed in as much air as my lungs could muster and let it out through clenched teeth. When finished, I did it again. Over and over until I felt the tension in my neck relax and my hands drooped at my side like spaghetti. My emotions were all over the place these days and I hated every second of their incessant torture. I needed to get control of myself before I screwed all of us and made a mistake that could cost Peyton her life.

I needed to calm the hell down.

The others discussed the bus schedule to decide when they should return since there was no way Savannah was parting with her dad's RV, and I let myself drift away from their voices. Over Jayden's broad shoulders, I could feel River's eyes on me, and I stabbed my fork into the omelet on my plate, pretending to eat so he wouldn't worry further. When I couldn't sit still any longer, I pushed the plate away and rose.

The chatter stopped, and everyone turned to face me.

"Billie?" Abigail asked.

"I'm going up to my room," I said. "I need to clear my head."

That same darkness I saw before invaded River's features, and I struggled to smile his way. He wasn't buying it, but I was glad he respected my wishes enough to let me have a breather from the group. His hand brushed against my thigh, and he winked. "I'll come up after breakfast."

Nodding, I said good bye to my friends and bolted for the elevators. My heart pounded in my chest as I waited impatiently for the numbers to reach the penthouse floor, and when the doors opened, I stumbled out of them like a psycho on a mission. Inside me, the shadows swam in circles, and I fought to keep them at bay until I got into my room. I needed to let them loose and I needed a release.

All the magic I held in me was tearing at the edges of my skin like daggers. The magic the High Coven taught me to command. I was about to do the unthinkable and yet, I couldn't stop thinking about it at all.

These women raised me when Beatrix bailed, and I was going to repay them by stealing from them. What kind of person did that make me? What kind of witch?

Guilt threaded my blood cells and as I stood in the middle of the hotel room, I did the only thing I knew how to do well. I let my magic consume me.

Chapter Thirty

The next hours passed in a blur. I spent the remainder of the day holed up in my room and trying not to freak out over what I was about to do to the coven. This was the right choice, and deep down I knew that, but I still couldn't get myself to get with the program. I think what bothered me most was that in the end, at least in the coven's eyes, I would be just like Beatrix. A traitor they would need to lock away.

My body felt as though someone beat me with a baseball bat and my head still throbbed, but after a long shower, I was feeling like myself again. Well, at least I looked like myself, the feeling part was something else altogether. Scrubbing my face with my hands, I gazed out the enormous windows that lined the wall of the suite and let myself drift off into the city. The sun had already set, and a thousand lights illuminated the streets below. The hotel was smack-dab in the center of the financial district, and the ghostly windows of the skyscrapers mocked me with their glares. This city used to be everything to me, and now, it had become everything I despised.

Confusion and discomfort burrowed into my soul as I worried about what I would do next.

I couldn't stay in Stamwick, not when I didn't trust my own coven, and it wasn't like anyone would welcome me back after I stole the book. Going back to Shadowhurst was always an option, but if I did that, I was definitely choosing a side, and I wasn't sure I was ready for that. Though, after everything, the choice was already made for me. Maybe that was the part that bothered me most, not being able to decide for myself where I belonged.

Where was my home in this world?

I had no idea.

Perhaps the High Coven would catch me red-handed and lock me up next to Beatrix. At least then I wouldn't have to face the high priestesses and the imminent disgrace I was about to unleash on the coven. And I wouldn't have to face myself. If I was being honest, that was who I wanted to encounter the least. Since my decision to steal the book and betray the coven, the shadows hadn't stopped wriggling inside me, and I was afraid to find out what that could mean. They always responded to my emotional turmoil but now that was I was completely destroyed, they had grown stronger and much more volatile.

Life's a piece of shit.

My phone lit up in my lap and I growled as I picked it up, half-expecting the hunters to call again. My face lit up when Marcus' number flashed across the screen, and I pressed the answer button so fast, the phone almost slipped out of my grasp.

"Marcus? Is Peyton awake?"

There was silence on the other end, and then Marcus' voice boomed over the line. "I'm afraid not, Billie. I was calling to see how you're doing on your end. Are you ready for tomorrow?"

Tomorrow was when I was to steal the Book of Darkness

and somehow, ready was not even in my vocabulary at that moment.

"I'm good to go," I lied. *You're so not good to go...* "A few of the hunters are coming back to help you with the shifter situation."

"That's not needed. We can handle our own."

A flash of anger rushed me, and I breathed into it. "We are in this together, Marcus. All of us. That includes the resistance. I know it might come as a shock, but I don't want anything to happen to the shadowers under your roof and if there's something my friends and I can do to help, we will do it."

"You're certain?"

"Hundo P," I said, channeling my inner Peyton. "Marcus, I need you to trust me. I know I'm a witch and I know the last thing you want to do is let me help, but I'm trying to do the right thing here."

"I know," he whispered. His voice grew softer, and I could feel his smile through the phone. "The leaders and I have been talking and I think we can all agree that we're rather surprised with your help on this. We expected this to go much worse than it had. We're grateful for your assistance."

"As I said, it's the right thing to do."

"I feel we may have gotten off on the wrong foot."

I blinked my eyes rapidly and sat up straighter. "How so?"

"Well, all this time, the shadowers despised the witches and the feeling was more than mutual. It seems to me that the problem isn't us but those we let lead us. I hope that with you on our side, we can right some wrongs and create something different. A new future for all of us."

My lips curled up and I smiled in earnest for the first time that day. How I wished that we could do exactly what he was saying. The High Coven led the witches with an iron fist, but they were way wrong about the shadowers. The shadowers weren't evil, at least not most of them, and they certainly didn't deserve to die at the hands of my kind. Most of the shadowers I met at the resistance were lovely people who never hurt a human or did anything to step out of line. The lies the coven spread about them to justify the hunts made the hair on my arms rise, and I grit my teeth as I considered everything I've done to follow their rules. For an instant, Evanora's face flashed in my vision and my stomach turned. Somehow, I had become just like her, fighting against the coven for the wrongs they dealt to the shadowers. Her delivery may have been atrocious, but in the end, she was trying to do what I was attempting as well. To stop innocent lives from being taken.

Was that a lot to ask?

I didn't think so.

"Oh, Billie?" Marcus asked and I shook the trailing thoughts from my head. "I've been thinking about your magic while you've been away."

"My magic?"

"Yes. Those dark shadows that you seem to be able to control. I think I might have an idea that will interest you."

WHAT THE HECK, MARCUS? You lead with that! "You know something about the shadows? Please, anything you can tell me would be great. I feel like I'm going crazy here. No witch I know has this kind of magic, and it's scaring the crap out of me."

"Just breathe, kid." Marcus chuckled. "I have nothing concrete, but I've been looking into it, and I may have stumbled on something that will help you understand all of it. But we should discuss this in person."

"What? Why?"

"I would be more comfortable if I had more time to confirm my suspicions before I get your hopes up."

Cock tease. Seriously.

I sighed. "Okay, fine. But when I'm back, you and I are talking. ASAP."

"Of course. Now, I won't keep you longer. You need your rest and I need to get back to the shadowers. It seems after the mess the shifters are causing around here, my presence is required everywhere."

"Sucks to be king." I laughed. "Have a good night, Marcus."

"You as well."

He hung up and I let the phone drop from my hands. Finally, someone had information that could clarify what was happening to me and what these shadows that plagued my magic were. I was sure the high priestesses would know, but since I couldn't ask them, Marcus was the next best thing. The guy was pretty freaking old, so he must have some idea. I couldn't believe it, after tomorrow, I would not only have the book and a shot at saving the soul suckers, but I might understand what was going on inside my body. The day was starting to turn around and I hopped off the couch, lunging for the tray of room service I ordered with a renewed appetite.

I was half-way through the meal when a knock sounded at my door and I stopped mid-chew, hesitantly getting up to check who it was. I couldn't remember ordering room service again, but in my delirium, there was no telling how much of Savannah's dad's money I was willing to spend in one night. My stomach growled as I walked to the door. *Let it be the quiche, let it be the quiche.*

Another knock sounded and I picked up my pace. "Coming!"

Swinging the door open in anticipation, my stomach jumped in my throat as green eyes invaded the hallway. River's lips parted to say something, but I didn't let him talk. I threw my arms around him, breathing in his woodsy scent as I clung to him like a Band-Aid.

"Good to see you too," he whispered against my ear.

Hesitantly, I pulled away from him. "I missed you."

River smiled and my worries crept away, hiding in the dark holes of my soul again.

"You're freaking out, aren't you?"

"Is it that obvious?"

"With you? Yes." He wrapped an arm around me and tugged me close. "Wanna talk about it?"

I shook my head and frowned. "Yes. No. I don't know." *Good job using your words.*

"...Is that a maybe, then?"

"It's a 'maybe later'. I'm all over the place right now. But I'm glad you're here. Wanna watch another movie?"

River's face dropped and he grimaced before turning me to face him. "Look, babe. I know you need a break and trust me, I wish we could just stay in this room and hang out, but we need to get ready for tomorrow. It's a big day."

"I can handle it. You don't have to worry."

"I know you can, Goldilocks." He half-smiled and lightly tapped my shoulder. "But it's not just you here. Sav and I want to help and you're going to need to let us. Hunters don't work alone."

"I'm a WITCH!" I said, a little louder than I intended.

River didn't seem to mind, and his eyes scanned my face as he grabbed my hand to tug me to the door. "Not right now, you're not. Right now, you're a hunter. So let's go."

If I knew anything about River, it was that resisting him when he had his mind made up was futile. It was something the two of us had in common. Something I would have normally liked, but at that moment, it was annoying the hell out of me. He continued to pull me out of the room, and I exhaled loudly before following him out. One last glance back to the hotel room, I slumped my shoulders and we made our way to his room where I was certain Savannah was waiting. Hopefully, the jerk had more clothing on this time, or I would not be able to concentrate on anything at all.

We marched down the corridor and each step sent shivers down my spine. Not only was I going to commit the worst crime against my coven, but I was planning the damn thing in detail. It looked like criminal behavior ran in the Stonewall family. How wonderful.

Chapter Thirty-one

"So, the coven's library is here? On this floor of the townhouse?"

Savannah's shrill voice made me want to throw up in my mouth, and I laser-focused my attention on the drawing to keep from punching her face in. She'd been drilling me for hours and I was over it. Savannah circled the small room on the rough sketch of the townhouse I mocked up a few times in red pen. *We get it, Barbie, you can draw circles. UGH.*

I grimaced and pointed to the drawing. "This is the only way in or out. There're no windows, so I'll need to go down the main stairs to get to the library."

"And you're sure there won't be other witches there with you?" she asked.

"No, I'm not sure," I growled. "It's not like there's a schedule. Anyone can go in whenever they want."

She looked up at me. "That will be a problem."

The only problem I see is staring right at me...

"She's right," River chimed in. "We need to make sure

you're in there alone. Is there some other way you can get in and out undetected?"

I shook my head. "I'm telling you, it will be fine. I'm going with the 'I missed you guys and had to come visit' sob story. Once I'm inside, I'll wait until the high priestesses aren't around and sneak in. No big deal."

River's face flushed, and he rubbed the back of his neck. My eyes traveled down the length of his body, spending way too much time ogling the rise and fall of his chest as he moved. I licked my lower lip, then pinched my thigh. *SNAP OUT OF IT! Get this over with so you can get out of here already.* Crashing my lips into a line, I furrowed my brow and snatched the drawing off the table. I knew every twist and turn in that townhouse, and I was sure I could get the book out with no one noticing. If someone spotted me, I would simply do the same thing I did when I was a kid and got caught red-handed playing with something I wasn't allowed to touch. I would lie.

The hunters always took everything so seriously and I was sick of it. This entire night was turning into a disaster. I was meant to be resting up for tomorrow so I could put on a convincing performance for the coven, but instead, I was trapped in River's hotel room while he and Savannah grilled me over and over.

I rubbed my chest, shaking my gaze away.

"This is a very big deal, Billie," River said, his tone serious. "We have to know where you are at all times in case something happens. Can you keep your phone on so we can hear what's going on?"

I laughed. "Oh, yeah, excellent plan. Let me just walk around with *that* red flag waving. Not happening."

"So, what's another solution?"

"Hmm," I fake rubbed my temples to mimic a thinking pose. "Let me see... How about I go in there like I've done for most of my life, get the book, and walk the hell back out? That sound good to you?"

Savannah chuckled and cleared her throat, looking back to the drawing in my hand. "Okay, so River and I will be right here." She pointed to a spot outside the sketch with her dumb pen. "If anything happens, you call right away, and we can bust in there. We'll be close enough to the main entrance to get there fast, but far enough from sight that no one will spot us. When you have the book, meet us over here." She drew another stupid circle on the paper.

"Great. Thanks. Can I go now?"

River reached for me, and I met his gaze. "You sure you're ready to do this?"

Not. At. All. "Yep. As ready as I'll ever be."

It seemed that lying was all I had to go by these days.

The next morning, I left the two of them in the spot Savannah ferociously circled on our map and marched down the street toward Sebyl's townhouse. The sun was shining brightly this morning and its rays warmed my cold bones as I rounded the corner and stepped onto the familiar street. Rows of town-houses stretched before me, each one as pristine as the next. This was one of the oldest neighborhoods in Stamwick and you could smell money as you walked down the street. I always wondered how Sebyl could afford this place, but had a pretty good inkling that magic had something to do with it. Either that or she was secretly loaded and forgot to tell the rest of us about it.

Memories of playing on this street ran through me and a sickening heartache burst in my chest. I was about to do something I never thought was possible. I was about to betray my coven.

I squared my shoulders and walked up the flower-lined stairs that pointed to the entrance of the townhouse, fishing my phone from my pocket as I climbed. My hands shook and the nerves in me pounced at my throat, but I willed them away, hiding them the same way I hid the lipsticks I stole from the pharmacy when I was younger. Looking down at the screen, I noticed four texts from River and sighed.

"Go away, babe," I whispered and swiped them off, opening a new chat box.

Hey, it's me. You at the mansion?

Three dots bounced as Vic typed her message. *I'm here. What's up?*

*I'm downstairs. Surprise *confetti ball emoji*.*

The dots appeared again, then disappeared. I waited another few moments and began to type when the door swung open and Vic pounced on me. Her arms wrapped around my shoulders and her legs dangled in the air as she hugged me. *Man, she's short.* I chucked and pulled her away. "Guess you're happy to see me?"

"Are you kidding? So happy! Come on!"

She stepped aside and I walked in, throwing one glance down the street again to make sure River and Savannah weren't following me like hounds. When I was convinced the coast was clear, I followed Vic inside and closed the door behind me.

The townhouse was exactly as I remembered, with a narrow hallway that stretched down the length of the house and several closed doors on either side. This was nothing like the Chandler home. While theirs, or mine now, was modern and open, Sebyl's townhouse was cramped and full of antiques that lined every inch of the hallway. There were shelves of books on each wall and narrow tables full of crystals, candles, and herbs filling the stretch of the long corridor. Each of the door frames that led to the rooms the head witches occupied was covered in dried herbs, under which runes pressed into the wood. The smell of burning patchouli and dragon's blood rushed into my nose, and I pressed my palm to my hand to keep it out. Something about being away from this place for so long overwhelmed me, and I tried to remember if it was this claustrophobic when I lived here. It likely was and I simply didn't notice. Seemed I didn't notice a lot of things in those days.

Vic tugged my sleeve and pulled me down the hallway with a wide smile. "Come on, I just got here. The other junior witches are already in the dining room. You have to meet the new ones! They're so intense! It's hilarious."

She bounced from heel to toe and nudged her head toward the dining room.

More memories flooded my system, most involving my own interactions in that same room with the coven. For such a tight space, we sure got a good number of witches into the townhouse from time to time. The full moon gatherings were always my favorite because everyone and their mother would show up. Seriously, there were a lot of family members here, and the strength of their familial magic used to bring me so much happiness. It was as though I could steal it for myself. I often imagined being a part of a long line of witches, but unfortunately, all I had was Beatrix and that wasn't quite as glamorous. That was why I stuck to the high priestesses like glue and why the junior witches hated me. Well, everyone except Vic. She was pretty cool most of the time.

My gaze landed on the small, carpet-lined stairs leading to the upper floor where the high priestesses had their rooms. "Are they here?"

Vic shook her head 'no'. "Off on some secret mission. You know how they are."

I really had no idea how or who they were these days but kept my mouth shut.

"Let's go," Vic urged me forward. "Say hi to everyone."

Invisible magnets pulled me with her, and I had to bury my feet into the dusty carpet to stop from following. Everything in me wanted to forget the hunters that waited outside and stay in the townhouse. It was as if I was bound to this place with chains. I tugged my hand back and Vic skidded to a stop, turning back to me with worry. "Everything cool?" she asked.

"Yeah," I said. "Totally. I'm just not in the mood to socialize right now. You get it, right?"

She pursed her lips and smiled.

"You mind if I wander around for a bit? Maybe see my old room or something?"

I expected her to fight me, but Vic grinned and wrapped her arms around me again. Her thin arms twisted over my waist and I could feel the bulge of the stake she carried against my thigh. At that moment, I wished I could tell her everything I knew about the lies the High Coven spread, but that wasn't an option. Vic was too entranced by the world we used to share. She belonged to a family I was jealous of, a mom that was always around and a grandmother wiser and older than dirt. If I told her what I knew, she would never believe me, and my heart hurt thinking of the day when we were no longer on the same side. Somehow, I got the feeling that day would come sooner than expected, especially once I worked the blocking spell and the priestesses got wind of what I was up to. My head pounded and I swallowed the pooling saliva in my mouth.

My choice was made, but that didn't mean I had to like it.

"Come find me when you're done running down memory lane," Vic said and let me go. "I'm really glad you're back, Billie."

You won't be for long.

I waved good bye to her and waited until she was gone to creep down the hallway. At the end, a small opening emerged, making way for an iron spiral staircase leading down to the library. My pulse quickened as I wrapped my fingers around the railing and took the first step down. The metal was cold against my skin and hairs stood straight on my arms with each step I took. By the time I reached the bottom landing, it froze me solid.

Stepping into the library, my lips parted, and I looked over the room in amazement. It was as I left it, books lining the rounded walls with perfectly cracked spines and the energy of magic in every corner. Shelves crammed every inch of the room; some full of books and some filled to the top with potions and spell casting supplies. In the center of the library, the small table I used to take notes on called my attention and I strode toward it, running my fingers across the oily wood with a smile. Memories flooded me and they were so real, I could almost see Luna across from me at the table. Her auburn hair twisted into loose braids and crystals lined her delicate face, staring at me in judgment. She moved and bells jingled on her dress, making me giggle the way I did when I was a child. The memory shifted and Luna's violet eyes bore into me just as my phone vibrated.

I raised it to my face, illuminating the candle-lit room with its modern glare. When River's face popped on the screen, I sighed and declined the call.

Shaking my head, I made my way to the books, scanning them to find the one I needed. Each spine brought back more memories and each one ripped me into pieces. My eyes watered and I blinked so fast, I thought I would pass out. I tried to focus on the books, but everything blurred in my vision. Text blended, melting into a heap of words I couldn't understand.

In my hand, the phone vibrated again, and I checked the messages, finding the latest one from River. *Call me back. Now.*

I scoffed and tossed the phone into my backpack.

My focus was back on the mission, and I trailed my fingers along the books, checking every single one. When I finished, I checked again, but none of them looked like what I needed. There were so many books here, but I was sure I remembered correctly. The Book of Darkness had to be here, it had to. I checked again, panic rising in my chest when I came up empty.

The book wasn't there.

Chapter Thirty-two

*T*his couldn't be happening. I ran over every single book again, hoping to find the grimoire but came up empty. How did I get this wrong? I was sure I saw it in my memories and standing here in the library with a blank stare on my face made me feel like a complete idiot. This was the reason we came here, because of me, and I had led us astray. *Great going, Billie. Just stellar.*

Fast, sharp breaths drifted through me as I panted in a crazed panic. I couldn't have been wrong, and I refused to believe it. The High Coven got their hands on a spell no modern witch could fathom, and I knew it had to be from that book. Somehow, I felt it in my bones.

My shadows tugged at my heart in agreement and I glanced around the library again, gaze landing on the potions to my right.

What if it's masked?

I ran to the row of potions, reading over the names on the linen tags tied to each bottle. If they hid the book, I would find it. No one knew more about hiding objects in plain sight than me. I thought of my grimoire sitting in the hotel room and smiled, the masking spell I used on it that morning was a piece of cake, and I prayed the coven performed a similar spell here in the library. If they did, I still had a shot.

Reading a few more tags, I snatched a bottle off the shelf and popped open the lid. The scent of lilac and mugwort tickled my nose, and I inhaled it deeply. This would have been easier if I knew the general area the book could be in, but since I was working blind, I needed to think on my feet. Hide and seek it is. I frowned and spread the potion over my palms, clapping my hands three times to activate it. The potion spread down my soft skin, penetrating me with its energy. I shut my eyes and accepted the elements it offered, letting the magic intertwine with my shadows. The greedy bastards latched on for dear life and my body shook from their force.

With my eyes still closed, I stretched my arms to the sides and let the shadows creep out of me. As they left my body, I felt a sense of relief mixed with sadness, missing their presence immediately. I swirled in a small circle, pushing more shadows out and covering the entire library in darkness. My pulse raced and I could feel sweat drip down my back as I let go of more magic. One by one, the shadows riled against the books, clinging to them like honey. My knees weakened and I readied myself for the next step. Whatever concealment the High Coven had in here, I was about to suck it into myself, vacuum up their magic as though it was nothing but dust. When I did this with my own grimoire, the spell didn't cost me a lot of energy, but I had the feeling that this time, I'd be knocked on my ass and taught a lesson. Breaking a spell set by the high priestesses would take a lot out of me, and I hoped that it would be worth it in the end.

My eyes snapped open, and I breathed in, sucking in the air in the room and the shadows into my body.

They rushed toward me, eager to return to the cage I kept them in for once. My body convulsed as they hit me, pushing their way through and tearing me apart. Tears streamed down my face, and I struggled to stand, dropping to my knees while the last of the shadows returned to me. My eyes slammed shut and my head rolled backward as I fell to my back in the middle of the library.

Jagged breaths filled my lungs and I rose on my elbows, scanning the room.

It looked the same. The books sat along the shelves with their ancient spines taunting me, and I was about to give up all hope when I saw it. There, lodged in between two unsuspecting tomes, the tiny horns of wet moons stared back at me.

A wide grin spread across my face, and I hopped to my feet, rushing for the book.

Pure happiness burst in my gut when I wrapped my fingers around the binding and pulled it out. The leather was coarse against my skin, and I ran my hand over the etchings in its surface. Wet moons and protection runes surrounded a small amethyst that lay indented in the front cover. I gasped when I touched it, the realization of what lay in my hands taking form. I couldn't believe it. The Book of Darkness, one of the very first grimoires of my kind, glared at me with such force, it could level a building.

"What's going on here?" a light voice sounded from the base of the staircase, and a breath lodged itself in my throat.

I turned to see Vic's gaping jaw, her hands cocked on her hips and questions swimming in her eyes.

"Vic!" I yelled out, "This isn't what it looks like."

"Really? Because it looks like you're about to steal from the coven."

Okay, so it's exactly what it looks like. "I need this book, Vic. You don't understand."

"Explain it to me then." She arched a thin eyebrow my way and tapped her foot.

My heart raced so fast, I could feel it against my sweatshirt. How could I begin to explain this to her? Vic was a solid member of the coven, and anything I said now would dig me into an even deeper hole. There was no way she would believe what I had to say, but I needed to try. I had to get out of here.

"Listen, the coven lied, Vic. Like a lot. About so many things. It would take me hours to fill you in, but I've been working with some people to help make everything better. Do you know that spell they're working on to draw out the soul suckers?"

Vic nodded but didn't speak.

"Well," I continued, "long story short, we can't let them go through with it. The shadowers aren't what the high priestesses said they were. They're not monsters and they're not evil. They weren't even created the way the coven said they were. It was all a freaking lie!"

Her face paled and for a moment, I thought I had convinced her. Every hope died when she threw her hands up and a puff of purple dust flew at my face. *Is this chick trying to knock me out?* I ducked out of the way, barely avoiding the hit. Clutching the book close to my chest, I rolled behind the table and pressed my back against the legs. "Vic! Come on! You have to believe me!" I yelled out, keeping myself as hidden as possible.

"You're a liar!" she shouted and hit me with more of her magic.

I cowered under the table to avoid the hit, but some of the dust found its way to my legs and I lost all feeling from the waist down. *For the love of!* I crawled to the other side of the table and peeked around it. A few steps away from me, Vic was powering up for another hit and I anticipated that this one would leave me completely paralyzed. Panic filled me and my eyes darted around the room for a solution. Hesitantly, I lowered the book, tucking it under the table for safekeeping. My legs dragged behind me as I crawled and rose a shaking hand to a blue bottle at the edge of a bookshelf. My fingers wrapped around it, and I snatched it down before Vic noticed.

As I turned, she was pummeling her way toward me, magic dancing between her fingertips. Her hair blew over her face and the menacing look in her eyes told me she was not playing. Vic was out for blood, my blood.

"I'm sorry," I whispered and threw the bottle as hard as I could.

It landed at her feet, the glass shattering, and I closed my eyes, shielding my face from the explosion. Black powder burst from the bottle and encased Vic's small body from head to toe. It was so dense, I couldn't make anything out but when I heard a scream followed by a thud, I knew I hit my target.

Panting, I cowered against the bookshelf until the powder dispersed, leaving a passed-out Vic on the floor. Without pause, I snatched another potion from the shelf and crawled toward her. My legs were still Jell-O, but I pushed on until I was lying over her as she slept. With my teeth, I uncorked the potion and dripped it down her lips, using my other hand to close her mouth. Vic choked but swallowed; her eyes still shut.

I breathed out in relief. When Vic awoke, she would remember nothing.

Dragging myself across the floor, I picked up the book and shoved it into my bag. As I wrestled with its heavy weight inside, I noticed three more missed calls from River and dialed his number. My heart was still beating like a drum, and I tried to control my breathing when he answered.

"Hey, I got it," I said, breathless.

"You need to get out now!" he screamed on the other end. "We have to get back to Shadowhurst."

"I'm working on it. What's going on?"

River took a deep breath in and his voice cracked when he spoke. "The High Coven found the resistance house while we were gone. No one saw them coming, Billie. They... They..." He took another breath. "Tyler is in a coma and Abigail is badly hurt. She's in the ER right now. Savannah is freaking out. We have to go back."

My throat closed up and I punched my useless legs, begging for them to work. Before I could ask him to give me more time so I could actually walk out of the damn townhouse, River's voice filled the line again. It was deep and pained, and I knew without hearing the news that whatever he had to say would destroy me.

"Marcus is dead," he finally uttered.

A sharp pain jolted through my legs, and I let the phone drop on the floor. My head fell back, carrying my body with it, and I slammed to the hardwood floor beneath, feeling no pain. River's words registered in my mind and I pressed a hand to my chest in some pathetic hope of making the heartache subside. How was I supposed to survive any of this?

Chapter Thirty-three

By the time my stupid legs started working again and we made it to the hotel, my brain filled with so much dread, I couldn't move. I shoved whatever clothing I could find and tossed it into the open bag on the bed absent-mindedly while trying not to vomit on the floor.

Why didn't I prod Vic more when she said the high priestesses were gone on a mission? I should have known better. People got hurt and it was all my fault. Again. I was growing tired of being the idiot that stood in everyone's way, and even though we got the book, it did little to make me feel better. The High Coven knew where the resistance house was, and there was nothing to stop them from attacking again. *Is there even a point to this book anymore?*

I eyed the dreaded tome suspiciously and crammed it into my backpack. Knowing the priestesses, they wouldn't stop after this one victory and the spell on the soul suckers would still be well underway, but I couldn't think about that at the moment. Marcus was dead. Not just hurt, but dead. And somewhere in a hospital bed, Tyler and Abigail fought for their lives. Everything was broken and I didn't know where we could go from here. The spell had to be stopped, but now, we had even bigger problems. Ones I wasn't sure we were prepared for.

The resistance house would need to be evacuated, though I was certain the remaining leaders were taking care of that as I packed.

Dumb, useless witch. I cursed myself and shoved a pair of leggings into the bag.

"DAMN IT!" I screamed, tossing the bag on the floor and spinning on my heels.

As I turned, my forehead collided with something hard and I wobbled backward, rubbing my temple and looking a baffled River over.

He rubbed his own head where we collided and forced a smile. "Rough day?"

I scoffed but didn't answer.

"Hey, it'll be okay," he whispered and stepped closer to me. "Tyler will be fine, and Abigail is already recovering."

"And Marcus?" I sniped. "Is he recovering too?"

River shook his head and his eyes darkened. He closed the distance between us, gathering me into his arms and pressing my head to his chest. My arms fell at my sides, and I urged myself not to move, but my traitorous body had other thoughts, and before long, I found myself wrapping my arms around his waistline and letting him hold me.

After a few long minutes, River pulled away and his eyes locked on mine. "Please, talk to me."

His emerald eyes had so much pain in them, it made my mouth dry up. Everything in me wanted to stay in those eyes forever and I acid rose in my throat when I thought about what I had to do next. River was not going to like this one bit. I wrestled from his hold and squared my shoulders.

"I'm not going back with you," I announced.

"What?"

"I have to stay here with the coven. If I return, we'll be in the dark again and I can't have anyone else get hurt because of my actions. Staying here is the only way. I can convince them to take me back and earn their trust again. I'll put the book back, and no one will know what happened. Then if they're planning an attack, I can warn all of you so you can prepare."

River crossed his arms over his chest and growled. From the look of his face, I could already tell a fight was coming and prepared myself to argue. "Yeah, that's not going to happen."

Cocky, son of a... "Not asking for permission here."

"I'm serious, Billie. You're not staying with these people. It's not safe and I'm not letting it happen."

"I'm sorry, I don't remember needing you to approve my actions," I bit out.

"That's not fair."

"Yeah, well, life's not fair. Deal with it, hunter."

His lips curled into a half-smile. "Listen here, witch. We're a team, so if you're going to be making decisions that affect me too, I get a say in them."

Slack-jawed, I stood before him torn between wanting to hug him and punch his face in. I had no concept of what a relationship was like, but whatever it was, I wasn't used to thinking of someone else when it came down to life decisions. In all honesty, I wasn't used to making life decisions at all. Up until my move to Shadowhurst, the High Coven told me what to do and I did it, no questions asked. Now, I had people that looked to me for answers, and I had no clue how to handle it.

What if I made the wrong choice and they all paid the price? I couldn't live with myself if that happened.

Tears flooded my vision and as I blinked, they streamed down my cheeks. River's hands cupped my face, forcing me to look at him and the sight of him made every emotion in me rise to the surface.

I sniffled and swallowed down more tears, placing my palms over his rough skin. "I'm the worst person. Ever."

"What are you talking about?" River asked in the same tone he would have used if I just told him the sky was green.

"I stole from the coven, River. *My* coven. These people raised as their own family and I stabbed them in the back like it was nothing. Like they were nothing."

"You had every reason to do that; it doesn't make you a bad person."

Another sob escaped me. "Doesn't it, though?"

"No, it doesn't." His face was stern and serious, and I slunk down in his grasp on me. "I know how you feel, I really do. When Evanora showed up at the farm, I wanted to set the world on fire. I mean, what kind of parent does something like that? But I didn't, and you know why?"

I shook my head.

"Because of you, babe. Because I knew you needed me and I couldn't let you get hurt, not when I could do something about it. Just like you did what you did to save your friends. It doesn't make you a bad person, Billie. Actually, it's kind of the opposite."

"But the High Coven—"

"The High Coven made their choice. It was the wrong one."

Flashes of Sebyl's face appeared before me and I shook them off. Green eyes ripped through me, and I swallowed hard. Despite wanting to collapse, I followed River to the couch, letting the plush leather engulf me. His gaze dropped to his lap, and he rearranged his seat to grab something from the pocket of his jeans. When he held his hands out to me, a small box was perching in his open palms. My eyes grew and I looked between it and him. "What's this?"

"Just open it," he said and nudged the box toward me.

Hands shaking, I took it and snapped the lid open.

A gasp escaped me when I peered inside. The simple, black jewelry box lay flat in my hands, and inside was a beautiful silver pendant on a delicate chain. Swirling lines in a teardrop shape created a cage of sorts, and as I turned it over in my hands, I noticed two small crystals rolling inside. One blue and one green.

"Sapphire and emerald," River said, reading my confused glare. "Like you and me."

My hand brushed against my lids and then reached for him. He leaned in, letting me touch the side of his face where his bright green eyes burnt into me. Sapphire for the blue in mine and emerald for the green in his.

I looked to the pendant and sniffled my nose, running my finger across it. The crystals caught the light and sparkled in their silver cage, and my heart swelled when I looked at them. "Where did you get this?"

"I was hoping to surprise you for your birthday next week," River said. "I had it custom made for you and believe it or not, Savannah helped me with the design."

This was too much. My head swam and I tried to stay focused on the pendant, but my eyes danced over the room like a wild animal looking for a way out. I didn't even remember my birthday, but River had everything planned out for it and I wondered when he had time to get this made.

"Wait," I said, pausing my rapid spiral into anger. "Is that why you've been MIA lately?"

River's brow furrowed and he reached for my hand, intertwining his fingers in mine. "Not entirely."

"Spill it, hunter," I hissed.

"Okay, so this is probably something you already noticed, but the whole shifter thing, it's getting intense." He waited for me to nod then continued, "I've been trying to figure it out, but it's been hard. Sometimes, there's this whole side of me that bursts out and it scares the crap out of me, Billie. It's like I can't control myself and I was so scared that I'll hurt you. Everything has been crazy, and I worried I'd trip my shift and if you were nearby and I did something..."

His words trailed off and I squeezed his hand. "You wouldn't do that."

"How do we know that? The other shifters at the resistance said when they shifted, it was like they weren't themselves anymore. Like some animal side took over."

"You can't judge yourself based on them," I said. *Furry bastards.* No wonder River had been so pissed the last little while. Those ass hats were filling his head with nonsense. "I know you wouldn't actually do anything to hurt me."

"But what if I did? I couldn't survive that." His eyes wetted and he looked up at me through his lashes. "I love you, Billie. If I hurt you, I don't know what I would do then."

Those three little words hung in the air, and I opened my mouth as though I could swallow them whole. The entire time, I was busy worrying over the coven, he'd been dealing with something so much bigger. The panic in his voice told me everything I needed to hear, and guilt overtook me. This boy, this thoughtful, beautiful boy worried about my safety while I was pushing him away to deal with my own shit. Instead of helping him understand his shifter side, I left him alone. What kind of person does that to someone they love? *Wait, WHAT? Did I just admit that I loved River? Oh, Goddess.*

My lips parted and I met his gaze. "I love you too," I breathed out. My palm reached for his face, and he pressed his cheek into it, closing his eyes. His head tilted and he brought a soft kiss to the soft flesh of my hand, breaking me into pieces.

The box shook in my hand and when I looked down, I realized my entire body was shivering. River reached for it, pulling out the pendant. "May I?"

He gazed to my neck, and I nodded, turning my back to him. Slowly, River brushed the hair off my shoulders and looped the chain around my neck. He tightened the clasp and ran his finger along my exposed skin, sending more shivers down my spine. His soft lips pressed to my shoulder, and I sighed as the heat of his breath brushed over my skin. There were so many emotions in me I thought I would burst into flames.

"I wanted you to have this because I know you've been worried about the stupid mate bond," he whispered in my ear and my body stiffed. "I thought if you had some part of us with you, you'd know that none of that matters to me. I pick you, Billie. I will always pick you."

Tears fell from my eyes, and I let out a small sob. My hand wrapped around the pendant, and I tugged it down, feeling the cool metal of the chain against my skin. "End game," I whispered.

"You know it," River said.

In a flash, I twisted myself on the bed to face him. My legs encircled his midriff and I squeezed myself against him as a fire lit in my belly. River tugged at my waist, bringing me closer to him until there wasn't an inch of space between us. He hoisted me upward and our lips crashed into each other in a blazing kiss. Every touch of his skin against mine sent me reeling, and when his tongue brushed against mine, the burning in between my thighs sent a new awareness through my body. I slid against him, riding his waist while I bit his bottom lip. River growled against my mouth, and I moaned in response.

His eyes shot up to glance at me and he dragged the ends of my hair, tilting my head so he could run his lips down my body. His teeth barred and he bit down softly at the small curve of my neck, kissing and biting and licking at the same time. My abdomen tensed and I pushed my hips against him as I rode out the pleasure his lips offered.

Running my greedy fingers over his chest, I slid his shirt off him. River's muscles tensed and he arched an eyebrow as if to ask for permission. He didn't need to ask, he had it in spades.

I threw my hands up and River raised the sweater over my head so gently, I could almost slap him for taking his time. When our eyes met again, the peridot hued glow of his eyes took my breath away and I pressed my lips to his in excitement. Inside, the shadows stood on attention but didn't budge, and I wondered if they were somehow used to River's shifter blood by now. *Weird.*

River's hands gripped my side and he swung us around, lowering my back to the couch and sliding himself between my legs. I moaned and the satisfaction on his face deepened. *Stupid, hunter.* My hips bucked against him, and River pulled away, looking me over. He licked his bottom lip and I reached for him, but he pushed me back. His fingers twisted over the loops of my jeans, and he yanked them off without bothering with the zipper. Thank the Goddess for elastic material.

When he lowered on top of me again, I all but screamed. My legs pulled him closer while I used my hands to nudge his jeans off. With only a few slivers of fabric between us, I was burning hotter than a race car engine and the heat of River's skin mimicked mine. Our limbs entwined and I brought my lips to his ear. "I want all of you," I whispered.

River's body froze and he drew back to look at me. His hand reached around my back, unclasping my bra and tossing it to the foot of the bed. A wild smile played on his lips, and I dashed my tongue over them, forcing him closer to me.

His hands cupped my face and he pinned me in place.

"I love you, witch."

"Right back at you, hunter."

Whatever worries I had before evaporated, and I could think of nothing else but this moment. Shadowhurst, the resistance, the High Coven. None of them mattered. All I saw was River. All I felt was him between my legs and all I wanted was for time to slow down so we could have this moment forever. As much as I doubted myself in the past, there was nothing about this moment that I didn't believe in. I trusted River simply for the fact that I trusted myself around him. He was the one choice I knew, without a doubt, I made correctly. River ground his hips into me, and I felt the pendant he gave me roll on my neck, forcing a smile to my face. I didn't need a mate bond to know I belonged with him. He was mine and I was his.

End game.

Chapter Thirty-four

The RV pulled into the Shadowhurst bus terminal, and the driver pumped the brakes so hard, I went flying off River's shoulder and into the leather seat in front of me. A red mark spread across my forehead, and I frowned, turning back to him.

"You okay?" he asked.

"Barely felt it," I said, rubbing my head.

He winked at me and squeezed the soft flesh of my butt. "I'll give you something to feel later."

Heat traveled down my thighs, and I was caught in an awkward spot that put me somewhere between longing and wanting to knock his teeth in. This guy got a rise from me, in more ways than one, and I wasn't sure how I'd be able to concentrate with him around. Reading my thoughts, he stood up and reached for the overhead compartment to get our bags.

"Come on," he said with a sneaky smile. "Let's get out of here before I do something that could get us arrested."

Waltzing down the wide aisle, he tugged both our bags like they were filled with feathers and disappeared into the street below. My legs still shook from our breathtaking hours together in the hotel room and I shuffled them down the aisle like I was auditioning for a zombie movie. Clutching each armrest, I finally made it halfway down when my gaze caught Savannah reclining on the plush seat close to the front.

Her back was straight, and she stared at my neck with narrowed eyes.

I pressed a hand to the pendant River gave me and looked back at her. "Is there a problem?"

"Nope," Savannah said. "Looks good on you."

If I didn't think I'd get a concussion from hitting the floor, I would have fainted. My jaw unhinged and I looked her up and down, waiting for the next smart-ass remark. When one didn't come, I walked to stand beside her.

From the corner of my eye, I saw River pop his head back in and when he noticed me beside Savannah, he shook it in question. I waved him off. I wasn't some damsel in distress that needed his help every few minutes. A lot has changed for River and I, but that part would always stay the same. He got the clue and ducked away again, peering over his shoulder as he walked.

"I'm kind of done playing games with you," I said when I turned back to Savannah. "And I'd appreciate it if you laid off flirting with my boyfriend."

"I know. Sorry."

Holy Batman suit! Did Savannah just apologize? Sure, it felt half-hearted, but this was the only time I've ever heard her say the words, so I was confused as heck when she spoke again.

"Listen, I know we started rough..."

I raised an eyebrow and she chuckled.

"Okay, fine, more than rough," she added. "And I know it was mostly my fault."

Another eyebrow danced.

"FINE! All my fault. But I wanted to clear the air before we go."

She gestured to the seat next to her and I slid in against my better judgment. The leather made a crunching sound when I sat down, and I gritted my teeth together. My back pressed against the seat, pulling me into the shackles that held me at Savannah's side. At the wheel, the driver gave us a death glare and Savannah jerked up from her seat, holding her hand up for him to move along. He began to speak, but the look she gave him sent him on his way in no time.

No surprise there. Everyone feared Savannah. Everyone but me.

"Talk," I bit out.

She raised her arms and leaned back on the window to have a better view of me. "I don't like you, Billie." *Excellent start.* "You come strolling in here with your stupid witchy magic and I gotta tell you, when I first met you, I wanted to kill you. Even before I knew you were a witch."

"Okay..." *Not okay.*

"And then River started hanging around you and it made everything worse. I really care about him, Billie. Like a lot. Since we were friends, and he was giving you all that attention, well, I don't know, it tore me apart."

I knew how she felt. Each time Savannah got close to River, I was ready to kill her. If she had feelings for River her entire life, seeing me with him must have felt pretty similar. I didn't want to understand her point of view, but I couldn't help myself. We loved the same guy and only one of us got to have him. That shit must have hurt.

Savannah looked past me. "Anyway, when he told me about that thing," she pointed to the pendant, "I knew it wasn't some little crush he had on you. River never dated much, so I didn't know how to handle it. I thought I was losing him, and it just made something snap. So, I may have been a bit of a jerk and tried to piss you off. And, well, you know how that played out."

I sure do, jackass. "So why tell me this now? What changed?"

"Look, whether I want to admit it or not, you're doing a lot for us here. And the others trust you, so you can't be all that bad." *Wow, really rolling out the compliments here...* "I think when I saw how River reacted to you asking him to leave with the others, it kind of clicked. I never had him. We're best friends, but that's it for us and it hurts like hell, but I have to deal. Plus, he like totally laid into me and threatened never to talk to me again if I didn't cut my shit out."

"That must have been awesome." I chuckled.

"You have no idea. That guy is so intense these days."

I lowered my eyes to my lap. "It's the shifter blood."

Savannah shifted in her seat, and it shocked me to see her grab my hand. Her skin was so cold, it felt like ice wrapping around me, but I didn't pull away. This was the only time we carried on a conversation where neither of us was at the other's throat and I would not be the one to ruin it. No matter how uncomfortable I felt, I needed to hear her out. For the team and for River.

"Hey," she whispered, and her tone was so soft, I did a double take to make sure it was real. "He'll be fine. He's got two bad bitches on his side, so whatever happens with the whole shifter thing, River will live through it."

"You know, you're not so bad when you're not trying to sabotage my life."

Savannah threw her head back and laughed. "I'm awesome and don't you forget it."

She slid out of the seat, climbing over me, and flashed a smile before stomping down the aisle. Her tight curls bounced behind her as she walked, and I watched her back retreat from me in amazement. This was the longest conversation Savannah and I had, and it wasn't as horrible as I imagined it being. In fact, I started to believe that I could trust her, and the thought jarred me senseless. Maybe Savannah wasn't as nasty as I thought her to be and there was a chance of us being friends one day.

When she reached the stairs to get off the bus, she flashed her teeth my way. "So, you gonna come do this spell blocking thingie or are do we live on this bus now?"

All right, maybe not anytime soon.

I curled myself out and took after her, legs picking up strength as I walked. On the side of the street, River waited with all our bags at his side and a grateful smile on his face. His bright eyes searched my face and I shot him a thumbs up before climbing down. Beside me, Savannah marched with an assured stride, and I tried to match her confidence. Eyes stared us down as we made our way to River, but I ignored everyone in our path. Each step led me closer to the sordid future that awaited me, and for the first time, I wasn't scared of it at all.

Chapter Thirty-five

Magic swam in my vision and its powerful energy tapped at the back of my mind like a woodpecker. Tap, tap, tap. Tap, tap, tap. I shook my head, dropping my focus long enough for it to drop out of my peripheral. Legs shaking, I spread them wider across the center of the pentagram on the floor and turned back to the book.

Somewhere outside, the moon glowed in the sky and a few howls let out. Damn shifters. Don't get me wrong, I was happy to have them patrol Savannah's farmhouse while I performed the blocking spell in her parent's basement wine cellar, but their loudness continued to shift my attention from the job. In my hands, the Book of Darkness sat with the pages turned to the reversal spell. Finding the correct spell was easier than anticipated, and the original witch that wrote it laid out the terms for the reversal easily enough for me to understand. Though shadowers were not created until years after her life, she wrote this particular spell to target anyone with dark magic, and it was simple for me to figure out which substitutions the High Coven would put forth to use the spell on soul suckers.

All they needed was a drop of soul sucker blood to direct it, and I was pretty sure they had that by the bucket. No one captured and killed shadowers like the coven, and my heart broke for the poor sucker that ended up being the donor for their little plan. Knowing the high priestesses, it was not a humane bloodletting.

I read off the steps to complete the spell again and looked around, unable to believe we got lucky enough to find it. I supposed even the witch that created it needed a backup plan. Magic always required a balance and a spell this powerful was no exception. If it backfired, the witch performing it could die and her coven had to possess the means to reverse the magic and return the energy to the earth before it overtook her.

Hopefully, that wouldn't be an issue this time.

I shuddered thinking about my magic going haywire and our entire plan falling apart. We've come too far to stop now, and as the howls of the shifters echoed in the distance, my nerves hitched.

We were running out of time.

To my right, backed against a wall filled with dusty wine bottles, stood River, Savannah, and Jayden. Beside them, the leaders of the shadower resistance took their place, holding guard over the basement entrance. With half our team incapacitated, the room felt empty, and my chest ached when I thought about those that couldn't be here. *Get your shit together. You're doing this for them.* I took a deep breath and checked the spell again. "I think I'm ready."

"You're sure this is all you need?" River asked, tossing a vial of Peyton's blood my way. I caught it with one hand and nearly dropped the book in the process.

"That and the black tourmaline," I answered and gestured to the five large crystal points on each end of the pentagram. "The tourmaline will act as a block, and I'll use Peyton's blood to pull soul sucker energy into the center rune. After that, it's just a matter of my magic cooperating."

"And you think you're strong enough to handle it?" Savannah asked.

I knew she didn't mean for the comment to be snarky and was genuinely concerned about the reversal spell working. Still, her words stung because she was right to ask the question. I wasn't sure I was strong enough to take on any of this. The witch who wrote the spell was much more powerful than me, and it was meant to be used by a full coven. The odds stacked against me, but I'd be damned if I didn't try this.

In my peripheral, I noticed Mel and Raiden exchange concerned looks.

"What's up, you two?"

Mel turned to me, shrugging her shoulders. "We're just wondering when you will start. The moon is full, has been for a while."

Before I could answer, Lorelei crossed the room to stand between us.

"She will start when that vial in her hand pulls on her magic," she said, making me see that the mind reaper knew more about this than she let on. "If the High Coven performed the spell already, Billie would sense it in Peyton's soul sucker blood. It would call to her. Since that hasn't happened yet, she can't begin the reversal. Is that about right?"

I smiled and nodded in agreement. "Yep. Can't reverse something that hasn't been done."

"So, we wait?" Jayden asked.

"We wait."

Waiting was the last thing I wanted to do, but I didn't have much of a choice. Lorelei was correct in her explanation. For me to complete the reversal, the initial energy tracking spell had to be performed and since I felt nothing off Peyton's blood,

I knew the High Coven hadn't gone through with it yet. What were they waiting for?

My blood iced over, and a shiver spread through my bones. What if I got this all wrong and the spell they were planning on using wasn't the one we thought? Or worse, what if they had something else up their sleeve now that the location of the resistance house was compromised? The leaders evacuated the house, but there was nothing to say that the High Coven didn't know where to find the shadowers in this town. For all I knew, they were out there right now, hunting them down while I stood like an idiot inside an onyx lined pentagram waiting for Peyton's blood to activate the pull.

More howls rose outside as the shifters made another round across the perimeter of the farmhouse. Their loud screeches carried into the basement, dying down in a beat. My body froze and my eyes flew to Mel and Raiden. "Something is wrong."

"I can feel it too," Raiden said. "They haven't stilled for hours, and now, I can't feel them outside at all."

He started for the door, but Lorelei pulled him back and shook her head. "No one move. We have company."

The mind reaper's hair trailed behind her as she moved to the only entrance leading to the basement. Her shoulders squared and Mel and Raiden joined her on either side. Behind me, River, Savannah, and Jayden stepped in to cover my back.

My head pounded and I clutched the vial in my hands so tightly, I thought it might burst. Feet planted firm, I trained my attention on the door and listened.

Outside, footsteps sounded on the stairs and my mouth dried. Magic swirled inside me, and I squirmed against it as it fought to get out. The door flew open, and the familiar scent of bergamot and patchouli drifted in, attacking my senses.

NO! They're here.

I took a step forward and River mirrored my move, positioning himself to flank my side. His chest rose and fell as he trained the tip of a knife at the door. Behind us, I heard Savannah knock an arrow.

Bells jingled in chorus and Raiden growled at their sound, puffing out his chest protectively in front of Mel. The seconds felt like years, and by the time Sebyl's blunt haircut peered through the doorway, I could have sworn I'd aged. Her sharp gaze drifted over the shadower leaders and landed on me, a grin tugging at her lips. Behind her, Theodora's bright blue hair emerged and darkness unlike any I've seen before washed over her features. My mouth opened and closed, but I seemed to have forgotten how to use it. When Rhiamon and Luna appeared in the doorway on either side of Sebyl, I all but fainted.

The disappointment on their faces made me want to crawl into a dark hole and stay there forever.

"Hello, Wilhemina," Sebyl said, her words stone. "Interesting group you have here."

She looked to Savannah and Jayden and grinned like a cat waiting to pounce. When her dark eyes landed on River, I stepped in front of him, grazing my fingers against his side with caution. Sebyl's face scrunched in disgust as she looked us over and beside her, the other high priestesses sighed in unison. "Couldn't track the hunters down, could you?" Sebyl asked sternly.

"Priestesses, please," I begged. "You can't go through with that spell. Innocent people will be hurt!"

"They are not people!" Sebyl roared. "They are animals!"

A low growl boomed in Raiden's chest and I was relieved when Mel warned him against attacking. Her muscled arms pulled on his and though he continued to growl, the shifter stayed still.

"NO!" I yelled, straightening my back. "You lied! About

everything! Does the rest of the coven know how the shadowers came into existence, or would that throw a wrench in your plans to wipe them off the earth?"

Sebyl's mouth pulled into a tight-lipped smile. "Child, you have no idea what you're getting in the middle of. There is still time to right this." She stretched out her hand. "Come with us, Billie. Come home."

My skin boiled and I fastened my fingers around Rivers before facing her again. "I am home."

The high priestess grimaced before looking to the other three.

"Very well," she whispered and stepped aside.

I had only a brief moment to register the fear that crept over when her slender body cleared the doorway and twenty head witches rushed into the basement.

Chapter Thirty-six

Bolts of lightning flew past my head and hit a row of wine bottles behind me. I ducked down, shielding my face from the explosion. The bitter scent of fermentation wafted over me, and I gagged as the cold liquid spread over my hair and neck. My eyes shot up, taking in the head witch that attacked me. Her plump figure drifted toward me, and lightning danced between her fingers as she readied for another blow. When her thin lips curled into a sinister smile, I tried to recount her name but was unsuccessful. Not that it mattered at the moment, I would end her no matter what she was called.

The witch threw her hands forward and lightning flashed in the air.

My body swerved to the side, dodging the hit. In front of me, I could see her skin pulse with energy as she pulled on the elements of the crystals adorning her neckline. My heart raced while I watched her. She was strong and capable, but I had a few tricks up my sleeve she wouldn't expect.

Before she could fire again, I let my shadows loose.

They rushed toward the witch, wrapping themselves

around her ankles, and pulling her under. A guttural scream left her lips and she hit the concrete with her back. I flipped my palms up, guiding the shadows up her body until they covered her fully. Her body convulsed, arms shooting up to her mouth to stop them from covering her face, but it was no use. My fingers curled and I tightened my hold on her, blocking her airways. Thrashing, the witch tried to scream, but the more she opened her mouth, the more my shadows crept in. They swarmed inside her, attaching themselves to her body like dark leeches, and I dared to smile. Her body shook again, then slowed as she took her last breath.

I called the shadows into me and watched in horror as the witch's head lolled sideways, her eyes devoid of life.

"Incoming!" River shouted and I swung my head his way.

He ran toward me, arms pumping at his side and dodging the bodies that filled the wine cellar. Magic exploded behind him, and he leaped forward, tackling me to the ground. His body froze and he pinned me down as purple dust spread over us. "River, NO!" I screamed, forcing myself to get out from under him. My hands shot up and a black shadowy shield formed over us seconds before the dust reached our bodies. Narrowing my eyes, I watched the shadows inhale the magic and swat it out of existence. Another second and River would have been paralyzed and unable to move.

Carefully, he climbed off me and rolled to his back, breathing hard. "Close call," he said. "Thanks."

"Watch out for the purple dust," I warned. "It'll knock you on your ass for hours."

We were on our feet in no time, facing off three more head witches. My gaze flowed over the cellar and heartache filled my chest. Not too far, Savannah and Jayden took on a head witch each. Their battle cries rose through the basement, and they slashed their weapons, kicking and screaming as they attacked.

Bottles burst around them, sending pools of wine and glass to the floor. The witches held their own, but I could see their energy depleting and their hits weakening by the minute. A ball of fire rushed at Savannah and she swatted it off with her blade as one would handle an annoying fly. The terror in the witch's eyes was palpable, and at that moment, I felt sorry for her; taking on Savannah on a good day was a tough task, but today, she was all violence and weapons. A truly worthy opponent and a hunter through and through. Beside her, Jayden slashed the abdomen of the witch he faced with a machete, never dropping his cheeky smile.

In my peripheral, the cement floor cracked, and vines crept up from the opening. I took a couple of steps, throwing my shadows at the witch controlling them and knocking her over. She flew across the room, landing in a pile of bottles with a crash.

"You got these two?" I asked River, pointing to the two remaining witches flanking us, and he nodded. "I'm going to help Mel and Raiden!"

River's determination was a force to be reckoned with and as he ran to attack, the glow of his eyes lit the room. His muscles bulged and his torn shirt flowed behind him as he jumped up, landing between the women. Their eyes scanned him as though they were looking for a weak spot, but I knew they wouldn't find one. River's shifter side was so close to the surface, he was more animal than man and I was confident he would handle them.

Forcing myself to leave his side, I ran for Mel and Raiden. Or at least what I assumed were Mel and Raiden. Somewhere in the attack's midst, the shifter couple transformed into their respective animals and their beauty took my breath away. They towered over seven witches, snarling the sharp rows of teeth that protruded from their jaws. Raiden was spectacular and the lion he possessed was nothing short of amazing. Glistening fur fell from his hide, and it took everything I had not to reach out to touch it. He dug his talons into the floor and roared. *Don't pet the lion, moron.* I turned my gaze to Mel, a gasp escaping my lips. Raiden's partner crouched next to him, her hips swaying from side to side as she prepared to jump. Her lioness body was so full of muscle she looked more like a truck than an animal, and I could tell right away she was the perfect mate for Raiden. They were a brilliant pair. Brilliant and so very terrifying.

The witches they cornered whimpered and backed away, but that only gave the shifters more room to attack. Everyone knew you can't run from a lion, and something told me my friends did not need any help in this fight. Still, I threw my power outward, leveling out two head witches to give them a head start. Raiden's massive head tilted my way and he growled under his breath before charging.

Screaming ensued and I looked away as the beasts tore the witches apart. *You're welcome, I guess.* I sighed and scanned the room for the high priestesses.

Deep in the crowd, Lorelei had joined River and they fought side by side to take down witch after witch as they made their way through the room. Their movement blurred and I urged myself to look away, searching further. My head swung around, checking every corner of the room when I spotted them.

In the distance, Theodora's blue hair shined under the overhead lights, and she leaned in the same doorway they entered, with Sebyl, Rhiamon, and Luna at her side. Their faces were blank and their movements minimal, but what worried me most wasn't their lack of participation. It was the four sets of eyes they had trained on me and the shadows swirling over my body.

Sebyl's dark gaze landed on the glowing moonstone ring on

my finger, and she scowled, turning to whisper something to Rhiamon. At her words, the priestess reached behind and pulled a massive sword from the strap on her shoulders. Her teeth gritted and she aimed the weapon my way, a warning on her face.

I swallowed. *Shit.*

She took a step forward. *Double shit!*

Rhiamon marched toward me, and I peeled my feet off the floor until I was matching her stride. The shadows danced in the air between us and when she took off in a dead sprint my way, I set them loose. I had no intention of hurting her, but I wasn't about to hang around while she sliced limbs off my body.

The shadows wrapped around the sword and Rhiamon moved her arms with so much speed and precision, I had trouble getting a grip. Each time I jerked my wrist to send more shadows, she tore them down with the silver blade. In the distance, I glimpsed Sebyl's satisfied smile when it hit me. *They're trying to tire me out! Drain me until I can't fight back.* A grin spread over my face, and I nodded in Sebyl's direction. Her pathetic smile dropped and her face paled as I shot a burst of shadows toward her and the remaining high priestesses.

With one hand, I wielded the darkness around Rhiamon while she continued to slice and dice my magic, while with the other, I pushed the shadows over the priestesses in the doorway, forcing my magic to pick up speed. It swirled around them, encasing them in a tornado of night and death. I could hear their screams through the darkness and a low chuckle escaped me.

Take that, bitches!

My happiness was short-lived and before I knew it, a bright light shone from the spot in my shadow tornado where the high priestesses gathered. Its blinding rays shot through my magic, ripping it to shreds. My eyes widened and I fought to keep my grasp on the few shadows left, but they burst like a water balloon before me. Sebyl's angry gaze met mine and she marched in my direction with the other two on her wings. Before they could reach me, I thrust both my arms at Rhiamon and fired the last of my magic her way. The shadows burst from my hands, wrapping around her waist and raising her off the ground. I struggled to keep her up but there was no backing down now. I needed to get her away from me. With a scream, I jolted my arms up and willed the shadows to throw her across the room. She toppled to the floor, her sword rolling from her grip and landing at River's feet. In seconds, he gripped its hilt and pointed it her way in a warning. *Stay down.*

Relief flooded through me when she listened.

River's eyes locked on me, and I gave him a quick smile, turning to Sebyl and the others.

"BILLIE!"

River's scream tore through the room, and I didn't have time to turn around when a blast of fire smashed into my midsection. I catapulted backward, feet trailing across the floor as the hit knocked me on my ass. My head hit a wall and I saw stars. Dark spots invaded my vision and I blinked them away, trying to focus on the pain. Looking down, I noticed the embers on my ripped shirt and the charred flesh of my stomach and stifled a gag reflex. I felt like someone ripped a hole through me, which was fairly accurate. Someone basically did. My hands swatted at the embers maniacally, and every hit sent sharp pains down my back and legs. Saliva pooled at my lips as I panted, teeth chattering from the ache.

Above me, Sebyl outstretched her arms and locked hands with Luna and Theodora. Their magic invaded the cellar and I watched it in slow motion. All the noise dissipated and as they willed their magic over me, I knew I was waiting to die. The high priestesses' eyes rolled back until I could see only the whites of them. Their lips moved in unison as they chanted words I couldn't understand, and terror ran through me when their familiarity hit me. It was the same language Evanora used in the field when she tried to suck my energy dry. Dark magic.

My eyes blinked rapidly, and I took in fast gulps of air, trying to stand up with minimal success. My entire body felt glued to the floor and my arms drooped at my side like useless strings. I wriggled my fingers and called for the shadows, but nothing happened.

Oh, Goddess. Please... No...

Tears streamed down my face as the chanting increased and the emptiness in me grew. My chest jerked up and my heart beat wildly as magic thrashed beneath my skin. It pushed on the edges, throwing itself against my body to be free. The priestesses continued to chant, and I continued to wither away. My lids fluttered and my head fell to the side, heavier than an anvil. I couldn't move. I couldn't breathe. I couldn't—

"NOOOOO!" River's voice cut through the darkness that pulled me under and I snapped my eyes open. The hold the priestesses had on me burst and I jerked up, eyes widening while I watched River push Sebyl down and lunge for her. His legs wrapped around her, and he pinned her in place, Rhiamon's sword pressing to her neck. His chest rose and fell, and his teeth ground so loud, I could hear them from where I crouched. The glow in his eyes was intense enough to light up Sebyl's face, and for the first time since I've met the high priestess, I saw fear in them.

River raised the sword and was about to bring it down when I screamed for him. "River, stop! Don't kill her!" *Are you serious?*

The look he gave me mirrored what I was thinking, and I had to admit, I was as confused as he was. Why did I feel the need to protect her after everything the High Coven did? I couldn't explain it, but something in me yearned to spare her life and I was done second-guessing myself. The priestesses were evil, but I would not be like them.

I would not kill in cold blood anymore.

My hand raised and shadows crept around it. It wasn't until I saw them that I realized how much I needed those damn shadows in my life. They were as much a part of me now as any other magic I wielded, and their energy completed me in a way I've never felt before.

Sebyl's jaw ticked, and she looked over River's wide shoulders to snarl at me. "You're a monster," she hissed. "A disgrace to your kind."

Darkness descended over me, and I took a determined step toward River, resting a hand on his shoulder and pulling him away. Reluctantly, he climbed off Sebyl and stood at my side, our hands clutched together in a tight grip.

I squared my shoulders and looked to the priestess, pity on my face. "I'm not the disgrace here and I'll make sure the rest of the coven knows who you are. You hear me?" I looked back at them. "Even if it takes me a lifetime, I will find out all your lies and I will bring them to light. The witches will know what you did. The entire world will know."

Panting, I stepped back and pulled River with me. We gave Sebyl a wide birth as the other priestesses gathered her up, their eyes shooting daggers my way. They stumbled to the door, avoiding my friends that circled in on them. Whatever head witches were left alive hobbled up the stairs and out of view while my friends screamed profanities their way. Okay, it was mostly Savannah and Jayden doing the screaming, but still. A good exit is a good exit.

When they were almost out of sight, Sebyl flashed an icy glare my way. "This isn't over, Wilhemina. You've made your choice. This is war."

I threw my head back and laughed, shadows swarming around me for that extra dramatic flair.

"There was no choice, Sebyl," I bit out, training her with the same stare she gave me. "I did what was right and if it's war you want, it's war you'll get. Just don't forget who you're dealing with."

"No better than Beatrix. A traitor," she breathed out and turned to walk away.

As her back retreated, a warmth spread through my body, and I leaned on River's shoulder to watch her walk away. She was right, I was no better than Beatrix, but she was also wrong. I would never betray my kind. The coven had to be led by honest women, and they no longer deserved to be lied to. For my kind to survive, they had to pick a side and I would stop at nothing to make sure it was the right one.

One way or another, I would bring justice to the High Coven. I would bring the war Sebyl wanted, and I would bring freedom.

I looked around and smiled.

The high priestesses didn't stand a chance against me and my friends.

Chapter Thirty-seven

"Can't you just use your magic to clean this place up?" Savannah kicked a broken bottle to the side.

The wine cellar looked as though a hurricane ripped through it and we've been trying to tidy up the mess up for over an hour. The shadowers left soon after the witches departed to get the news of our success to the others, and it surprised me to find out they would continue to meet at the house in the woods. When I asked Lorelei about it, she said she was confident they could defend the perimeter if the High Coven attacked again and that no one wanted to meet elsewhere. I supposed I understood their reasoning. The resistance house was a home of sorts for the shadowers, and they would fight tooth and nail to hold on to it. Still, I wasn't happy with the risk they were putting themselves in. Going back to the place we all knew was compromised seemed like a stupid plan to me, though it didn't seem my opinion mattered much to Lorelei. I had to trust the leaders to do what's right by their people.

Savannah kicked another bottle and huffed in annoyance. "Seriously, wave a wand or some shit."

"No problem!" I yelled out. "Let me just get my trusty mice and talking teacups to spiffy this place up for you!"

She stifled a laugh and looked around at the destruction that laid before us. "My parents are going to kill me."

Fear nudged at me when I remembered what Jayden said about her family and how they treated her. If they came home to see this mess, she'd be in a heap of trouble, and I didn't want to leave her alone with them. I still didn't know the exact dynamics of the Michaels family, but I had the feeling that seeing their expensive wine collection destroyed would not go over well. I tightened my lips into a line and left River's side to stand next to her.

"They won't be home for a couple of weeks. I'm sure we can replace everything that broke by then."

That seemed to give Savannah some comfort, and her shoulders relaxed. She turned away from me, continuing to clean up, but I could tell her nerves were still sky high. I sighed and dumped a few shards of glass into a trash bag. Cleaning this place up would be tough, but I meant what I said to Savannah, we would make sure it looked untouched by the time her parents got back. It was what friends did.

I was on all fours and wiping red wine stains from the floor when River approached me. His wide shoulders blocked the overhead lights and the way his hair fell into his face made me want to press my lips to his. Leave it to River to look dashing as hell after taking on the High Coven, and I doubted my own destroyed looks matched his perfect stature. Looking down at my ripped shirt and the red stains the wine left in my hair, I was pretty sure I looked completely destroyed by comparison.

He held out a hand to help me up and I took it instantly, jumping to my feet and wrapping my arms around his waist. I smelled worse than I looked, but I didn't care; I wanted to feel him against me.

"Got another call," he said.

My heart leaped in my chest, and I looked up at him through my lashes. "For the love of! What the hell is it now?"

River chuckled. "Good news, actually."

Arching an eyebrow, I nudged him to stop playing around.

"Peyton's awake. She asked for you."

I was out the door before he could blink.

Peyton was laid out in the same room Marcus put me in when I passed out, though this time, it looked more of a hospital than a bedroom. There were beeping monitors all around the bed with wires running from them to Peyton's frail body. An IV unit full of clear fluid stood at the side with yet another tube leading to her arm.

As I neared her, tears flooded my vision at the sight.

My beautiful, stubborn friend didn't resemble someone I remembered. The fight she had in her was gone, and she was covered in medical gauze wherever her flesh peeked through the hospital gown. The parts that weren't wrapped were black and blue, and each time she moved, her face scrunched up like she was in more pain than she could handle. Even her signature dark liner was scrubbed clean, leaving her face pale and unencumbered.

I tried to smile when I reached her side, but my lips fell flat.

"Hey," Peyton said, her voice hoarse, "no crying."

"Peyton, I... I..."

"I said no crying, girl. Now, stop that shit and fill me in already. What'd I miss?"

She struggled to sit up and I rushed to her side, helping her rise and placing a pillow behind her. My eyes continued to register the bruises on her arms and legs, and I forced myself to peel my gaze from them to focus on her face. "Well, you missed pretty much everything," I finally choked out. "Good job."

A small laugh escaped her, and she wheezed immediately after, rubbing her chest over the tubes under her gown.

"River said you guys were pretty stellar with defeating the High Coven."

Of course, that had to be the first thing he told her. "Yep. Though I'm pretty sure they'll be back. Peyton, seriously, are you okay?"

She tried to laugh again but a wheezing cough replaced it and she heaved over her legs, shaking until the fit went away. As her small body shook, my heart broke into pieces. I couldn't believe those damn shifters did this to her, but now that we had the Book of Darkness and one leg up on the coven, I could concentrate on dishing out the ass-kicking they deserved. Lorelei assured me the resistance still had the bastards locked up and as soon as I left Peyton today, I would pay them a visit. *Let's see how they do against someone their own size.*

As if reading my thoughts, Peyton snapped her attention to me. "Whatever you're thinking of doing, don't. They're not worth it."

"I'm not just going to let them get away with this," I whispered. "They deserve to be punished."

"Oh, I never said they won't be punished, B." She smiled. "They'll get exactly what's coming to them, but it'll be me who does it."

"Peyton, no offense, but you're not in any condition to be picking fights."

She winced as though I just slapped her. "But I will be. And then it's showtime."

I didn't intend to take this away from my best friend, but I knew I couldn't promise her not to hurt the shifters. The anger in me was scratching at my heart and eventually, I would give into it. I might give her some time to heal, but if there was anything I could do to make sure the shifters were all but destroyed by the time she got to them, I would do it. A smile played at my lips as I pictured how good it would feel to knock every sharp tooth from their disgusting mouths.

"Hey, how's Tyler?" she asked, and I shook away my wretched thoughts.

"Still out," I answered with a sigh. "But the doctors say it won't be for much longer. I think they're basically keeping him under now until his body heals. Abigail is not impressed, as always."

Peyton laughed and my heart swelled at the sound. "Nothing new there. But hey, maybe now they'll be less tongue and more talk, huh?"

I shrugged. "One can only hope."

There was a rustle outside, and I jumped from the bed, running to the window to peer through the blinds. When I saw two mind reapers pass by, I relaxed. Lorelei had shadowers patrolling the perimeter on the hour, though it did little to put me at ease. If the High Coven was to attack again, we weren't ready. At least not yet. But we would be. Even if it was the last thing I did, I would get them all ready. It's what Marcus would have wanted.

A cold shiver wrapped around me, and I grimaced, thinking of the soul sucker leader.

"I'm sorry about Marcus," I breathed out, unable to meet my best friend's eyes. "He was a really good guy."

She was quiet for a long time, and I regretted saying anything, but when her small hand reached for mine, I grabbed it instantly. My fingers looped around hers, obliterating the tattoos she sported from view.

"He was amazing, and I miss him," Peyton said. "I wish he

was here to tell me what to do. I'm not ready for this, B. Not at all."

I knew what she worried over. There were very few soul suckers in the resistance, and most of them were quite young. With Marcus gone, the other leaders agreed to give the role to Peyton if she wanted it. The continuous support she showed for their cause built their trust in her and I had to admit, my best friend would be an amazing leader for the younger kids. She was kind and ferocious and exactly the type of person one would expect to lead her kind. In a way, Peyton was very much like Marcus, only feisty and with a lot more attitude.

Even though I didn't want her in any more danger, I knew she'd be perfect for the role, and I was proud of her for not backing away when it was offered. I was even more proud to call her my best friend.

It was strange how much had changed since I came to Shadowhurst. No longer did I doubt every decision I made. In fact, I made those choices bravely and stood by every one with defiance made of stone. But it wasn't because I trusted myself more, that trust was always there. The only thing that changed was that I now had people in my corner that I would do anything for. I had something worth the fight. Every choice I made wasn't for the sake of the High Coven, it was for something greater; something more important. I lived for those I loved and those that had my back and following that path could never steer me wrong.

I gave Peyton's hand another squeeze and scooted on the bed next to her. "You'll do great. I know it."

Her weak smile returned, and she leaned back into the pillow.

"So," Peyton said, "all fun and games aside, when were you gonna tell me you saw River naked?"

My jaw dropped and I ripped my hand away from her, but she pulled me closer. "How did you know?"

"Girl, are you kidding? You have that look on your face."

"What look?"

"The one that says, '*I got me some hunter action*'." She chuckled and traced a finger over the pendant on my neck. "I see the pup already marked his territory. Vomit much?"

Peyton made a gagging motion with her mouth, and I laughed, burying my flushed cheeks into my hands. Only my best friend would want to know about my love life with forty tubes stretching from her body and bruises all over her skin. But hey, this was how I loved her, so if it was details Peyton wanted, it was details she would get. I leaned back next to her, letting the soft cotton of the pillowcase wrap around me, and took a deep breath before telling her everything that happened in Stamwick. Sharing those moments with her felt like a dam opened inside me and before I knew it, I was floating over the bed, watching us interact. Cheer spread through my chest as I took in the sight of Peyton and me on the bed, gossiping like normal schoolgirls. This was why I turned my back on the coven and this was what I would fight for. For her, for River, and for everyone else in that house. For my family.

Chapter Thirty-eight

ildfires danced in the night and howls and cheers rose over me, dragging me into the party. There were shadowers everywhere and I walked among them with squared shoulders and a wide stupid grin over my face. A loud yell sounded close to me, and I jerked my head to the side to see children pretend fight next to their parents. Two shifters and a soul sucker from the looks of it. Their cheerful voices carried over the fires while the parents chatted and threw drinks back like they were chugging water.

I chuckled, turning to River, who stood at my side with his arm draped over my waist. "This is some rager."

"HA! You should have seen how excited Jayden was to come tonight. I swear, it's like the boy has never been to a party before."

I followed his gaze into the crowd, landing on Jayden surrounded by a group of mind reapers. He said something and everyone laughed in excitement, patting him on the shoulder. "I'm sure he hasn't been to a party like this before."

"Truth."

We continued to walk through the crowd, stopping occasionally to say hello to a few of the people we knew. It was odd being amid this many shadowers and not having a gut feeling tell me to vanquish them, and I loved it. People smiled when we approached and offered us drinks and snacks, and for once, I didn't feel like a shark on the hunt. Beside me, River made small talk in that cocky way I'd learned to love, and I leaned into his chest, nodding along with the conversations.

The fires balled brighter and brighter, and the yells of the crowd grew as we walked. Everyone was celebrating and their joy brought tears to my eyes.

I finally did something right.

"Hey, bitches," Peyton's cheerful voice grabbed my attention and I turned to see her and Morgan stroll up to us. They looked so comfortable together that I wondered if my best friend forgot to mention a few details during our catch-up session. Mostly, though, I was just relieved to see her out of that damn bed.

Darting my eyes from Morgan to her, I arched an eyebrow. "Hi, guys. I see you both made it."

Peyton nudged me with her foot and a deep crimson blush spread over her cheeks. *Get it, girl!*

"How long you guys staying?" River asked, catching on quickly.

"Not long," Morgan said. "We're bailing soon to go watch a movie."

The red in Peyton's cheeks brightened and she dropped her gaze to her feet, suddenly finding the laces of her shoes immensely interesting. I almost laughed out loud but kept my mouth shut for my best friend's sake. After everything that happened, she deserved this. As I looked her over, I realized that she wasn't wearing her usual attire and instead sported a long-sleeve red lace shirt and blue leather leggings. Her knee-high boots grazed her thighs and I had to admit, she looked absolutely badass in her outfit. Beside her, Morgan wore her token flowery tank, though this one showed a lot more cleavage than I was used to seeing from her. Judging from Peyton's continuous gazes toward Morgan's assets, I realized who the tank top was for. *Nicely played.*

I grinned and turned to River, my eyes running up the slim cut of his very tight jeans and the even tighter shirt he wore tonight. *I can't believe he's mine.*

A hand tapped my shoulder and I whipped around, running face-first into Savannah's chest. She buckled back and I readied for a fight, but when she smiled instead, confusion coated my face. "Cute top," she said, pointing to the army green band tee I chose for tonight. "Think I can borrow it sometime?"

What is happening right now? "Um, sure. If the girls can fit into it."

Savannah threw her head backward and laughed, landing a playful punch to my shoulder. I was still puzzled as hell when she looked down at my leggings and frowned. "Those you can keep to yourself."

And there she is.

I smiled and pressed myself closer to River, searching the crowd.

"Let's go find Raiden and Mel."

We left the others and made our way around the fires to a large gathering of shifters. Knots formed in my stomach as memories of Peyton in the bed flashed before me, but River's hold on my waist kept me steady. His back straightened as he led us to the pack, and they hollered when we approached. A few stayed away, but most of the shifters greeted us with warm embraces and compliments on our handling of the High Coven. Some still teased River about not having shifted, but I knew he didn't take it to heart. River was just as relieved about his shift not triggering as I was. It was one less thing we had to worry about.

Near us, Raiden's roaring laughter echoed, and I twisted to see him leaning on a tree with Mel clutched to his chest. Raiden was topless, something I came to understand was normal for him, and his khaki slacks sat low on his hips, showing off the V Mel was hungrily eyeing. He laughed again, and she reached her fingers through the loops of his pants to drag him into her. The long slit of her skin-tight maxi dress pulled up and I blushed as I watched their display. Mel's eyes met mine and she shrugged in that '*I don't know what to do about him*' way, which made me giggle. Mel and I had a lot in common thanks to the stubborn men we chose, and it made me like her even more. Okay, maybe the fact that she was a badass lioness had a little something to do with it. Who didn't want someone like that on their side?

We were about to make our way to them when Lorelei stepped in our path. The mind reaper's pin-straight hair was pulled into a high ponytail, which stressed her fae-like features and dragged my attention to the prominent bridge of her nose. Small diamonds adorned her skin around the eyes and forehead, and her flowing silver dress sparkled in the light of the surrounding fires.

When we locked eyes, she held her hands out to me, presenting a small leather-bound book.

"For you," she said, voice soft like a songbird. "It was Marcus'."

I must have looked bewildered because when I reached for the book, she clasped her palms over my hands and gave them a small shake. "It was his journal. I read it after he was taken, and I think there is some information here that you need to see."

No freaking way in hell! He actually found something? With everything that happened, I completely forgot that

Marcus said he had a hunch about my shadows and after he died, I assumed any information he had got buried with him. Yet here it was, lying in my hands and begging me to read it. I couldn't believe it.

"Thank you," I whispered. "I miss him, Lorelei."

"Me too," she said with a nod.

Lorelei stayed for a time while River and she talked about nothing that drew my attention. All I could see was the journal and my fingers wrapped around it, putting indents in the soft leather. When Lorelei walked away, I didn't even notice her leave.

"I'm going to go talk to Raiden," River announced and leaned into my ear. "Take your time and come join whenever you're ready."

"Wow! Thanks, Dad," I said with sarcasm coating my words. "Shocked you're letting me go on my own, what with my house arrest and all."

River threw his head back to laugh and his eyes were back on me in seconds. The feral look in them made blood rush to my face. "Small steps, love. Besides, with the Chandlers away on vacation for the next few weeks, I'll have plenty of time to take full advantage of that house arrest."

He winked and my cheeks burnt. *Smug bastard!*

Hands still on the journal, I leaned in to press my lips to his and agreed to join after I learned what Marcus found out. River wasn't even out of sight when my sticky fingers ripped off the string that held the book shut and I rummaged through the pages. Most of it was notes Marcus had taken on the daily activities at the house, and I felt wrong reading his private thoughts. I skimmed the pages, looking only for some hint of my name so I didn't overstep. Lorelei's name popped up on more than one occasion and my heart broke for the mind reaper. Marcus and she may not have been open about their relationship, but I knew they had something, and losing him must have hurt her more than the rest of us.

I was halfway through the journal when tiny fingers folded over my leg. Looking down, I saw a small shifter girl about five years old peering up at me through thick lashes. Her bright blue eyes sparkled in the moonlight, and I leaned down so I could talk to her face to face.

"Well, hi there," I said with a smile. "How's your night going?"

She gave me a thumbs up with her pudgy hands and tugged at my sleeve. "I have something to show you."

Still pulling, she wrestled me to my feet, and I tried to catch River's gaze before following her. He was deep in conversation, and I gave up getting his attention, following the girl without bothering to get his attention. Whatever this adorable kid had to show me trumped listening to Raiden's dumb jokes, anyway.

We walked through the crowd and when we reached a thick growth of trees, she continued to pull me behind her. My head twisted to see the party get smaller and the fires disappear from view. Panic rose inside me, but the girl continued to urge me forward, so I pushed it aside and took careful steps to follow.

Around us, the trees thickened, and the darkness spread, and when she finally stopped, I almost tripped over her tiny frame.

The girl looked up at me and in the night, her eyes shined brighter than rubies.

"What did you want to show me?" I asked.

Her bow-like lips opened but I couldn't hear what she said and when I leaned in closer, she turned from me and ran into the trees. I started after her, but something wrapped around my wrist and jolted me backward. Turning, a scream formed on my lips, but before I could let it loose, something hard hit my head and the world went black.

Nausea filled my gut as I fluttered my eyes and peeled the lids apart. My vision swam and I fought the urge to vomit as I brought it into focus. All around, darkness spread its icy fingers and I could feel a chill in the air that nipped at my skin. My legs felt like someone dropped bricks on them and I reached for my toes, hoping to bring some sensation back to my body.

As soon as my hands yanked forward, a loud rattle of chains echoed through the darkness, and my arms jerked back over my head.

What in the fae? I moved my arms again and the chains clinked against each other, sending fear to the bottom of my stomach. My stomach turned and I thrashed at the restraints until my wrists burnt from the metal rubbing into my soft skin.

Stilling, I tried to figure out where I was but all I could hear were drips of water in the distance followed by a silence that chilled my bones.

"Hello?" I yelled out and my voice carried through the space I was held in. Hello, hello, hello... It taunted me until it disappeared, and quietness took over once more. "Let me out! NOW!"

Let me out, let me out, let me out... Now, now, now...

"DAMN IT!"

Damn it, damn it, damn it...

I yanked at the restraints again, but they were clamped over my wrists and no matter how much I pulled, I couldn't get free. My entire body shook, and fear gripped me, but I struggled, calling for my magic and the shadows that awaited inside. My eyes clamped shut and I reached deep down, begging them to appear. As I felt their power, a sharp agonizing pain spread through my body and I pulled my knees into my chest, grinding my teeth against each other. *The hell?* I tried again and again until the pain knocked me on my ass. Something in here was blocking my magic, and without it, I would never get free.

Throwing my head against the cool stone at my back, I took a deep breath in and waited for the pain to subside. Around me, the sound of dripping water played a tune and I bit down on the inside of my cheek as the fight left me. Whoever trapped me here knew what they were doing, and my head throbbed as I thought what that could mean.

I wasn't getting out. Not without their permission, and somehow, I doubted it would be that easy.

# Chapter Thirty-nine

River

Come on, Billie. Where are you? I pushed through the crowd, throwing a shoulder at everyone who got in my way. *I swear, when I find this girl, I'm chaining her to my side.*

The fire rose over the people gathered near them, and I had to zig and zag to avoid getting pummeled by the excited shadowers that filled the clearing in the woods. Whoever thought it was a good idea to throw a party in the middle of the forest was a damn idiot. I growled under my breath as a group of mind reapers made their way toward me. They froze in their tracks, lowering their gazes to the floor.

Who's a pup now? Keep moving!

Another growl and they were on their way, giving me a wide birth.

There were so many faces, I couldn't scan them all but there was only one face I needed to see to calm down and I couldn't find her anywhere. Where could she have gone? It had only been fifteen minutes since I left Billie with that stupid book, and she said she'd come to find me when she finished reading it. Maybe she returned to the house? Why wouldn't she tell me she was leaving? This wasn't like Billie.

Another shoulder collided with mine and my eyes met Savannah's. Her curly hair was pinned up today and I wondered who she was trying to impress. *It sure as shit better not be me.* Teeth grinding, I tensed my jaw and faced her. "Have you seen Billie?"

"Not for a while." Savannah shrugged. "Why?"

"I don't know. She just disappeared and it doesn't feel right."

Savannah's face grew rigid, and she looked the crowd over, searching for Billie's face. When she came up empty, as I knew she would, she looped an arm under mine and urged me forward. "Let's check with the others."

We darted through the clearing until we saw Morgan and Peyton, who looked as though they were about to leave. Peyton opened her mouth to speak, and I shoved my hand in her face with more force than intended. It did the job and she shut her lips, staring at me in bewilderment.

"Have you seen Billie?"

Morgan looked to Peyton then back to me again. "I saw her go off into the woods with some kid. That was a while back though."

"Are you kidding me, Morgan?" I tried not to yell. I really did. "Why didn't you stop her?"

She cowered back from me, and I felt Savannah pinch my arm in warning. *Right. Don't bite your friend's head off. Got it.* I didn't get it and I wanted nothing more than to rip Morgan's head off but stayed put. *Try to look normal.* I forced a smile, but the look on Morgan's face told me it did not have the effect I needed it to have.

"I didn't think it was a big deal," she said. "The kid was what? Five? What's the worst that could happen?"

Images of all the worst things that could happen flooded my vision and my jaw ticked. I fisted my hands at my sides and tried to count to ten like my mom used to teach me when I spiraled out of control, but all it did was make me tense harder. Every muscle in my body was on fire, and I knew the only way I would calm down was if I found her. Now.

Next to me, Savannah grimaced and turned to the trees. "Come on, let's go get her."

We marched in unison, and I was sure I still looked like I would rip people's faces off because the crowd parted as we passed, giving us enough room to get through. When we reached the tree line, the knots in my stomach twisted tighter and I sped up my pace. Beside me, Savannah kept up and we barreled through the dark woods like one of her arrows. Night surrounded us and acid rose in my throat the deeper we got inside the trees.

"Billie! Come out now! Enough playing!" I yelled, my voice carrying over the darkness. "Billie!"

My arms shook and I threw a punch at a tree, letting the bark break over my skin. Eyes narrowing, I turned in a circle, checking every nook and cranny of the damn forest until I found my girl. The woods were as empty as my stomach was about to be, and I leaned against a tree trunk, battling the urge to retch over my sneakers.

Savannah's soft hand pressed to my shoulder. "We'll find her."

Will we? How? I wanted to scream, but no words came out. Something was wrong and while I couldn't put my finger on it, I knew Billie would never disappear like this. Sure, she was stubborn as hell, but it wasn't like her to vanish knowing how worried I'd be. Not after everything we just went through.

My eyes darted from side to side, and I looked between every tree when my gaze landed on something tucked under a pile of leaves. Heart racing, I ran toward it, Savannah on my heels. I bent over to snatch the item from the ground and my heart plummeted.

"What's that?" Savannah asked.

"Marcus' journal," I half-whispered.

My head pounded and my pulse beat through my chest as I clutched the leather notebook. Something was definitely wrong here. Billie wouldn't let this thing out of her sight, not when it had answers about the shadows plaguing her magic. Or maybe blessed it? I wasn't sure anymore, and to be honest, her damn shadows were the last of my worries. My gaze snapped to Savannah and her quickly paling face told me she was thinking the same thing I was. "Someone took her."

In the distance, thunder roared, and I could sense my bones grow cold in anticipation. A storm was coming, and it was coming fast. I crouched and let my hands fall to the ground, grabbing a fistful of leaves and crunching them into oblivion. Savannah said something, but her words didn't reach me. All I saw was Billie's face and someone else's hands on her as they dragged her away. Anger burst within me, and I felt every single blood cell rushing through my veins. My limbs tingled and my muscles tightened, and when I looked down, a faint green light illuminated the journal.

"Uh, River?"

I didn't look at her. I couldn't. Just as Savannah spoke, a pain like none I've ever felt before coursed through me and I fell to the ground, wriggling like a fish out of water. My skin felt too tight over my bones and when I heard the first crack, I threw my head back and screamed. The thunder mocked my screaming, roaring in the sky while I was helpless on the floor. Somewhere over me, Savannah gasped, and I tried to follow her voice. My vision blurred and the next crack of bones sent me into an oblivion of pain. A fire burnt in my gut, and I kicked my legs back, roaring again. I thrashed violently enough that leaves kicked up dust around my flailing body and covered me in their disgusting array of colors. I hated fall. Now more than ever.

Crack after crack, my body reformed, and the pain was so intense that I stopped feeling it at all. I was numb from what was happening to me, and I would no longer fight it. Whatever worked to make this go away so I can be on my way to find Billie. Her beautiful face formed in my vision, and I kept my focus on it. *I'm coming, love. I'll find you.*

She smiled and I fell into pieces. Several screams later, sweat covered me whole and when I tried to stand, I fell on all fours. I yelled for Savannah, but instead, a guttural growl left my lips. My eyes looked around the clearing, landing on her cowering frame behind a tree. From here, I could smell her fear and it called to me. Her body was encircled in a red glow and though she was hidden behind a wide tree trunk, I could see her clear as day.

What the hell is happening right now?

My back shuddered and I stomped my feet into the ground when I saw it. Thick gray fur covered my hands from top to bottom, but that wasn't the thing that scared the most. It wasn't even in the top five scary things at that moment. What petrified me to no bounds, scared me completely shitless, was that my hands weren't hands at all. They were paws.

Ready to dive into the next mystery to hit Shadowhurst? Last we heard, Billie woke up chained to a wall and River went through his first shift. That sounds like a complete disaster! What will happen to our two love birds? Will Billie be able to escape her captures? Can River control the beast inside him long enough to find her? Find out in Book Three of the Shadowhurst Mysteries: **Cavern of Lies**. CLICK HERE to read **Cavern of Lies** now!

You can also check out the cover and description for the Cavern of Lies below.

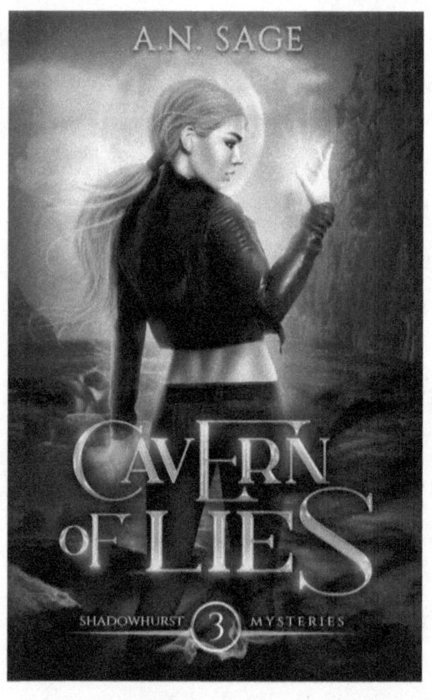

One minute, I'm partying. The next, I'm chained to a cave wall, and not on purpose.

As a witch, I have skills—skills that should get me out of this fine mess. Right?

That's under normal circumstances. There's nothing normal about my current situation. For starters, my magic has been blocked. Secondly, and slightly more concerning, no one knows where the shifters have locked me up.

All I can do is hope River will find me before the torture is too much to bear.

Just another day in the hell that is Shadowhurst.

·   ·   ·

CLICK HERE to start reading the **Cavern of Lies** now!

Haven't read the beginning of the story and wondering what's going on? **Witch of Shadows** will catch you right up! Read the first book of the Shadowhurst Mysteries here:

READ THE BOOK NOW!

Interested in finding out what happened to Beatrix Stonewall? Read the prequel novella Coven of Deception for FREE!

READ COVEN OF DECEPTION

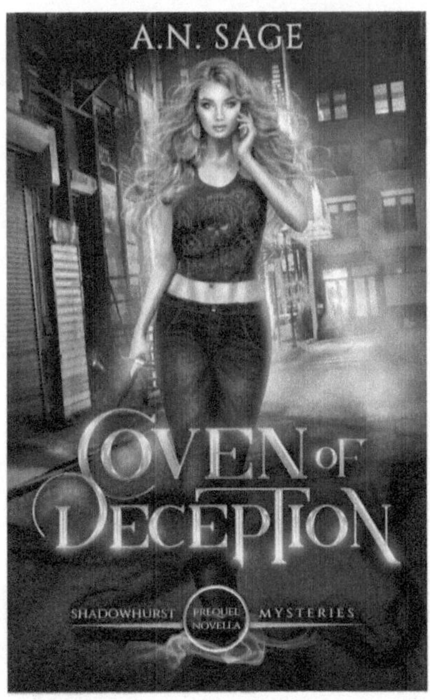

Who said fairy tales aren't real?

I have it under good authority, they're not only real, they can be a veritable nightmare.

Not only do I possess magic; I also belong to a secret coven of witches who've been living in plain sight.

First came the fun part. My powers manifested.

Next came reality. Trouble found me.

One minute, I'm living my life without a care in the world. The next, I'm dodging a mystery stranger who can't get enough of me.

So much for easing into this new life. It's time to see where these new skills will take me. Want to come along for the ride?

Start reading Coven of Deception by CLICKING HERE.

ACKNOWLEDGMENTS

All I can say is wow! Writing this book has been quite a journey and I am so proud of how it turned out.

As always, a tremendous thank you goes to my wonderful partner who stood by me through nights of wanting to rip my hair out when I hit a snag. Thanks for putting up with me!

To my parents, you never once questioned my decision to become a writer and I love you for it with all my heart.

Lastly, to my amazing readers. You make it all worth while and none of this would matter without you. Thank you for giving meaning to my words and thank you for giving up your time to read this book. You are the reason I keep writing and I'm forever grateful to you for that.

Stay magical!

ABOUT THE AUTHOR

A.N. Sage has spent most of her life waiting to meet a witch, vampire, or at least get haunted by a ghost. In between failed seances and many questionable outfit choices, she has developed a keen eye for the extra-ordinary.

Since chasing the supernatural does not pay the bills, she dabbled in creative entrepreneurship, marketing and retail management. A.N. spends her free time reading and binge-watching television shows in her pajamas.

Currently, she resides in Toronto, Canada with her husband who is not a creature of the night.

A.N. Sage is a Scorpio and a massive advocate of leggings for pants.

For more books and updates:

www.ansage.ca

Connect on social media:

Facebook Group:

facebook.com/groups/945090619339423/

Instagram:

instagram.com/a.n.sage/

Twitter:

twitter.com/ANsageWrites

Facebook:

facebook.com/ansagewrites
Pinterest:
pinterest.ca/ansagewrites
Goodreads:
goodreads.com/author/show/18901100.Alexis_N_Sage
Amazon:
amazon.com/author/a.n.sage

www.ingramcontent.com/pod-product-compliance
Lightning Source LLC
Chambersburg PA
CBHW050021120726
47903CB00006B/1859